EYES OF IRIS

EYES OF IRIS

JOSHUA A.H. HARRIS

atmosphere press

For my sons (Leomides and Helexios), nieces (Phaedra and Kepley), nephews (Maximus and Grainger), and their rising generation of innovators, explorers, and pioneers

There's always a story. It's all stories, really. The sun coming up every day is a story.

—Terry Pratchett, *A Hat Full of Sky*

The future influences the present just as much as the past.

—Friedrich Nietzsche

PALO ALTO, CALIFORNIA
AUGUST 10, 2023

PALO ALTO 1

Would he have called it a premonition, the dread Dr. Ernest Kairos felt that morning—the morning he met Iris—or merely the debilitating residue of a broken night's sleep? As a seasoned psychiatrist and research professional at Stanford University Medical Center, he likely would've disregarded the concept of forewarning as violating the rules of time. He might have said that omens are mere stories we tell ourselves after the fact, coincidences we infuse with irrational significance. Still, one must wonder: could he somehow sense the danger ahead? Anticipate the uncharted rapids just around the next bend?

In either case, it was time to get up. Bare feet to cold wooden floor, he rocked his head from side to side and removed his iPhone XL from its cradle on his bedside table. He opened a loving-kindness meditation app, placed his wrinkled hands on his pajama-clad knees, and took long breaths in sync with the disembodied voice echoing off the empty walls of his small bedroom: *may you be safe, may you be mentally well, may you be physically well, may you be at ease...*

"Mornings are the hardest," he reminded himself as he entered the bathroom, avoiding his red eyes in the mirror.

At breakfast—plain oatmeal, milk—he checked his email, reviewed his schedule, and pulled up his favorite self-help app, Chroma. Among other features, it had a color-coded calendar with specific intentions for each day. Thursday, August 10, 2023, would be a purple day, according to some unknown algorithm, indicating the intention of maximum compassion and openness to the world around him. Daisy, his AI counselor, popped up on his screen and asked about his mood. They chatted for a while; better than eating alone, he rationalized. He then toggled Chroma's reminder function to high and set his sights on a positive mental health day. Despite its automated nature, he often viewed the app as a necessary rudder for a ship that could otherwise easily find itself lost at sea.

At a quarter to nine, Dr. Kairos sat on a bench outside the hospital, attempting to put intention to practice. The early morning fog had quickly given way to crisp sunshine and marine breezes. He took the first sip of his daily Americano and rolled up the sleeves of his white coat, allowing the sun to penetrate the mottled skin of his forearms.

He closed his eyes and chased the floaters on his eyelids. They looked like strange, squiggly fish swimming in a hot orange current, but he knew they were, in fact, just a symptom of age-related degradation of his vitreous—his eyeballs' jelly-like substance—and the associated slumping of its interior surface. A few minutes passed before he realized he'd found the moment of peace—however fleeting—he'd been seeking all morning.

After triggering the hospital's automatic doors, he paused momentarily at the threshold, extended his arms out wide, and focused on the contrast between the sidewalk's early warmth and the climate-controlled, HEPA-filtered air inside. Three night nurses scooted by him on their way home; they nodded but didn't break stride. He was known as an eccentric. Standing like a crucifix in the entrance of the hospital was not a big deal, just one of those Dr. Kairos things. Tiny beads of sweat broke out on his brow as he reminded himself to try to stay positive.

***

Approximately an hour later, a nurse interrupted the mental wellness team's weekly meeting to summon Dr. Kairos to the psych ward. He was needed, she said, to assess a new patient as a potential 5150, the legal term for holding a mentally ill person against their will, pending further evaluation. Dr. Kairos located Dr. Simmons, a fresh-faced ER resident with the bright blue eyes of a Siberian husky, who informed him that the patient seemed to be suffering from delusional thinking—Dr. Kairos's area of expertise.

In fact, Dr. Kairos had written a bestseller on the subject, entitled *Who's Fooling Whom: Mitigating Reality Through Delusional Storytelling*. In it, he recounted his many years of collecting patients' delusions and shared his system of grading the accounts on a multidimensional scale like diamonds. His book concluded that all humans are necessarily delusional—just some more than others. The phrase that really struck a chord with the public appeared on page fifty-five: "Liberate your idiosyncratic reality." His publicist had even printed up hundreds of T-shirts with the clunky slogan—in alternative capital letters ("LiBeRaTe YoUr IdIoSyNcRaTiC ReAlItY")—emblazoned across the front. Dr. Kairos hadn't even really remembered writing it.

His book had earned him a spattering of critical acclaim, a flashing moment of fame, and a small, desperate following of wackadoodles begging him to analyze, endorse, or realign their variously distorted realities. His groupies eventually lost interest when they realized Dr. Kairos was no messiah and that he'd already said all he wanted to say in his book. He'd been the quintessential flash in the pan.

"She was admitted at 5:30 this morning," Dr. Simmons said, "with no apparent injuries, but she was at risk of going into shock, so I gave her dopamine and fluids, the usual. She's responding well."

"How did she get here?"

"She's a walk-in, or maybe a drop-off. Either way, she flew in solo."

"And?"

"At first, I thought she'd just partied too hard, had taken something she couldn't handle. But as I continued to interview her, she started sobering up and began telling me this super weird story. About ten minutes in, though, she looked me dead in the eye—caught me off guard. She must've seen what I was thinking."

"And what was that?"

"Honestly? I was thinking, 'This would make a killer movie.' She knew right then that I wasn't buying it, and she clammed right up."

"What was her story?"

"She claimed she'd been caught in some other body, tall with thick, gray skin—or something like that."

"Sounds like clinical lycanthropy."

"Whatever, dude," Dr. Simmons said. "It's been a while since I read up on delusional psychosis. Anyway, she's all yours. The name's Irisa, but she prefers Iris. I got that much at least."

As Dr. Kairos walked toward the room where Iris was being held, he noted his rapidly improving mood. The Americano's caffeine had kicked in, which always helped, but more, he felt eager and excited to hear this new patient's elaborate, deep-seated delusion. Purple, purple, purple, he cooed as he walked, let's see what this weird world of ours has on offer today.

"Good morning," he said softly, sliding into the room and letting the door close quietly behind him.

The overhead lights were off; the drawn curtains cast the room in shadows of gray and black. Dressed in a hospital gown and partially covered with a pale yellow sheet, Iris seemed to be sleeping. But as Dr. Kairos crossed the room, her toes twitched. He opened the curtains, flooding the room with citrus morning light.

She had light brown skin, her short hair—bleached white with streaks of blue and black—looked like it hadn't been washed in days, and she appeared to be on the short side, maybe 5'3". Her one exposed arm revealed a bulging bicep, and her unpainted fingernails were neatly trimmed. She had an eyebrow ring over her right eye, multiple earrings stringed around the helix of her left ear, and a small tattoo of the Greek letter psi (Ψ) on her neck, off-center as if purposely placed over her carotid artery. She wore no makeup. Her cheekbones protruded just enough to highlight her small, closed mouth and a gentle bump on her nose, just below the bridge, where it might've been broken years ago.

Even with the burst of light, she didn't move. But her uneven breathing suggested she was both awake and curious—or maybe just irritated. He waited for a minute, then two. She continued to play possum.

Dr. Kairos sat down on the comfy white chair situated in the corner of the room and pulled up her chart on his phone. Following a link to a Wikipedia article, he discovered a trove of information about her. Her parents, both immigrants—mother from Jamaica, father from Belarus—had met at UC Berkeley. They'd married and produced a daughter, Irisa ("Iris") Solovyov. In a tragic turn of events, her parents died in a car crash heading home from a party on a rainy night. Iris—only two years old at the time—had been properly secured in a car seat and had survived unscathed.

After the crash, Iris had bounced around the Bay Area's foster care system until her kindergarten teacher noticed she preferred reading books upside-down. The teacher quickly discovered that she read flawlessly in a mirror, could page through a book backward and retain every detail, and had no trouble speed-reading high school textbooks. Someone called a reporter, and the next week, she was on the front page of the *East Bay Times*.

The state placed her in the Ardmore Academy, a small boarding school for gifted children in the Sierra foothills. She'd graduated from high school at age thirteen and then earned a bachelor's degree from UC Berkeley in cognitive psychology three years later, the youngest student ever to do so—thus the Wikipedia article. At her present age of twenty, she was finishing up a graduate degree at Stanford in computational neuroscience. Dr. Kairos looked up from his phone at his patient's dyed hair, muscular physique, and piercings; never in a million years would he have guessed that she'd have such serious intellectual chops.

"Might as well open your eyes—I'm a friend, not foe."

"You're my mental health evaluator," she replied without opening her eyes, "so you should be unbiased, correct? Neither friend nor foe."

"How about we go with 'neutral, interested professional just trying to do his job'? My name is Dr. Ernest Kairos. Better?"

She opened her bloodshot eyes and looked him up and down. "You mean, 'Doctor Delusion'?"

"Some have called me that, though it's been a while."

"I read your book when I was eleven. For your sake, I hope you're a better psychologist than you are a writer."

She raised the back of the bed, pushed the sheet down to her lap, and pulled herself into a seated position. She'd destroy me in arm-wrestling, he thought.

"Are you an atheist?" she asked.

He smiled, took a small, leather-bound notebook out of the pocket of his white coat, and wrote down her name, the date, and the words "ASSERTIVE" and "DEFIANT" in capital letters.

"Don't you think we're getting a bit ahead of ourselves?" he responded. "I noticed in your background that you've studied quite a bit of psychology. Perhaps you can tell me what you're into—your specific areas of interest."

"So let me get this straight: you're going to ask me a bunch of softball questions to build trust. Then I open up, tell you all my problems, and reveal my 'delusions' so you can make your recommendation on whether I should be released or held here for seventy-two hours—all based on what you think is the most useful and relevant information contained in my statement."

"You could put it that way."

"One big problem: what you think is 'useful' and 'relevant'

may not fit my definitions of those terms." Dr. Kairos noticed that, unlike most patients in her situation, she consistently held eye contact—even to the point of making him uncomfortable. She continued, "So whose definitions are we going to use?"

"As I'm sure you understand, the world is filled with an infinite number of competing perceptions—both human and otherwise—all relative to the individual's perspective. The orangutan sees the orangutan world, not that of the blue-footed booby. I'm guessing you'd agree."

She answered with silence.

"But I can tell already that you and I have many similarities in our thinking—so maybe our definitions of 'useful' and 'relevant' might be more aligned than you presume. Maybe you can just tell me what you think is important, and I'll promise to be open-minded."

"Still not going to work," she said.

"So you wish to remain in the probing, potentially combative stage of our interaction? Dogs sniff butts and bark; we do the same, I suppose. But I'm sure you've studied 5150 holds, so you know I need some answers."

She was about to speak but then took a sip of water from a light blue, plastic cup fitted with a lid and straw. From his initial assessment, she didn't seem to be suffering from any form of psychosis. But then again, many of the most intensely disturbed patients can easily pass as mentally fit—that is, until you dig a little deeper.

"Can you just forget about this whole thing? I shouldn't have said anything to that other doctor, but I was still kind of messed up."

"You know I can't just let you go—legal obligations, administrative standards, professional liability...and of course there's always the remote possibility that I might actually care about you as a fellow human being. At a minimum, I'd like to make sure you're not going to leave here and jump in front of a bus."

"That's not how I'd do it. High caliber pistol to the head—most effective and least agonizing." She put her right index finger up to her temple and pulled the imaginary trigger. "Anyway, I simply experienced a drug-induced hallucination, that's all. We don't need to drag this out all day, okay?"

"Are you presently feeling suicidal?"

"Come on, Doc, you can do better than that." She looked over his shoulder at the sky out the window. "Simple questions beget simple answers. Do you seek simple answers?"

Dr. Kairos wrote "ARROGANT" down in his notebook. He considered the word for a moment—accurate, perhaps, in some ways, but far too judgmental and reductive, especially for a purple day. He crossed the word out, closed the notebook, and slid it back into the pocket of his white coat.

"Honest answers," he responded, "that's all I ask. Dr. Simmons seemed to think that you may have experienced something more than a bad trip, but I can't come to any conclusions until I hear more. If I discharge you based on your self-diagnosis, I'd be both lazy and negligent. And I'm neither of those things. I should think someone as smart as you would understand that."

"Wrong term."

"Hmm?"

"I'm not just 'smart.' I'm a genius. There's a difference—*genius*, from the Latin *gignere*."

Recognizing a potential opening—prodigies, even guarded ones, love to show off—Dr. Kairos asked, "*Gignere*, huh? Tell me more. I've never been good with etymology."

She looked at him skeptically but explained nonetheless: "The Latin verb *gignere* means 'to give birth.' The ancient Romans believed that everyone is born with a spirit that guides them through life; they adopted the word 'genius' to describe these spirits. Later, 'genius' became shorthand for people with exceptional abilities, like me, based on the belief that we must have singularly powerful spirits directing our lives."

"So do you think you have some omnipotent spirit watching over you?" It didn't sound like the "other body" delusion Dr. Simmons had described, but it was worth a shot.

"You're not going to nail me down that easily, Dr. Kairos."

"You can't blame me for trying."

"I can, actually." She smiled, just for a moment, before turning her attention to a loose thread on the hospital sheet in her lap.

"Fine, fine, you win," he said, "but tell me—I've always been curious—what does it actually feel like to be a genius?"

"Do you want my usual answer, the one I always give to you normals?"

"Normals?" he asked.

"Non-geniuses."

"Why do you presume I'm not a genius like you?"

She shook her head. "I read your book, remember?"

"Now you're just being cruel."

She laughed despite herself—it was like music to Dr. Kairos's ears—then answered, "I usually tell people that I comprehend and remember everything I experience, almost as if I've already done those things many times before. Then I tell people, 'like a preprogrammed computer,' and the normals always nod and say, 'Oh, I see.'"

"Oh, I see," Dr. Kairos said, though the lame joke was lost on her.

"But after last night..." she continued, almost to herself. "After last night...my genius feels..."

He waited a beat and then said in his most reassuring tone, "I've treated thousands of patients in my lifetime. Try me."

She crossed her muscular arms and looked up at the ceiling. "Words like 'transcendent' and 'terrifying' pop to mind."

"Tell me what happened. As you can imagine, I'm a very good listener."

"Part of me would like to—maybe you could help me clear a few things up—but I *don't* want to get locked away in a mental institution. I've visited quite a few, for classes and clinical trials—they just don't feel like home to me."

Dr. Kairos already knew he was going to let her walk. People who demonstrate the type of calm demeanor she was displaying can't be held involuntarily—no matter how deeply troubled they may be. Psych holds are for extreme situations, for patients who are out of control. Iris had control down pat. Plus, 5150 beds were limited and expensive. Admin would never accept holding her in her current, composed state.

"I'll make you a deal," he said, leaning forward, "just between you and me. Answer the 5150 questions and then tell me the *entire* story of what you experienced. If you do those things, I'll sign the papers and release you when we're done—but you have to tell me everything."

"Why would I trust you to keep your end of the bargain?"

Dr. Kairos felt a pang of sorrow for his young, guarded patient. He'd always found it so perverse, how the initially antagonistic patients often end up being the ones most eager to share, most starved for love and compassion. What a lonely world this could be.

"I think you already trust me," he said. "And as you know, recounting an intense event helps the brain process that experience—even for geniuses—especially when it is fresh in your mind. You need to tell your story—you and I both know that—and I'm offering you a perfect, no-strings-attached opportunity to do so. Why wouldn't you avail yourself to my expertise? I usually don't come so cheap."

"I guess it couldn't hurt, and maybe..."

He let the pause sit there between them.

"...maybe you could help me figure out what the fuck just happened to me. I know you're going to want to diagnose me as delusional, but what I experienced was something different. It was all so...real."

Real. All his patients felt it, knew it for a fact. Deeply delusional thinking could be so intense, so isolating, so cruel. His cardinal rule, though, was never to question the delusion until the patient is absolutely ready to readjust their perception of reality. They need to believe you're along for the ride until they're ready to think critically, analyze the evidence, and begin healing. Sometimes that could take years.

She sat quietly, inspected her trimmed fingernails for a moment, and then ran her fingers through her multicolored hair. Dr. Kairos knew she'd already made up her mind. She wanted to tell him her story. Without waiting for her answer, he began the 5150 questions.

"Are you likely to harm yourself if I release you?"

"No."

"Are you likely to harm other people if I release you?"

"No."

"Will you be able to take care of your food, clothing, and housing needs if I release you?"

"Yes, I can take care of myself." She took a deep breath and looked relieved. "I've been doing it my whole life."

"Now, your turn," he said. "Start from the very beginning. And give it to me step-by-step, moment-by-moment, don't leave anything out. If I think you're holding out on me, our deal is off, okay? It's for your own good."

"You sure? I've got both eidetic and echoic memory. It could take a while."

"Profound insights often hide among the most seemingly insignificant details. I'll make time for you." He pulled out his phone and cleared his calendar. "You've got me for the entire day, if necessary."

Instead of putting his phone back into the pocket of his white coat, he surreptitiously opened AudioFile, pressed *Record*, and set the phone, facedown, on the small table next to his chair. He'd started recording his patients' delusional accounts soon after the publication of *Who's Fooling Whom* in hopes of coming up with a sequel. At first, he'd asked his patients' permission, but he quickly discovered that many of his patients were too paranoid to cooperate. He eventually convinced himself that the benefits of his life's work outweighed his patients' speculative privacy concerns. "Ethics" could be considered just another delusional construct, he reasoned, though he never felt truly comfortable with that imperfect justification.

And now he felt quite guilty about not asking Iris for her permission. But he feared such a request would ruin their deal or, at a minimum, cause her to edit herself, knowing that her every word was being recorded. No, he needed this story, unvarnished and in its entirety. If it was half as astounding as Dr. Simmons had thought it might be, by the end of the day, he'd have a new, brilliant gemstone to add to his collection—perhaps even a crown jewel.

The following is a transcription of what Iris said that day, edited for concision and clarity—and to remove Dr. Kairos's responses and many prompting questions.

FILE A

FILE A.1

I've always slept like the dead. But then, about a week ago, out of the blue, my dreams started jolting me awake in the middle of the night—heart pounding, pouring sweat, and totally freaking out. They weren't nightmares, just snippets of commonplace experiences, set in some historic or prehistoric time. But the visions were alarmingly real—like those hyperrealistic paintings—you know, reflections-of-a-gas-station-in-a-chrome-fender type of thing. It was like I was actually there, in the flesh.

In the first one, I was a young, Italian woman in a blue dress sitting with a friend—sometime in the 1960s—licking melted *nocciola* gelato off my fingers in a beautiful piazza. I looked around and recognized everyone, the boy watching us from a distance, the shopkeepers, the kids playing soccer—and I could *really* taste the cream and hazelnut. When I suddenly awoke in my apartment, I bit down hard. Look, Doc, you can still see the purple semicircle under my fingernail.

The next night, I dreamed I was a young boy in a white robe playing a board game and eating dates with my brother. The board had three rows of ten spaces and instead of dice, we threw four sticks. I jolted awake and grabbed my phone. It took zero seconds to find out that I'd been playing an ancient Egyptian game called *senet*. I'd never even heard of it before. My stomach sank. So the strange game in my dream was... real?

Like I said, I remember everything I experience, so obviously, I'd normally recall learning a game. Could I have possibly absorbed the rules of senet while drifting off to sleep in front of the TV? Or maybe I read something about it when I was very young? And what about the two boys? And the

Italian woman? Were they "real" too somehow? It had certainly felt that way.

From then on, all my dreams contained similarly mysterious and vivid sensory material. Many lacked concrete details, like walking around in a nondescript desert following a herd of goats, stumbling around in a pitch-black cave and smelling smoke, or being strapped to a cradleboard in the middle of a snowstorm. But others were easy to decode, like when I was swabbing the decks of a wooden supply ship named the *São Miguel* and singing in fluent Portuguese, a language I've never studied. I awoke and confirmed I'd been on Vasco da Gama's expedition to India in 1497.

As you can guess, I started to feel a bit unsettled—a little unhinged. Why was this happening? What did these visions mean? I wasn't losing my mind, *per se*, but at one point I found myself wondering if some clandestine government agency had somehow downloaded a bunch of seemingly random information into my head, inadvertently producing my weird nocturnal visions. Ridiculous, I know, but I was grasping at straws.

I tried to act normal—hit the gym, focus on my studies—and hope that the visions would disappear just as they'd arrived. I decided they had something to do with my genius—that I absorb much more information than I'd ever thought possible, like one of those giant NASA antennas picking up everything that comes its way. And now, for whatever reason, all that data was just exploding out of my brain. No big deal. You get it, Doc, I was employing a "necessary delusion," as you say in your book—"a critical bulwark against insanity," as I recall.

But then, a couple days ago, after a particularly disturbing dream in which I inhabited the body of a Cherokee man walking the Trail of Tears, I decided that I needed a real explanation for what was happening to me. I just couldn't fake it anymore. So I grabbed my laptop and headed to the place where I do my best thinking, the Rose and Crown. I ordered a Guinness and my usual, an English breakfast. I'm a bodybuilder, hope to go pro someday, but sometimes you just gotta go for it, and for me, that means good beer and piles of bacon, grilled tomatoes, fried eggs, black pudding, buttered toast, and sausages.

I savored every bite, ordered another Guinness, and then spent all day reading everything I could find on collective unconscious, genetically inherited memories, reincarnation, past life regression, bio-cultural evolution, residual neural codes, parapsychology, metempsychosis, déjà vu, déjà vécu—anything that might help me explain all the alternative realities floating around in my brain. None of it seemed right. In fact, most of it seemed like complete bullshit.

One word, though, kept popping up on my screen: Ayahuasca. It's a centuries-old hallucinogenic brew used by indigenous Amazonian communities. I read a couple articles about "psychonauts," people tripping their balls off in search of answers to ever-elusive questions. Then I watched a video of some meathead from New York, deep in the jungles of Brazil, who thought he was communicating with his dead sister. I was about to turn it off, but then he turned to the camera and said, "Time found you, sister, lost you, then found you again, dear sister..."

He looked completely zonked, but still, his words struck a strange chord in me. I felt something I'd never experienced before: the video felt like some kind of sign.

FILE A.2

A few minutes later, I stumbled upon the website of a self-described Ayahuasca shaman named Clara Sol—a bit on the nose if you ask me—living right here in Palo Alto. Maybe it was the beers or just pure desperation, but I decided to call the number on my screen. A gentle voice, with a Hispanic accent, answered. After a few pleasantries, I told her about my dreams.

"So you're a traveler, very nice," she said in a singsong voice.

"It's actually pretty upsetting."

"Disruptions in the pool of reality can be painful, but they're also enlightening. Follow the ripples, and you'll discover many new things. Come to me, and I'll help you understand."

I almost hung up. As you might guess, Doc, I've never been a crystal-rubbing, voodoo mysticism, Mother-Earth-healing kind of person, but then I reminded myself that I had no other leads. I needed to be open to any type of information—spiritual, psychological, supernatural...even crackpot.

"Come tomorrow morning, early," she continued. "The moon is full, a powerful time for travelers."

And so that brings us to yesterday—though it feels like a lifetime ago—and how I found myself standing on the front porch of a small house in East Palo Alto, a bit hungover, as the early morning sun cast a skeleton of shade across the house's vinyl siding. Clara opened the door wearing a flowing purple gown with embroidered flowers sprouting from the hem. Two long, white braids framed her narrow, wrinkled face.

Thick shades covered all the windows in the living room, a few candles cast a soft, welcoming light, and Tibetan prayer flags hung from the ceiling. The room lacked furniture, just pillows, thick rugs, and blankets neatly spread out on the floor. Normally, I'd have found it all a bit much, but Clara's obvious sincerity allayed my cynicism.

She took me into her galley kitchen, where we sat and discussed the ceremony over a glass of basil lemonade. She laid the raw ingredients of the brew—bright green *chacruna* leaves and stringy Ayahuasca root—out onto the table, showed me pictures of ceremonies from a pile of dog-eared books, and told me how she'd learned everything she knows from her own indigenous tribal leaders, who still lived deep in the jungles of Bolivia. This was clearly not something she just picked up on YouTube.

"This is your medicine," she said, handing me an old rum bottle containing three inches of a thick, reddish-brown, and opaque liquid. "It will help you find your way."

I held the bottle up to the sun, spinning it once to watch the tiny fragments of leaves and roots swirl. "Should I be afraid?"

"We'll start slow and gentle with you, my sweet, troubled traveler." She took the bottle back, poured a small dose into a red enamel pot, and set it on the stove. "And I'll be here the whole time."

"Does it taste good?" I asked.

"Like a panther in the darkest corner of the jungle."

I held my tongue.

Back into the living room, she lit three sticks of *palo santo*, passed them over my head while whispering prayers, and then handed me a small wooden bowl carved with twisting lines like DNA. I took it in both hands and sipped at the inch of warm brew inside. It tasted awful, like dirt and bitter leaves. She told me to drink it quickly.

FILE A.3

Clara began to sing, whistle, and chant. These *icaros*, she had told me, would provide a touchstone, a way to get home. Eventually, she incorporated a small drum, a leaf shaker, and a rattle. As the drugs kicked in, her *icaros* faded away, and I started to feel very alone. Filaments of white emerged from my eyes and wound themselves around my body—a spider's cool silk wrapping me up tight. I didn't panic; there was nothing I could do; I was dead already, or maybe not yet alive. Eventually, Clara's voice began resonating like a tuning fork in my chest, calling me back to myself, back to her living room. When I returned, she was cleansing me again with *palo santo* smoke.

"You travel well, *mi hija*," she said, handing me a second, larger dose of the thick brew in the same wooden bowl.

Instead of feeling still and contained as before, I felt intense movement and began opening out. I vibrated in a giant chamber, peering into the mouths of hundreds of tunnels chiseled into rock. I chose a tunnel, passed into it, and sped into darkness. I emerged into a new cave with even more tunnels. This kept going—the pace and intensity increasing rapidly—until I began to feel divided into many concurrent beings, standing in many different chambers, and choosing many tunnels simultaneously.

Again, I followed Clara's *icaros* back to her living room. My head lay in her lap, and she was stroking my sweaty hair. I had no idea how much time had passed. She let me rest before pouring a megadose of the brew into the wooden bowl.

"It's time for you to find what you're looking for," she said, handing me the bowl.

After taking the third dose, I vanished—for lack of a better word. I became untethered, unplugged, undone—I don't know.

I felt nothing, not bliss, not devastation, just a simple, pure, endless emptiness. Buddha would've been very fucking proud.

Sometime later, I inhabited a shimmering mote of stardust landing on a shoreline. As in my first vision, I remained cocooned in stillness for days, weeks, years, eons. Then quite suddenly, I was pulled into a simple chain, and later I hooked into the lattice of a sugar molecule. We sought out others and began organizing ourselves into stacks. As we split and evolved—learning to self-propel and developing metabolic pathways—my consciousness became infused into an ever-widening swath of life. From that one tiny grain of stardust, I became a component of hundreds, then thousands of light-sensing, hunger- and sex-driven multicellular plants, animals, and fungi.

I know what this sounds like to you, Dr. Kairos: this patient has studied the origins of life, and then she tripped her little ass off. And I can't really blame you for questioning the microbial stuff—it sounds a bit crazy—but then I started catching brief glimpses of human experiences, a parental grunt, a broken toenail, some strange gristle between my teeth.

Remember those dreams I couldn't figure out—the dark cave, the unknown desert, the snowstorm from a cradleboard? As those moments came back into focus, I realized I was witnessing scenes from prehistoric times—but more than just witnessing, I was experiencing them through actual human senses. As I'd suspected, my nocturnal visions had been real.

As I bounced around, I started to understand; I was related to all these strangers. I saw that we shared some common material from that first mote of stardust. We were family, and our connection dated all the way back to the very first days of life on Earth. I started calling them my "stardust relatives."

Once I'd put those pieces together, I felt completely relieved. I now understood my dreams, so I could just relax and enjoy the ride. As I continued, I revisited the Egyptian boy, the *nocciola*-loving Italian woman, and the Cherokee. And

I met many new stardust relatives. With most of them, I could only observe, only see things pass before their eyes like a time-traveling tourist, but with others, I felt much more present, at times even on the cusp of actuation.

Then, nearly imperceptible at first, a thumping began to resonate in my ears. I pushed toward it, toward the rhythm of her heartbeat, her *icaros*. I could hear her chanting and the drumbeat. I followed her songs into a long red hallway. I was going home. I ran until I came upon a red door, which opened onto another red hallway. I encountered another red door and threw it open. Another hallway.

As I ran through a seemingly endless series of doors and hallways, I began to worry—and Clara's *icaros* started to change. The beat became distorted and irregular—more like discordant sonar pings, impossible to trace. I was losing my way, but there was nowhere else to go but straight ahead.

Then I hit a black door. It had a sign taped to it, which read: "Remember your future." I thought it sounded like a joke I'd write to myself, a clue from another life. So I didn't hesitate. I grabbed the handle, pulled the door open, and stepped through, eager to go home.

FILE A.4

I awoke. As my eyes adjusted to my dark surroundings, I noted a series of thick wooden boards, about a foot above my face. For a second, I thought I was in a coffin. Death made sense given the black door. Perhaps Clara had murdered me? Or cast a spell? Maybe she was burying me alive.

Out of the corner of my eye, I noticed a strange wall to my right. I felt a thick blanket on top of me and realized I wasn't in a coffin, but rather in a bunk bed—the bottom bunk, I presumed—shoved up against a stone wall. To my left, I perceived open darkness. The air was cool and dank, like I was in a cave.

As I lay there—frozen in that new stardust relative's body and staring up at those oppressive wooden boards—I felt uneasy, worried. Wherever I was, it wasn't home, and it didn't feel right. I had no choice but to wait and see—and to hope I'd soon skip out of that experience. But something told me I wasn't going anywhere anytime soon. This new circumstance felt more concrete, more hyper-tangible, than any of my other visions.

Some overhead lights flickered on. I heard multiple grunts—guttural protests, it seemed to me, neither animal nor human, from what I could surmise. The body of my stardust relative quickly turned away from the light before I could gather any other details about my surroundings. It curled up, facing the stone wall. More strange sounds began quietly echoing off the hard walls of what seemed to be a large—even cavernous—room.

Something felt off about that whole scene. I wanted to touch the stone wall. If I could just run my fingers across it, I'd know if this experience was real. The hard surface looked wet, but it might've just been worn smooth and slick by years of contact, like a flight of old stone stairs leading down into a medieval dungeon.

But I couldn't move my hands. I recalled the rules—I couldn't control my stardust relatives' movements—and felt a moment of calm. This was just like the other visions. Perhaps I was in some long-forgotten prison in Russia or a mining camp in the High Sierra. I'd spend time here, observing, then I'd move on—with luck, very soon—toward home.

But then, as when you overcome the brief paralysis of waking from a deep sleep, a hand buried under the blanket—a hand that was previously outside of my realm of consciousness—became reality. I—the real me—twitched my right index finger. My heart raced as I registered the kinesthesia of that movement in my own brain, something that had never happened with any of my other stardust relatives. I gently flexed my other fingers and then lay still for a second to process the fact that I might be more of an actor here, not merely a spectator.

I slowly drew my hand up and out of the covers and began to reach for the wall. But the instant my hand came into my field of vision, I froze, and my heart caught in my throat. My skin was *gray*, almost like an elephant's hide, and the back of my hand was covered in short, black hair. My four fingers were elongated, approximately twice as long as normal—narrow, too, but muscular, with chapped knuckles—and my thumb was nearly as long as my fingers with an extra joint, like those people with triphalangeal thumbs.

I made a fist and opened my hand again, hoping to see a change, but everything remained the same. It felt like I was wearing a virtual-reality headset, playing some sci-fi game—only I was pretty sure this was reality-reality, or some version thereof. I gagged, almost threw up, but held it back; I had no idea where I was, when I was, or *what* I was.

I reached out, touched the stone wall, and was overcome by another wave of panic. I could really feel it—as though I was one hundred percent inside that body. The wall was as cold and hard as I'd imagined, but it wasn't wet; its shiny appearance seemed to be the result of years of greasy skin rubbing against it.

I thrust my hand back under the blanket, pulled the covers over my head, and lay perfectly still. The darkness felt momentarily safe. My morning breath, on the other hand, smelled like death. The grumbling noises around me grew louder along with the sounds of feet shuffling. I prayed to every god that ever existed that I'd wake up somewhere else soon. But that was not to be.

FILE A.5

As I lay silent and still, I felt an itch on the bottom of my right foot. I instinctively reached my bizarre hand down my long, foreign legs and relieved the itch by scratching the heavily callused skin on the ball of my foot.

What I discovered, however, provided the opposite of relief: I only had three toes. They were wide, long, and powerful, like they could crush a small bird. I ran my fingers over my three thick toenails. Contrary to my normally well-maintained nails, the edges of these toenails felt thick, rough, and sharp, almost like talons. I wanted to scream, but I was afraid of making any noise. At that point, I remember thinking: there were never any human species with feet like these—this must be a hallucination.

But then, I clearly recalled Clara seated on the floor of her strange, warm living room, the *palo santo* smoke and the Ayahuasca ceremony, and the bitter, muddy taste of that strong, musky brew in my mouth. My unclouded awareness of that other world seemed to negate the idea that this was all in my head. Both worlds seemed equally real, equally crisp. I knew my old life without any gaps—I could remember every detail—while at the same time, everything in that highly disturbing, bunk-bed reality felt entirely authentic: my new body's strange, sickly-sweet odor; the odd coarseness of the blanket on my skin; and the awful furry, dry-mouth feeling on my teeth and tongue, like I hadn't brushed in...well, maybe forever.

I ran my hands slowly up and around my bulging calves; the word "muscular" doesn't even come close to describing them. My skin was stretched tight against the hard muscles and ropy tendons of these new legs of mine. Underneath, I could find no fat. As far as I could tell, I wore no clothes. My hands slid up to my ripped thighs and started to reach for the area you'd guess would be next, but before I could explore my alien genitalia, I suffered an immediate, mind-blowing headache.

In response to the excruciating pain, I pressed my rough palms into my eye sockets and squeezed my forehead with my long fingers. I've heard migraines can make people want to kill themselves; this pain felt worse than death. Maybe I was actually dying. I needed help, so I twisted toward the room and stuck my head out of the covers. All of a sudden, the pain turned to a dull ache, like a dial somewhere had been turned down. I learned later, that was, in a sense, exactly what had happened.

I took a moment to survey my surroundings. The area before me was more cave than room, though the floor was made of rough wooden planks, and dim, square lights set into the stone ceiling cast faint shadows all around. I'd been correct in thinking I was in a type of bunk bed, though the beds were stacked four high, one right on top of the next. Whoever constructed the bunks made them extra long and left just enough room to roll over, but not enough to sit up. I counted three rows of five—for a total of sixty beds. My bed was in the back corner, pressed against the wall.

The whole scene looked like a bizarre, windowless military barrack. All the bunks had already been vacated, except mine. I looked around and noticed a group of tall figures slowly walking away from me, gathering near a distant, open doorway.

Just then, my headache came back, and I felt an urge—I eventually began calling them conformity urges—to get out of bed. I threw the blanket off, stood up, and the headache instantly and completely disappeared. How could my head start hurting so intensely so quickly? And how could the pain stop so abruptly? It seemed physically impossible. Bile, with its sharp taste of alarm, rose from my stomach, coated my throat. My heart pounded in my ears. I again felt like I might be dying. Was I having a panic attack? I steadied myself against the bunk, closed my eyes, and tried not to pass out.

I took a deep breath. Then, in that strange way your mind reaches for old, reliable comforts in times of great need, I thought of Arthur Dent in *The Hitchhiker's Guide to the Galaxy*—my favorite book of all time. The Ardmore Academy required all new students to read it upon admission. I was seven then. I read it repeatedly, backward and forward—a couple times upside-down. During my first semester, I even slept with my dog-eared copy under my pillow for comfort. Back then, Arthur Dent's adventures into the unknown galaxy seemed a lot like my own lonely, strange journey—new town, new school, and many new, strange, and unreliable characters.

And now, standing in that mysterious cave-dorm, I felt like I'd been thrust into a completely different, but nonetheless equally mind-bending story. I recalled one quotation that I'd written in permanent marker on my canvas pencil bag, so long ago: "All you really need to know for the moment is that the universe is a lot more complicated than you might think, even if you start from a position of thinking it's pretty damn complicated in the first place." On the other side of my pencil case, I wrote the most famous quotation from that book in big block letters, "DON'T PANIC," surrounded, of course—because I was still a little girl—by black-petaled daisies.

I opened my bizarre, new eyes and decided to take Douglas Adams's advice; I'd resist panicking and try to embrace the complexity of this unanticipated turn of events.

FILE A.6

Taking a quick look down at my gray body, I noticed that much of it was covered with short black hair, my breasts were almost nonexistent, and my upper-body physique easily matched my ultra-muscular legs. Standing there naked, I felt no shame. Somehow, I knew that nudity was normal here. I checked in between my legs—definitely female.

When I pushed up on my toes and stretched my hands into the air, a bolt of deep exhilaration shot right through me. I'd only ever dreamed of inhabiting a body as exquisitely balanced, muscular, and toned—as finely tuned—as this one. Whoever I was, I ate only what I needed, I didn't skimp on exercise, and I certainly wasn't hungover—maybe never had been. I lowered my weight back onto my heels and flexed my quads, biceps, and glutes as though I was in a bodybuilding competition. I remember thinking: well, this might not be so bad.

I wanted to look around a bit more, but that ridiculously painful headache quickly returned, coupled with an urge to catch up to the group. I resisted for a millisecond, but the headache came on like a hammer to my temple. As I walked toward the group at the far end of the room, the pounding dulled to a throb and then disappeared altogether. I began to understand what was happening and gave the headaches a name: obedience migraines.

I easily caught up to the group as they remained clustered around the room's one narrow doorway. My peers were waiting patiently—for what, I had no clue. But no one pushed forward. All of them just gradually moved toward the exit. I joined at the back. I realized that my previous estimation seemed correct; there were about sixty of us in total, all naked as the day we were born.

Looking closer at individual members of the group, I noticed that we all looked quite similar, with minimal variation in body type and height—skinny and strong and about six and a half feet tall. Everyone had the same three-toed feet, gray skin, and black body hair. I noticed too our outsized craniums, strong necks, and broad shoulders. And we were all females, approximately the same age, though some seemed a bit younger and slightly less wrinkled than others.

We seemed human-esque—bipedal, opposable thumbs, forward-facing eyes—but obviously we were far from *Homo sapiens sapiens*. Out of pure scientific instinct, I gave us a new name, *Homo sapiens griseos*, gray humans, or just "griseos" for short. I thought about *elephantus*, because of the coarse hair and thick, gray skin, but I didn't want to go the animal route. Griseos seemed better; maybe we were highly evolved, and I just hadn't figured it out yet.

But then, maybe not, I quickly began to suspect. First, I started listening to the griseos "talking" to each other all around me. It was language, to be sure, and I could understand it—I was fluent, in fact—but it seemed quite rudimentary. At that moment, most of the griseos were repeating one word—actually more like a long grunt, something like, "*Ghuuuuuuu*," which came across as "Move." They repeated it over and over again, but not in an impatient way, not like what you'd hear in line for a slow-moving supermarket checkout stand. No, they said it in a flatly declaratory manner, as in, "We're currently moving forward in this line."

I eventually started thinking of these types of statements as being conjugated in the "present obvious" and discovered that they used this tense nearly all the time—not great conversationalists, as you'll come to understand, Doc. It seemed to me that even if they had the vocabulary, they still wouldn't have anything interesting to say.

"Move...move...move..."

Then I heard a variation: a griseo next to me conjugated

the verb and said, "I move...I move...I move..."

Some of the griseos ahead of her shifted slightly to the side to allow her to inch closer to the door. They began to repeat, "She moves..." but they didn't call her by a name, just "she." Eventually I learned that they didn't have names. The griseo who cut the line walked outside next, while the rest of us waited patiently—with one griseo stepping through the exit approximately every thirty seconds.

"*Ghuuuuuu...ghuuuuuuu...ghuuuuuuu...*" the monotone chorus resumed.

I thought about trying out my new voice and vocabulary but concluded it would be safer to just stay quiet. I figured I should wait for a more opportune moment to begin to ask the many questions racing through my brain.

Then I heard my mouth form the words, "*Ghuuuuuuu... ghuuuuuuu...ghuuuuuuu...*"

FILE A.7

Which brings up an important topic, one I'm sure you'll find interesting, Dr. Kairos: the configuration of my brain in that foreign body. On the one hand, I retained access to the entirety of my normal mind—that which belongs to me, Iris, the body-building genius currently sitting before you. I felt my "self" fully there, with no diminished capacity or other restrictions on my overly active cerebral cortex—lateral, divergent, and convergent thinking, all systems go. The only part of "me" that was missing? My present body—this corporeal collection of hydrogen, carbon, nitrogen, and oxygen atoms—sitting up in this hospital bed right now.

But I wasn't alone in that foreign brain. The griseo mind that had existed before I showed up was still present. We were like copilots, but more intimate than that because I could also read her mind. I'm not sure I got access to her whole persona, but I got a pretty good lay of land. As the day progressed, I learned that this other brain—my g-brain as I started calling it—knew how to do many things my Iris-brain didn't. And it was surprising—and totally cool—that I instantly understood their language. I discovered, too, that I could sense her emotional state, which was consistently subdued, and her basic instinctual processing.

I soon realized, however, that I couldn't tap into any of her memories or thoughts of the future. I wondered if these types of thoughts were off-limits to me or if they just didn't exist. I concluded at the time that the griseos were simple beings, that they leaned more bovine than human when it came to intelligence. I figured out later that—like everything else in that world—things were much more complicated than they first appeared.

I needed to rationalize this split-brain situation, so I told myself that I had a previously undiscovered form of dissociative identity disorder, with my two separate identities coexisting contemporaneously and without conflict. My Iris- and g-brains operated seamlessly inside. It got even easier when I realized—and I'm not trying to be a bitch here—that my g-brain had left plenty of room for my genius-sized Iris-brain to move in and make myself comfortable for a while. It was like my griseo roommate had been living in a five-bedroom mansion all her life but had never quite made it out of the maid's quarters.

So back to that first morning: a few minutes later, when I neared the exit, I rose onto my toes—relishing again the extraordinary equilibrium of that body—and glanced over the remaining griseos' shoulders. Outside stood a portico, flanked on both sides by open trenches. Six squatting griseos, three on each side, were pissing and shitting into the trenches. When one would finish, the griseo waiting in the doorway would take her spot.

I thought for a moment about turning around and climbing back into my bunk. Maybe I could claim a sick day? I began to turn away, but an obedience migraine flared up inside my skull, and an urge to stay in line rotated me back toward the door. I also realized that I really did need to relieve myself, and soon.

A moment later, I was alone in the vast dorm room, and it was clearly my turn. At a minimum, I wanted to wait until the other griseos had vacated this all-too-public defecation station before I stepped out to do my business. I stayed in the doorway for a moment or two, but the headache quickly grew unbearable. I can't do this, I thought.

Fortunately, my g-brain took over as our shared body stepped out of the dorm and into the portico and got down into a perfectly balanced squat. I noticed pink waves of some type of opaque solution pulsing at regular intervals through the trench and then watched as my waste—round pellets, like a deer—dropped quickly and easily out of me and into the magenta stream flowing below my bare butt. Upon completion, I stood up and walked toward the group of waiting griseos. I guess we don't wipe here, I remember thinking.

FILE A.8

Obviously, what I'm describing here will seem fantastical to you, Dr. Kairos, but I just want you to listen as I continue—listen for the intricate details, the far-out yet plausible oddities, and the extraordinary twists and turns my story takes as I recount my time in that strange place. Could a patient suffering from a delusional disorder come up with a narrative such as mine? I'm confident it was real, but I'm also willing to listen to your diagnosis—so long as you stick to our agreement and let me walk out of here when I'm done telling my story. I know I'm not mentally ill, but I also recall that old saying about crazy people thinking that the rest of the world has gone insane.

But, you know, Doc, maybe the whole sane/insane inquiry should be thrown out the window. Maybe our collective "reality"—our ontological baseline—varies so constantly, so widely, that it doesn't really exist at all. Like your old theory that everyone sees the world through their own set of complicated and delusional lenses. Who, really, is to say whether an apple is truly an apple?

Anyway, after the bizarre bathroom experience, I exited the portico and found myself milling around with the other griseos under a large, canvas canopy—a staging area of sorts, or maybe, more accurately, a pen with no fences. Peeking up, I noted that our spartan living quarters—the underground dorm, the toilet portico, and this odd staging area—sat alone in a shallow, barren valley. It looked a lot like a movie set for some dystopian survival movie.

"*Ghuuuuuuu...ghuuuuuuu...ghuuuuuuu...*" we mooed apathetically as we exited the covered area and began sauntering down a wide, sandy path.

We walked as one naked mass with no obvious leader:

heads down, gray shoulders bumping gently into gray shoulders, hands brushing against neighboring hands. There was no discernable wind, so I could really smell our collective body odor. I tried not to be too grossed out. And I could sense that my g-brain had a very different reaction to the smell. She registered a feeling of comfort and security.

Wanting to avoid attracting attention, I followed the other griseos' example and kept my eyes down. We were clearly in some type of desert environment, though the early morning air did not feel particularly hot, just pleasant. On either side of the path, I noticed sparse vegetation: squat, spiny bushes; clumps of dry, tan grasses; and a few small cacti here and there. I searched the ground for signs of any animal life other than us—bugs, snakes, lizards—but saw none.

Soon curiosity got the better of me, and I began to steal furtive glances at my surroundings. None of the griseos reacted to my quick peeks. It seemed like no one had noticed that I was there, that I had taken up residence in that body. They were, it appeared at the time, innately incurious beings. I brought my head up, cautiously at first, and looked around. I noticed a deep auburn light all around us. The desert plants cast only slight, almost imperceptible shadows. The morning's orange light reminded me of the dark, smoky days here in Palo Alto during bad wildfire seasons.

I looked for the sun and found it behind me, hiding just above the horizon, partially obscured by a band of agitated red-brown haze churning in the distance. I once saw a wild video of a Saharan sandstorm, in which an utterly calm market scene was quickly and brutally swallowed by an angry, dark wall of swirling sand. The cloud in the distance looked like that, except some mysterious force held the roiling miasma at bay. I scanned the horizon and found that we were completely encircled by this curiously contained sandstorm.

Above the ring of brown, a lighter, thinner layer of yellow gave way to a bowl of blue sky directly above us. It was like we were inside a giant eyeball, surrounded by a dilated brown iris, and looking straight up through a perfectly clear pupil at a brilliant summer day. The air felt as clear and clean as any I'd ever inhaled. Nothing, it seemed, penetrated our protected area. I surmised at the time, and confirmed later, that we were inside an enormous climate-controlled dome, which covered an area the size of a large city.

I walked along with my griseo companions, strides relaxed and even-paced just like the rest. But the internal me, my Iris-brain, had kicked into overdrive and was racing to process every fresh observation of this strange, new, inexplicable world. I could only assume that I was still on planet Earth, but there wasn't much to go on. We could've been on Mars for all I could tell—except maybe for the familiar, terrestrial-style vegetation and the circle of blue sky high above.

For a moment, I considered the possibility that I might have stumbled into some prehistoric realm, one that had escaped discovery by present-day scientists. Were these griseos some version of a missing link? Or some ancient branch of evolution that had mysteriously died out? I even thought for a moment: perhaps those stories about aliens inhabiting the earth long before the dinosaurs were actually true. Anything, it seemed, was possible.

But then I thought about the lights in our dormitory, the bunk beds, and even the toilets. They seemed to be derived from human technology. I looked again at the massive protective dome surrounding us, recalled the note on the black door in the red hallway ("Remember your future"), and began to put all the clues together: I was, somehow, visiting a stardust relative in the future. Don't panic, I reminded myself.

We rounded a bend in the path, and I could see much more of the territory protected by the dome. Directly below us, multiple groups of griseos—or herds, as I began to call the clusters of sixty or so beings—were filing in and out of a sprawling, single-story building. About half a mile beyond the flat building sat twenty-four all-glass structures, approximately six stories high and illuminated from within by bright purple lights. Large hovercrafts zipped back and forth between the large, busy structure below and the glowing glass buildings.

As we headed down a set of wide switchbacks toward the single-story building, my fellow griseos started chanting their word for food. Of course, I realized, breakfast in the cafeteria.

FILE A.9

As we entered, a herd of griseos to our left stood up in unison and exited through a door on the opposite side of the large, open room. I noted that they looked very similar to my herd. In fact, everyone in the cafeteria looked pretty much the same. We were all naked—except for a busy group of griseos dressed in simple blue gowns, who were serving and clearing tables—and we all shared nearly identical builds. I was again struck by one anatomical detail—our unusually large heads—but had, at the time, no way of guessing why that would be. As I glanced around, I observed some obvious differences, like a scar on a cheek, a missing earlobe, a rash on a forearm, but otherwise, I thought, we looked like sisters—like hundreds and hundreds of sisters.

When we sat down at the recently vacated set of tables—just enough room for all sixty of us—the blue-clad griseos brought each of us a metal tray. Breakfast consisted of a hard, white square and a cup of warm, cloudy liquid, which I soon began calling monotony milk since it tasted like flour-water and was the only drink we were ever served. The griseos at my elbows dipped their brick-like squares into the monotony milk and gnawed away at the edges. I did the same. The solid substance slowly softened up. The meal in its entirety was nearly tasteless. We didn't have any obvious manners—we smacked, chomped, and slobbered—and no one seemed to care.

As we ate, I took a closer look at my tablemates. Their teeth were stained and worn, but straight, with no obvious missing teeth. Their faces looked somewhat human, though their mouths were wider and their ears bigger. They all had small, dark eyes, narrow and set close together, with a big shelf of a brow jutting out above them. The hair on top of their heads was thick and short. I reached up and ran my fingers over my own face, ears, and hair. They say beauty is in the eye of the beholder, but this felt like a stretch to me.

We were mostly quiet as we ate, with one or another of us mooing "food" at odd intervals, but then, about halfway through the meal, something surprising occurred. The griseos began to converse—well, kind of.

First, a griseo across from me said the word for "ceremony," and a few of the others nodded their heads. One repeated the word, which sounded like *Ooolooo*, and then added a time reference, which my g-brain translated for me: seven days.

"*Ooolooo...ooolooo...ooolooo...*" they chanted in unison.

"Praise the gods," one griseo said—something like *Maaalaaa*—as the *Ooolooo* chant began to die down.

"*Maaalaaa...maaalaaa...maaalaaa...*" they all repeated.

Gods? I wondered. The word was definitely plural but disclosed nothing else.

A few griseos then chimed in, "*Baaabooo*," which roughly translates to "exciting" in English, though excitement doesn't exactly capture the spirit of the word. I sensed some slight anticipation mixed with a noticeable measure of anxiety. As with all griseo emotions, my g-brain's experience of this *baaabooo* felt muted and controlled—watered-down, somehow.

After all the "excitement" had diminished, we thanked the gods again with another round of "*Maaalaaa*" and then stretched our right hands up to the sky and kissed each knuckle on our left hand. Of course, at the time, I couldn't make heads or tails of this strange gesture, though it was obviously connected to our worship of some mysterious collection of gods. And that was the extent of our uber-stimulating breakfast conversation.

After breakfast, we boarded a driverless hovercraft. Inside, there were two long benches facing each other and banks of tinted windows. I walked to the back and sat down. When I thought we'd reached capacity, more griseos piled in. We scooted our muscular butts close to each other, and then closer still. We were all sweating, skin on skin. Eventually my entire herd squeezed in, a feat I hadn't thought possible just moments before.

I felt quite claustrophobic. Not only was I trapped in that foreign body in that foreign land, but now I was being packed like a sardine into that unknown vehicle, headed for god-knows-where. But when I looked around at my fellow griseos and assessed my g-brain's reaction, I perceived nothing but blank contentment and unquestioning calm. I took a deep breath and, as before, allowed my restrained g-brain to take the lead. Everything is fine, its vacant tranquility assured me, there's nothing to worry about.

In fact, during the entire time I spent with the griseos, they only broke from their unwavering passivity one time, which I'll get to soon enough. Aside from that, I never saw any sign of heightened emotion—positive or negative—about anything. They were docile in a way I'd never imagine any human—or humanoid, I guess I should say—could ever be. At the time, I thought they must be innately passive, or just lacking in basic emotional vocabulary, but as I discovered later, there was nothing innate or natural about their quiet, obedient demeanor.

FILE A.10

"Work...work...work..." the griseos repeated in a slow, easy murmur as the hover transport vehicle entered the expanse of glowing purple buildings. For a second, I resisted joining in just to see what would happen, but a conformity urge pushed me into quietly chanting along with my cohort.

In the back of my mind, I heard the seven dwarfs singing, "Heigh-ho, heigh-ho, it's off to work we go." I couldn't help but smile. Oddly, the zygomaticus muscles in my cheeks quickly started to burn. Were we not even allowed to smile here?

The floor blinked red three times, the hovercraft came to a stop, and we spilled out onto the sandy street. I followed the others into one of the tall glass buildings through a large opening that resembled an industrial-sized garage door. Two herds of griseos already stood inside, tightly packed together. My herd was the last to arrive.

After we'd all scrunched in, the giant door came down and sealed shut with a whir and firm clank. A thick spray began to emanate from the ceiling, and the floor filled with a warm, amber liquid. The griseos just splashed the liquid with their oversized toes and milled around. But I wasn't feeling that vibe. I wanted to get the hell out of there. I held my breath and moved to the back, looking for an emergency exit. But of course, there weren't any.

When I couldn't hold my breath any longer, I took a deep breath and found that the mist smelled and tasted vaguely like cinnamon, with just a hint of bleach. The liquid at our feet rose to our ankles and then began to drain away through tiny holes in the floor. The sprayers above turned off. I looked at the gray skin on my arms, legs, and chest and noticed a moist sheen. It seemed we'd just been decontaminated.

For the umpteenth time that morning, I told myself to relax. I'd just have to wait and see how this all was going to play out. It's not like I had any choice; I hadn't seen any ruby slippers, magic wardrobes, or obvious time machines lying around. But in that moment, I remembered Clara's instructions and listened for any hint of her *icaros*. Maybe she'd been calling me back this whole time, and I just hadn't been listening. I closed my eyes and really listened.

Instead of Clara's voice or drumbeats, I heard a loud bell ring three times. I opened my eyes and saw three sets of large double doors sliding open just in front of us. Through the middle door, I could see an enormous room filled with tall, leafy plants, almost like banana trees. The room's bright light shined out on us, casting my neighbors' faces in an eerie, purple glow. I also noticed an intense, tropical aroma flowing out from the room, striking given the arid, mostly odorless quality of the outside air. Flanking the verdant room, the other two doorways opened to reveal wide staircases.

I wanted to explore the lush room directly in front of us, but when I stepped in that direction, I felt compelled to pause. As an experiment, I took one more step toward the enticing purple light and the huge green leaves. A familiar ache bloomed inside my head. I relented, allowed my g-brain to take the reins, and we quickly fell in line at the base of one of the staircases. As I sidled up to the other griseos in my herd, I felt a little shot of dopamine hit my brain. The stick and the carrot, I recall thinking as I followed my herd up the stairs. But how?

At this point, I noticed I'd been walking next to a particular griseo for most of the morning. It wasn't like we'd been connected at the hip, but I kept finding her by my side. She had a small black mole on her left cheek and another on her forehead. A long, jagged scar, like a lightning bolt, marked her calf. Most notably, though, she was missing her left pinky and ring finger. I assumed she'd seen her share of hard times and was probably pretty tough, so I nicknamed her "Perseverance."

And now, here she was, next to me again as we rounded the first landing. As we climbed, other griseos split off into vast, glowing rooms. I counted six floors, just as I'd estimated from the hill above the cafeteria. Our herd had been assigned the two top floors. Perseverance and I, along with a few other members of our herd, turned right and entered an antechamber lined with clean, white smocks and wide-brimmed hats. We donned the smocks and hats and walked into the main room on the top floor.

It felt weird to get dressed. Strange how quickly I'd gotten used to being naked and unashamed. But then, I thought, we humans have always habituated to communal norms, in ways both good and bad.

FILE A.11

The room was about the length of a football field and about half as wide. Hundreds of long, elevated metal boxes stood in neat rows, filled with tiny, gelatinous blue beads and topped with abundant greenery.

In contrast to the lobby, staircase, and antechamber, the ceilings, walls, and floors of the grow-rooms were made of a seamless, transparent material. From certain dizzying vantage points, I could see all the way down to the bottom floor. And the walls were so clear and clean that when I looked out at the landscape, it felt very much like I was standing outside on a precipice overlooking this strange new land. Every square inch of the translucent, luminous material emanated a subtle, diffuse purple light. As I adjusted my hat, I thought about our small, tapered eyes; they seemed perfectly evolved to accommodate this ubiquitous light.

I followed Perseverance's quick strides to one of the metal boxes, out of which grew squat bushes covered in large, red berries. Perseverance began weeding out a few small shoots around the base of the plants. I did the same. We then collected two curved, white bowls from hooks on a nearby glass wall, strapped them to our waists, and began picking the ripe berries. Round and plump, they looked and felt like cherry tomatoes, but they were seeded in a tight, external pattern like a strawberry.

We moved down the long metal box, Perseverance on one side, me on the other. We didn't talk. We didn't look at each other. We just picked. I watched my fingers as they quickly tested each berry, twisted the ripe ones from their calyxes, and left the unripe ones for later. Never once did I squeeze too hard. Never once did I separate the calyx from the plant. And we moved at breakneck speed. I glanced over at Perseverance's rapidly moving hands; her missing fingers didn't seem to hinder her at all. I felt like I'd chosen an apt nickname.

As we continued down the long row, I began to want to eat one of the berries. I wasn't hungry, just curious. I mean, how often do you get to taste something that no one else in the world—this present world, I mean—has ever tasted? I'd likely experience another obedience migraine, but I figured I'd be able to pop one in my mouth before the pain got too bad. I kept picking and dropping berries into my basket until I found the perfect one. It seemed plumper and redder than the rest, like it was calling out to me.

I picked all the berries around it, building up the courage to just go for it. Perseverance had already moved on to the next plant on her side. The headache started before I'd even made my move. I picked the berry and weighed it momentarily in my hand. The headache intensified. Perseverance kept picking. I opened my mouth and tried to shove it in, but my body didn't obey. My head quickly turned away, and my otherwise dexterous fingers dropped the berry, which fell to the ground and rolled out of sight.

I considered crouching down to pick it up, but, by that point, my head felt like it was being split in two, and the urge to stay on task became impossible to defy. When would I learn? I quickly moved on to the next bush. I tried to catch Perseverance's eye, to see if she had any reaction to my lapse in protocol, but she didn't meet my gaze. As usual, her face betrayed no emotion whatsoever. As my headache subsided, I decided to stick to the rules for now, for any act of rebellion, no matter how small, seemed too painful and—pardon the pun—completely fruitless.

When our wide bowls were brimming with the beautiful, shiny red berries, we walked to the center of the room, where approximately twenty clear pipes descended from our penthouse grow-room all the way down to the ground floor. Perseverance opened a hatch, and we carefully poured our berries down a sloped chute into one of the pipes. Through the open hatch, I heard a faraway machine begin to hum. All the equipment seemed relatively sophisticated; that said, I felt certain that you could easily lose a finger or two around here. As the last of the berries disappeared, my mind skipped to a different kid's movie: were we the Oompa-Loompas in this story?

As Perseverance closed the hatch, I realized just how much I really wanted to taste one of those damn berries. And I was getting tired of being manipulated. If we were the Oompa-Loompas, then where was Willy Wonka? Because I wanted to have a word or two.

Perseverance mooed, "Work...work...work..." and my g-brain answered in kind as we walked back toward another row of bushes. It would be days—and in *much* different circumstances—before I finally got to taste the sweet flesh of those illicit berries.

FILE A.12

As the morning wore on, the artificial light in the grow-room changed from purple to orange, which then faded to yellow. Toward midmorning, the light system turned off completely. I looked outside and saw that the sun had cleared the dusty sandstorm surrounding the dome and now shined directly into the room. A ventilation system kicked on, causing the leaves all around us to flutter in the gentle breeze. I closed my eyes and registered the warmth of actual sunlight and the circulating air on my skin. It felt, just for a split second, almost normal, almost like I was home.

Throughout the morning's luminous transition, I watched in amazement as tiny buds on a row of nearby plants grew fat and then blossomed into bright pink flowers right before my eyes, like a time-lapse video. As soon as the flowers opened, I heard buzzing. Approximately twenty metallic bees flew into the area and began to pollinate. The mini-drones resembled real bees in terms of anatomy—head, thorax, and abdomen—but their bronze exoskeletons made them shine like midday fireflies.

The sun continued to climb the strange dome above us. But then, oddly, the daylight momentarily dimmed, like when a low-flying airplane passes in front of the sun. Initially, I thought nothing of it. A cloud perhaps, my mind automatically rationalized. But when I looked up, I saw nothing but blue sky. Just then, I overheard Perseverance mumbling something. I listened closer. In a very hushed tone, she thanked the gods, *"Maaalaaa."* She then held her right hand up to the sky and kissed the knuckles on her left hand, just as we'd all done at breakfast. I looked around and noticed other griseos doing the same.

"Maaalaaa," I intoned. Better safe than sorry.

At about noon, the entire building flashed green three times. Perseverance and I dumped two full loads of berries down the chute, hung up our smocks and hats, and joined our herd as we headed downstairs, murmuring, "Food...food... food..."

The outside air felt like the inside of an oven. Fortunately, we all knew exactly where to go, so loading up took very little time. As before, we all scrunched together on the benches, but I now felt less bothered by the cramped quarters. My claustrophobia from earlier had already been replaced by the spark of something akin to camaraderie.

As we entered the cafeteria, my stomach rumbled loudly. I prayed that lunch would include some of those berries we'd been picking, or at least something tastier than the hardtack and monotony milk we'd been served at breakfast. But my prayers went unanswered.

In fact, every meal I had with the griseos consisted of the exact same fare. It wasn't entirely awful, though. I found that each meal delivered the perfect amount of energy—with no indigestion, food comas, or acid reflux. It was like the ideal fuel for our finely tuned bodies. Of course that didn't stop me from daydreaming now and then about biting into a breakfast sausage and taking a swig of Guinness down at the Rose and Crown.

The afternoon routine closely mimicked the morning's activities, only this time Perseverance and I picked a variety of citrus fruit, something akin to a skinless blood orange. Incredibly, the fruit seemed to have sprung from the very trees those miraculous, metallic bees had been pollinating just a few hours earlier.

How could that be? I wondered. I theorized then that it had to do with some type of genetic modification, and I found out later that I was right. Not only did each citrus tree produce dozens of oranges a day, but they also produced them already peeled. As Perseverance and I repeatedly filled our bowls with the fleshy, red-orange fruits, I ran through everything I knew about genetic manipulation. I remembered reading an article in *The Lancet* about the pros and cons of a technology called "CRISPR"—you know, Doc, where they flip DNA switches to edit genetic expression. The authors foresaw everything from curing cancer and producing record harvests to causing devastating, irreversible changes to the human genome.

I weighed one of the oranges in my hand. Then I inspected the lean, gray hand holding it—genetic modification seemed likely in both cases. And as for the body I inhabited, some human-nonhuman interspecies crossbreeding was likely at play as well. Sounds crazy, right? But scientists, here in 2023, have *already* created viable chimera embryos with DNA from both humans and macaque monkeys. Who knows what we'll be capable of in just a few decades, much less centuries? A little gray skin will likely be child's play, wouldn't you say, Doc?

But from what I'd witnessed thus far, the griseos could not be capable of such scientific endeavors. They couldn't even formulate full sentences. So where was all this incredible experimentation taking place? And by whom?

As I mulled various theories, the sun sank below the thick ring of brown haze, and the translucent walls of the vertical farm lit back up. Afternoon slipped into evening, and the building shined with the light of a seemingly eternal sunset—the photographer's "golden hour." Even Perseverance looked majestic, in an alien goddess kind of way, with rose highlights and stark shadows drawing the beauty out of her strange face. She and I continued to harvest until our section was completely clean of fruit. As at noon, three flashes of a green light marked the end of our afternoon shift, and we headed downstairs.

I tried to get a read on my g-brain. Was she tired? Feeling accomplished after this long day of work? Bored? Frustrated?

Looking forward to a day off sometime soon? Instead, I registered only a sense of flat calm, a deep indifference, like her mind was a ghost town—all the infrastructure still in place but only tumbleweeds rolling through the streets.

Because of the rapidly descending darkness, I expected the outside air to feel chilly, but it was instead perfectly pleasant, like a lovely summer evening after a hot day. The last moments of filtered sunlight cast faint shadows on the ground. In contrast, the circle of clear sky directly above us had turned a crepuscular shade of violet. A smattering of stars looked down on us as we boarded the hovercraft.

As we sped away from the vertical farm, I thought of home. I wondered when, or if, I'd return. Compared with my other visits with stardust relatives, which felt so transitory—like a show you know is going to end—this griseo experience felt so oddly permanent, like real life, like *my* real life. For one thing, I wasn't just a spectator here; I was a full-blown participant. That was definitely different—and very unsettling.

But also, everything in that future world seemed to be happening in real-time, not in snippets or flashes, not in dreamtime. I hadn't realized it before, but my other time-traveling experiences had lacked a certain chronological reality—the real, inexorable tick-tick-ticking away of time. Strange as it may sound given the circumstances, I'd already caught myself getting bored a couple of times—but picking fruit and berries for hours on end, even on the first day of your new life in a bizarre future world, can quickly prove quite tedious.

More than all that, though, everything there felt so visceral, so tangible—the plumpness of the fruits we picked, the texture of the hardtack in my mouth at lunch, a bead of sweat dripping down my enormous gray brow—it all felt so damn real. I feared that, somehow, I'd actually become a griseo and would never return to my "real" life—this, my Iris life. I thought of Clara again, silently begged her for a sign, and listened for her voice. I heard nothing but the low, mechanical hum of the transport vehicle.

A few minutes into the ride, the griseos around me began to coo, "*Haooohaaa*," their word for warmth. I looked out the window and noticed we were headed away from the cafeteria and our dorm. The energy in the hover transport vehicle became somewhat elevated, though for griseos, that was only a matter of the slightest degree. Though I couldn't be sure, it seemed we were going someplace special.

We traveled across an empty stretch of desert, gaining elevation along the way, and soon pulled up to a cluster of small, white, windowless tents nestled at the base of a large, crescent-shaped butte. The tents reminded me of a field hospital or an old pioneer camp. As I stepped out of the transport vehicle, I could see in the distance many similar configurations of tents—one for each herd, I assumed—dotting the butte.

The butte was situated next to one edge of the dome, so when I turned around, I could see the entire expanse of our protected territory. The vertical farms sat in the middle of the central plain and had begun to glow purple again. I looked beyond the glowing sprawl and saw, in the distance, the outlines of five large cafeteria buildings—not just one, as I'd assumed that morning. Above them, a constellation of dimly lit structures spanned the rolling hills on the other side of the dome. They were, I realized, the portico-entrances to the many scattered sleeping quarters that housed the griseo population. Dozens of zigzag switchbacks cut the face of the hills like a lightning storm. I did some quick math and estimated that as many as five thousand griseos likely lived and worked under that one dome.

The refrain of *haooohaaa* intensified, and my fellow griseos began to fan out along lighted paths toward the tents, each about the size of a large canopy bed. I allowed my g-brain to lead our shared body to our designated tent. A curtain magically opened as I approached, revealing a long metal pod—like a coffin, but with rounded edges. The pod also opened automatically, and I climbed in.

When the lid closed, the pod began to fill with warm water. I talked myself out of panicking. If they wanted to kill us all, there were many more efficient ways of doing so. A pillow inflated under my head as the water level rose, keeping my face just above the waterline, and I felt somewhat reassured.

Swirling lights appeared above me—seemingly inspired by the northern lights, if I were to guess, only these swathes of color were hypnotic. As my eyes followed the trails of red, green, and orange, I began to feel superhuman—energized, confident, and invincible—but also as soft as a sleeping baby—vulnerable, soothed, and, above all, loved. Maybe it was the mesmerizing lights, or maybe it was something in the water, some exquisitely balanced mix of transdermal drugs, I don't know, but I'd never really felt so optimally comforted, so completely peaceful and reassured.

At some point, I realized there really *was* something in the water, many things in fact, tangible, slick, and active, moving and caressing, teasing and exploring, stimulating and then slowly but firmly penetrating—I'm telling you this, Dr. Kairos, because you asked for the entire story—"profound insights frequently hide among seemingly insignificant details," if I'm not mistaken—and because I'm not shy about sex. Anyway, when I tried to figure out what was making me feel so good, I discovered that I couldn't move a muscle.

In that blissful, paralyzed state, I multi-orgasmed like I'd never thought possible. It was insane. I have no idea how long it lasted because time disappeared in my pure euphoria. Eventually, sadly, the pleasure probes—or whatever they were—retreated, the light show ended, and the liquid drained. As the lid opened back up, I recovered my ability to move. I considered staying, hoping for a second session, but the now-familiar pain in my head returned and a conformity urge quickly forced me up and out.

My herd and I all exited our little tents at the same time and formed a loose ring on a flat spot near the hover transport vehicle. "*Haooohaaa...haooohaaa...haooohaaa...*" we repeated quietly, our collective post-coital bliss softening our voices into whispers. We then got down on our knees and chanted *Maaalaaa* repeatedly, thanking the gods. Then, as before, we each held our right hand up to the sky and kissed each knuckle on our left.

As we sped back toward our cafeteria, I dubbed the pods "ecstasy coffins." But it wasn't just sexual; every aspect of my being, psychological, emotional, intellectual, artistic...everything felt like it'd been perfectly stimulated, soothed, and coddled. I wish I could've brought one of the coffins back with me. I'd either become the richest woman in the world or I'd just plug that sucker in, and you'd never hear from me again. Probably the latter. It was just that good.

FILE A.14

At dinner that night, my herd grunted again about the upcoming ceremony, but provided no further details, just expressed that same measured sense of excitement and anxiety from before. One of the griseos indicated that the ceremony was now more like six days away. We all agreed and got back to gnawing away at our hardtack.

So frustrating, I thought, we're so damned limited. I wanted to learn more, but no matter how hard I tried, I couldn't ask a question—any question. I guessed at the time that they must have become so bored, so regimented and incurious, that, over generations, the vocabulary needed to formulate a question had atrophied until it was gone. It didn't sound quite right, but it was all I could come up with.

A few minutes later, one of the griseos at our table suddenly stood up and showed us her protruding belly.

"Pregnant," she said, flatly.

Now that was something I wasn't expecting.

Other griseos at the table answered, "You pregnant." The mother-to-be sat back down, and we all continued eating.

After I got over the griseos' lack of excitement about this news, I began to wonder what an infant griseo would look like. Gollum, perhaps? No, that was too mean—and inaccurate; Gollum had giant eyes and scrawny arms.

I took a second look at the pregnant griseo and recognized her. She'd sat right across from me in the hover transport vehicle at the beginning of the day. She'd struck me as the youngest of our herd, but I hadn't noticed any sign of pregnancy. Could I really have missed the telltale bump? Especially given that we were all so fit and naked? And she wasn't just a little bit pregnant; she looked ready to pop.

As I finished up my hardtack and monotony milk, I began

connecting a few unsettling dots. I recalled the pollinating metallic bees and the seemingly impossible appearance of ripe, peeled oranges just a few hours later. I thought about the ecstasy coffins and all their expertly calibrated probes. The bees and the oranges, the coffins and that pregnant griseo's belly—no, I thought, that's not possible. But what did I know about impossibility at that point? I checked my own midriff. I felt as un-impregnated as ever.

"*Maaalaaa*," I whispered, resisting the urge to smile.

The pregnant griseo's announcement raised a cavalcade of questions in my mind. Where did all the griseo children live? And what about the males? Had they been replaced by the ecstasy coffins? No males would mean what? Infanticide? Or maybe they controlled every aspect of the splitting cells in each embryo? Nanotech-sperm? And the elderly griseos? Was there a Florida dome? All I'd seen were young to middle-aged females.

Toward the end of dinner, two griseos dressed in tan gowns approached our table. The pregnant griseo stood up. She seemed, remarkably, even bigger than before. We all muttered, "She pregnant...she pregnant...she pregnant..." as she turned and waddled away. She didn't say goodbye to anyone— no hugs, no tears in any griseo eyes. She just left with the two escorts. One of my tablemates said something like "Mothers' Home," and the others agreed.

When we got back to the dorm, I collapsed into my bunk. My g-brain curled our shared body up into a tight ball, with our back pressed against the stone wall. So I'd been right; the worn look of the wall I'd noticed that morning had indeed been created by years of touching, in this case, by many greasy, griseo spines rubbing, night after night, against the hard stone.

I was exhausted, but I resisted sleep and focused all my remaining energy on thoughts of life back home. My dreams had gotten me into this mess—perhaps they'd also prove to be my ticket home. This became my routine during my time with the griseos, but each morning, I'd awake to the same greasy stone wall; the thick, wooden boards just inches above my wide, gray forehead; and the morning grunting of my fellow griseos as they rolled out of bed to face another day of work in the vertical farms.

FILE A.15

For the next few days, we followed the same schedule. I tried to stay calm, but of course there were moments when I completely freaked out about being there, triggered often by the smallest details. Most notably, the ugly talons on my three toes posed a real and consistent mental challenge for me. Those thick, ragged toenails—I so desperately wanted some heavy-duty clippers and a nail file. Or, even better, I just wanted to look down and see my own decently manicured, five-toed feet. And also, though my body always felt clean after our daily pilgrimage to the ecstasy coffins, I would've killed for five minutes with my electric toothbrush. My molars were literally furry. For the most part, however, I just tried to go with the flow and keep faith that eventually I'd return home.

I mentioned feeling momentarily bored on that first afternoon, but I had no clue, then, how completely, mind-blowingly boring griseo life would prove to be. Hours and hours of the same damn thing, over and over. It drove me crazy. How did they do it? Did they want anything beyond that mundane, workaday life?

No matter how hard I tried to find answers close to home, I couldn't get anything out of my g-brain's flat psyche. And at times, I wanted to reach over and grab Perseverance by her shoulders—shake her until she'd tell me something, anything, about herself. But, like I said, I couldn't even formulate a simple question, and all I ever heard from her, from any of them, were the same simple grunts over and over—those same ridiculous declaratory statements repeated ad nauseam.

But then, too, I had to ask: what did the intensity of my boredom say about me? I'd never quite realized just how much our attention economy had wired my brain for constant stimulation, had altered my ability to sit still, work quietly, just enjoy the pleasures of simply existing for a little while. I couldn't believe how much I missed my phone, computer, and TV—no Instagram or TikTok, no texts or emails, no old movies, no streaming sitcoms, reality shows, or binge-worthy dramas to scratch the itch, fill the void. Just long, slow days spent in near-complete silence with my dull griseo compatriots.

For a day or two, I convinced myself that I'd been gifted the perfect opportunity to start meditating. I've read some Thich Nhat Hanh, and I once watched an entire seminar on YouTube about mindfulness and being "omnipresent," so I figured I knew enough to get started. I quickly realized, though, that my minimal theoretical knowledge did not translate to any form of actual practice, and that it would take a lot of time and real, hard work to undo my calcified expectation of endless entertainment and information. My mind simply could not be stilled.

As I watched them move peacefully through their days, I began to think that maybe the griseos were not so dumb after all—were in fact *more* evolved than we are. Maybe they were the high priestesses of calm, a special unit of nuns inhabiting this strange domed convent. There certainly was something very monastic about their lives—except, of course, for their daily dose of ultra-soothing machine-sex. Sorry, Doc, I guess I'm kind of stuck on that detail. Anyway, they barely talked, had no possessions, and quietly went about their humble lives, eating only what they needed to sustain their exceedingly healthy bodies and accomplishing basic, manageable tasks throughout the day. And, of course, they spent significant time expressing gratitude—thanking the gods for this and that throughout the day.

But that's where my rationalization of their religiosity and potential intelligence started to crumble. The griseos' prayers were nothing more than rote mantras to some unidentified, nondescript collection of "gods." I looked everywhere but found no temples, statues, or shrines. No stories to illuminate these gods. Their religion lacked complexity, was held together only by blind devotion.

And their near-constant piety struck me as odd—misplaced even—given how hard they worked every single day and how little they got in return: our bunks were cold and hard; our toilets, little more than a flushing ditch in the ground; and we were never served anything other than monotony milk and hardtack—breakfast, lunch, and dinner. With all the food we were producing in those vast vertical farms, it just didn't seem fair.

And how was I to reconcile the clear disconnect between the remarkable technology of that world—the metallic bees, the highly advanced farming techniques, the enormous dome—and our base level of existence? While the whole nuns-in-a-convent thing had initially been interesting to consider, as the days wore on, I became increasingly uncomfortable with the obvious signs of exploitation. At times, Marx's "religion is the opiate of the masses" ran on a loop in my head.

On my fourth day with the griseos, we awoke to near-total darkness in the dome. From what I could tell, the sandstorm had intensified, covering the entire dome with a deep brown haze. There was just enough light to get around, but it was so gloomy in there. The entire landscape looked so bleak, so dead, and the artificial glow of the vertical farms turned downright eerie in that daytime darkness.

The sky was dark the following day as well. By the third day of gloom, I felt increasingly restless, irritated, and hopeless. Any temporary peace I'd managed to maintain about being stuck there had shriveled in the brown darkness. Every night before bed, I mined my memory for exact details of my apartment in Palo Alto, the lab I work at, my favorite gym, and even the Rose and Crown, hoping to trigger whatever inscrutable time/space mechanism had transported me to that monotonous future. I also relived every moment of my interaction with Clara, the Ayahuasca ceremony, and my visits with stardust relatives. Maybe I'd missed some key detail, some critical clue. But no matter what I tried, nothing worked. Each morning, I awoke distraught, discouraged. During those long, dark days, I just let my g-brain take over the mechanical operations of our body while I brooded.

In my desperate state, I could no longer ignore certain obvious questions and gnawing suspicions. Along with the feeling of exploitation, I just couldn't get over the blanket lack of autonomy we all experienced. I'd stopped testing the obedience migraines and conformity urges because there really was no point—they were one hundred percent effective one hundred percent of the time. But I'd had enough. It was completely ridiculous; one misstep and, bang, you're devastated by an excruciating headache and made to get back in line. I desperately wanted to know who was manipulating us. And how? And why? I felt imprisoned by my own mind. And I just couldn't ignore the fact that there had to be someone somewhere pulling all the levers.

Pay no attention to that man behind the curtain! I thought. Funny how little I knew then.

FILE A.16

A day or two more like that and I would've completely lost my mind. Was this really going to be my life forever? But then we emerged from our cave the next morning to completely clear skies. Even the persistent ring of brown haze on the horizon had disappeared. As we descended the path to the cafeteria, I observed the sun's early light reaching out onto the wide plain below. The image of a tiger stretching its paws after a long nap sprung into my mind. I couldn't quite believe it; I felt renewed, refreshed—rejuvenated, even. Strange how linked they are, mood and weather, eh, Doc?

After breakfast, our hover transport vehicle drove right past the vertical farms, sped out to the edge of the dome, and pulled up to a large portal. I was surprised at first, but then I recalled that the ceremony was scheduled for the following day. Sunny skies and a break in the routine—I began to feel downright cheerful. We exited the main dome into a tunnel made of the same clear material. We zoomed along for about ten minutes before entering a similar, but smaller, dome, which covered a wide, flat playa.

The hover transport vehicle pulled up next to hundreds of tall cages, all neatly arranged in concentric circles. Each cage—empty at the time—had a sturdy metal platform, a cylinder of widely spaced gold bars rounded at the top, and a tall gate—something like a cross between Tweety Bird's cage and those used by divers to observe great white sharks. At the center of the circles of the cages stood a huge, round altar—think Super Bowl halftime show—with sets of stairs leading up to it.

Two large vehicles with open beds filled with produce from the vertical farms awaited us at the edge of the configuration of cages. We grabbed familiar white baskets and began carrying loads of fruits and vegetables from the vehicles, through the rows of cages, and up to the altar. As we worked, the air turned crisp and cool, like the inside of a refrigerator. Later, another herd of griseos showed up to help, and then another. Fully loaded cargo vehicles arrived throughout the morning.

We ate hardtack and monotony milk out on the playa for lunch—a picnic with the griseos, who would've guessed? And then we got back to work. The last few vehicles contained only flowers: big blooms akin to roses, only the size of my griseo cranium; towering and nearly transparent orchids that shimmered purple in the dying light of the day; and piles of giant, heavenly scented gardenias. By the time we were ready to head back, the altar looked like an enormous, surreal, still-life painting by some long-dead master.

The next day, I awoke to the sound of chanting. As we lined up for the latrines, instead of "Move...move...move..." my fellow griseos cooed the word for ceremony, "Ooolooo...ooolooo...ooolooo..." and I was happy to join in.

After breakfast, we were shuttled out to the ceremony site. We exited the vehicles and began to fan out, walking toward our preassigned cages. My g-brain knew exactly where to go. As we wove our way through the curved rows, I began to notice something remarkable. Many of the griseos started skipping or galloping. One broke into a full-on sprint, waving her arms in the air. Some did flips. Some cartwheeled. Many stopped to roll around on the ground, bathing in the white dust of the playa.

The chant of "Ooolooo...ooolooo...ooolooo..." grew louder, real emotion pouring out. Then some of the griseos started screaming their heads off—a terrible, pig-like squeal. I wasn't sure what was going on, but one thing was obvious; the impassive, droning griseos had transformed into...I honestly don't know how to do it justice. Like Friday night, and the factory whistle had just blown, but that sounds too tame. It was more like hundreds of coked-up ten-year-olds bursting out onto the playground after a month of rain. I know that sounds weird, but it *was* weird—wild-rabid-animal weird.

I sensed a new, unbridled energy blowing up in my g-brain. I was very curious, so I let the original owner of our shared body take control. She swung our arms side to side, stuck our tongue in and out like a Māori warrior, and then kicked our legs up in the air like a Rockette. She stopped and shouted "*Ooolooo*" so loud it hurt.

A heavy bass beat, emanating from somewhere above, began to resonate throughout the dome. We griseos stumbled and danced and somersaulted our way to our designated cages. When we climbed in, each in our own cage, the gates closed and locked automatically. The cages were generous enough to allow for our wild gesticulations. Many griseos arched their backs and rolled their heads around and around in circles. Others turned to face the altar, gripping the bars, running in place, eyes wide, faces spasming.

I looked to my left and saw Perseverance's cage right next to mine. She smiled at me. What a strange sight. Was it friendly? I wasn't sure. Rhesus monkeys smile when anxious. Other primates show their teeth to demonstrate anger, aggression—a readiness to fight, to compete. What were we griseos to each other? Sisters? Companions? Rivals? I still had no idea.

I smiled back but she'd already turned away. I kept smiling and wondered why the muscles in my face didn't hurt like before. In fact, everything felt so loose and free—no obedience migraines or conformity urges here. We were in full-on, free-form party mode. I laughed—such a strange sound, the griseo laugh, but it felt so good. Of course, in retrospect, I see the irony of finally feeling free while locked inside our own little cages.

The drumming intensified, and thunderous soundwaves shook the bars of the cages, the sand on the ground, and even—I could've sworn—the giant dome above. Each deep boom made my gut ache with a strange, wonderful pleasure.

All around me, griseos stomped their feet, shook their heads violently, pulled at their hair, nipples, and ears.

We all started pointing up as an area of the sky began to tremble. A narrow slit opened in the skin of the dome. As the edges receded, the material of the dome wrinkled, like we were in a giant, swollen abdomen, and a surgeon high above was pulling it open. The hole in the dome grew into a huge oval, allowing the intense heat of the real outside world to rush in.

Two aircraft descended into the dome, the aperture closed, and we began to shriek, howl, and bark like dogs. The ships looked like massive metallic pills with no obvious form of propulsion. One was approximately the size of an aircraft carrier. The other was about a quarter of the size of its counterpart. They flew silently and shined like mirrors, reflecting distorted views of our cages back to us.

We yelled, "Welcome gods...welcome gods...welcome gods..." And I remember thinking: so the "gods" are *real*?

The larger aircraft swooped down over our heads, hitting us with a thrilling blast of air and kicking up a rooster tail of dust. We spat, cheered, and rubbed the dirt into our sweaty, naked bodies. The ship came to a stop directly over the altar and opened an enormous cargo door.

The altar shuddered for a moment, and then, incredibly, began to lift off the ground. Thousands of pounds of produce and the huge structure of the altar itself simply floated straight up into the belly of the ship. When its cargo doors closed, the ship lit up in a stunning kaleidoscope of colors—reds, yellows, and blues flowing from nose to tail—and circled the dome.

"*Maaalaaa...maaalaaa...maaalaaa...*" we roared. I watched the ship and its mesmeric colors as it zoomed around the interior of the dome, and I wondered: what exactly were we so thankful for? My g-brain was filled with pride for our offerings to the gods. She was thankful too, I sensed, for their endless protection. That sounded all wrong to me, but I decided to just let it go for the moment. The large ship's exterior eased into a soft, red glow and then exited the dome with its bounty.

FILE A.17

An ethereal flute-like melody backed by a highly synthesized rhythm echoed throughout the dome. The remaining ship flew gracefully above us—diving, spinning, and hitting multiple loop-the-loops in time with the music—and we swayed back and forth in our cages, enjoying the airshow. Then the ship began flying in circles, slow and low, right over our heads. We stood on our tiptoes and extended our arms as high as we could—hoping to reach it, to touch the divine.

At first, I thought this might be a farewell flyover, but then the ship stopped, and a small circular port opened. One of the griseo cages rose off the ground, just as the altar had before. The griseo squealed with delight—and the rest of us watched jealously—as she flew up into the ship. The cage fit perfectly into the opening, and the portal closed. My g-brain repeated "chosen" in our head.

"Gods' Home...Gods' Home...Gods' Home..." we all began to chant as the ship cruised around again. With each passing moment, our chorus grew louder until we were shouting at the tops of our lungs.

I couldn't tell if we were being assessed or teased, but I didn't really care. I could tell by my g-brain's excitement that becoming one of the chosen was the ultimate prize, an unrivaled privilege—like winning the mega-millions lottery. For my part, I figured any place called "Gods' Home" would have to be better than the griseos' no-frills work camp, and I was ready for an upgrade.

The ship passed right over the top of our cage, a mere ten yards away. I joined with my g-brain and, together, we waved and jumped. I felt like a fan at a basketball game freaking out for a free T-shirt—though the stakes here seemed significantly higher.

But it was the cage right next to us, Perseverance's cage, that lifted from the desert floor. She jumped, laughed, and cried with joy as she disappeared into the portal. The ship moved on, and my g-brain registered devastation.

I watched the ship pick up three more griseos on the far side of the circle of cages, and I started to feel real disappointment. What was wrong with us? I wondered. Didn't we work just as hard as the others? Then the ship came back in our direction, and my hopes were rekindled. From what I could sense, there was only one spot left. I let my g-brain take the lead, for she was an old pro at this, and our shared body held nothing back. Waving and screeching, she put every ounce of manic energy we had into getting noticed.

And somehow, her freak-out worked—or, at least, that's what I thought at the time. Our cage shifted in the sand. And then we were airborne, flying above that flat plain and all those caged griseos. I fed off my g-brain's ecstasy. We'd done it! We'd won! After all the years of toil, we were finally headed to Gods' Home.

Just before entering the ship, I looked down and saw a griseo from my herd climbing out of her cage. They'd been released. The ceremony was over. The unlucky griseo looked defeated, shoulders slumped as she stepped down onto the sandy ground and started walking toward the waiting hover transport vehicles.

Then she turned and glanced up at me, and for a split second our eyes met. I wondered how long she'd known the griseo me. I waved goodbye, smiled, but she didn't wave back, didn't return my smile.

FILE A.18

My cage had entered a solid tube. I felt its smooth edges all around me, about three inches from the bars of my cage. The remnants of the ceremony's frenzied energy still coursed through my veins. It was hard for me to stand still in the pitch dark and wait. As the seconds ticked past, though, I noted my g-brain sliding right back into her normal passive state.

I held onto the bars as the ship accelerated. As you can imagine, Doc, I was dying to see the view, but the black tube stayed in place. Now I felt like a bird in a covered cage. Eventually, I felt the ship slow to a stop. A minute passed and then another. I knocked on the tube. No answer. I began to sweat. Where was the welcome party? I ran my fingers up and down the curved wall of the tube, looking for a latch or some other type of release mechanism, but found nothing. We six griseos had been chosen by the gods, but chosen for what?

The complete darkness began to play tricks on my eyes. Imaginary stars illuminated my peripheral vision. I kept turning around and around to see them, to catch them before they disappeared. I felt dizzy and disoriented. I thought I might pass out or throw up. I kept losing my balance, falling backward, forward, side to side. I banged my head on the solid bars of the cage and thought, this can't really be my reality. But then I started wondering if "reality" was even a real word. I tried to say it out loud but registered only my own strange griseo grunting.

I began to doubt that I'd ever return to my normal life. How did I get so far away from home—stuck in that strange time, in that strange body, in that blacked-out cage? Who am I now? I wondered. Just a transient spirit? And who was I before? Just a momentary collection of insignificant stardust?

My g-brain was no help. Her frenzied persona had disappeared. She'd begun to simply repeat, "Gods' Home," waiting patiently—faithfully—for whatever lay ahead.

Just when I thought I couldn't take it anymore, a cloud of the familiar, cinnamon-scented decontamination vapor filled the dark tube. I felt surprisingly reassured; at least something was going to happen. Starving to death in utter darkness isn't on my bingo card.

Then multiple padded pistons emerged and dug into my midsection, momentarily demobilizing me, and a needle poked me right in the butt. I reached around to resist, but the mechanism was gone in an instant. My mind flashed to one terrible Halloween and a haunted house with hands coming at me from every direction, grabbing my ankles, ass, and boobs. I'd punched and kicked my way out of there. Standing in that cage, I felt the same tide of anger. I began banging on the side of the tube as hard as I could.

But whatever drug I'd been given rapidly took effect and melted away my concerns, replacing them with indifference, lethargy, and, more than anything, incredible hunger. My eyelids drooped, my face relaxed, and I rolled my head around, enjoying the deep stretch of muscles and tendons in my neck. I was suddenly too tired to remain standing, so I sat down in the dark and started dreaming about all the different kinds of food I wanted to eat.

A few minutes later—or was it hours?—my cage shuddered and began to drop out of the black tube, startling me to attention. I was still hungry as hell. I got to my feet and held onto the cage's bars as it descended into a small, brightly lit, and windowless room. I waited for my pupils to constrict and looked around, hoping to find something to eat.

Two griseos stood to my left, and three to my right, including Perseverance, who was right next to me as usual. Still in our cages, we had been arranged in a row against one wall. The room looked like an empty operating room, glistening white and spotless. I looked across the room and saw six wide shelves.

And on the shelves? Piles of food—and I don't mean jugs of monotony milk and stacks of hardtack. Someone had heaped a smorgasbord of fruit, vegetables, bread, nuts, and some items I wouldn't even dare categorize onto six metal trays about the size of a baking sheet, one for each of us. Peering through the bars of my cage, I instantly recognized the berries and the citrus from the vertical farms and got really excited. Would we finally get to taste the fruits of our labors? Were we actually about to become gods?

The bars of our cages detached from their bases and then disappeared into the ceiling. We remained on the elevated pedestals like a display of doped-up Oscars, awaiting instructions. Perseverance momentarily swayed back and forth to my right. She looked as high as I felt. She said, "Food," and I repeated it. The others joined in: "Food...food...food..."

We stayed put, though, not knowing if it might be a trick—a trap or an illusion. We griseos were conditioned to obey, not to make decisions—even simple ones. But I needed to put something in my mouth ASAP. I thought, what's the worst that could happen? An obedience migraine? I'd already survived quite a few of those. And now it seemed the rules might've changed. The glistening pile of colorful food was definitely worth the risk.

So I stepped off the base of the cage, walked straight to the tray in front of me, and picked up one of the red berries I'd been craving since that first day in the vertical farm. When I brought it to my mouth, my body didn't rebel—no loss of dexterity or involuntary head-turns, no headache, no urge to refuse. Quite the opposite, in fact; this is what I was supposed to do. I bit down, and the flesh dissolved into the most luscious liquid I've ever tasted. Maybe we *were* gods now; the berry sure tasted like ambrosia. I ate ten more in an instant. The other griseos realized that they'd better get in on the action. They came over, and then we were all standing at our trays, stuffing our faces.

I pounded down three enormous biscuits filled with a tangy red filling. I ate a pile of the peeled citrus fruits I knew from the vertical farm, and then I moved on to giant, indigo grapes, chunks of purple grapefruit, and handfuls of some strange chocolates that fizzed like Pop Rocks in my mouth. There was no meat—in the back of my mind, I still yearned for the Rose and Crown's English breakfast—but with so much delicious food in front of me, I wasn't about to complain. To wash it all down, we had large bowls of thick brown ale, honeyed and milky, topped with a creamy head and laced with something that smelled and tasted like lavender.

The griseos next to me chomped and slurped. We were like pigs at the trough. When a tray of food started to look a little empty, it'd float up—like magic—into an opening in the ceiling and a fresh, full tray would descend in its place.

My hunger was limitless. I remember wondering how my griseo stomach could accommodate so much food. Did we have multiple stomachs? I started contemplating everything I knew about ruminant digestive systems, but then I thought, do I really care? I just wanted to eat. I was like an artist in the zone, totally absorbed in the act of consumption.

I remember telling myself, isn't this, in the end, the only, *real* purpose of life? What else is there? Worms, wolves, whales—every organism's first line of code is simply to eat as much as it can.

FILE A.19

I quickly lost track of myself and my surroundings. I have no recollection of finishing that first meal. I do remember a wide, plush seat—like a futuristic La-Z-Boy—emerging from the floor. It conformed to my butt and legs with something like thick memory foam and later reclined into an ultra-soft bed.

I awoke on my back, feeling groggy and disoriented. I remembered dreaming that I'd continued eating and drinking many hours after I'd passed out—but then, too, those visions felt more real than dreamlike. How long had I been out? Had I been eating while asleep? Or fallen asleep and woken up to eat multiple times?

The white light in the room was too bright, so I kept my eyes closed. I was exhausted and needed to pee. But I felt too weak to move. I couldn't hold my pee any longer, so I just let it go. I felt no wetness, just relief.

I may have fallen back asleep; I don't know. Keeping track of a timeline in that white room was impossible. In any case, sometime later, my La-Z-Boy lifted me into a seated position. I could barely focus my eyes. Through the haze of my blurred vision, I could see that three of my fellow selectees were passed out cold. The other two were back at their shelves, hunched over and eating. But there was something very different about them. I rubbed my eyes—my vision cleared a bit—and looked again: somehow, they'd all gained an incredible amount of weight.

I looked down at Perseverance, who was strapped to her bed right next to me and fast asleep. Her obese chest and stomach rose and fell heavily with each breath. Her mouth hung open, and a thin line of drool spilled down her cheek. Much of her abnormally swollen body was covered in berry juice, breadcrumbs, and smears of chocolate froth—evidence, it seemed, of many frenzied meals. I also noticed that she had a large tube sticking out of the side of her torso and another, smaller one that disappeared between her chubby legs.

I then looked down at my own body and couldn't believe what I saw. Like the others, I'd gotten very big. How long had we been locked up in there? And just how many "meals" had we consumed? I couldn't remember much after those first few moments of eating. I wanted to get up and find someone with some answers, but I was strapped to my La-Z-Boy contraption. When I looked down, I saw that I too was covered in old food and had a colostomy tube and a catheter coming out of my enlarged body.

When I reached down to pull the straps off my legs, I felt a needle poke me in the ass, straight up through the seat of the La-Z-Boy. My whole body instantly relaxed. My eyelids grew heavy again. My mind turned to goo. My insatiable appetite returned. Why would I ever want to leave this place? Where else would I want to be? I've got all my needs taken care of right here. Fresh food descended onto the shelf in front of me, and despite the faintest echo of an alarm ringing in the back of my head, I began shoving fistfuls of fruit and bread into my mouth and slurping down a thick, neon orange shake. Then came another long period of being almost completely blacked out.

As I sit here now, I can only recall some snippets of that time; they're detached, out of order, like flipping through random photos on a phone. Mostly, I just remember flashes of pain: my gut burning with inflammation; the muscles of my jaw aching; my mouth lined with bleeding sores. Seconds later, however, I'd receive my shot, feel the drug-induced hunger wash over me, and go right back at it, eating and eating until I couldn't eat anymore—and then, I believe, eating even more.

Toward the end of that strange time, I began to lose myself. When I'd surface for a moment and could gather a thought or two, I'd focus only on the drugs and food. Craving and con-sumption—they became my everything. I stopped thinking about my past, my future, or how I was going to escape. I even stopped thinking of home. I just needed my drugs and food.

FILE A.20

I awoke—truly awoke—in a semi-recline. There was no food, and my head felt clearer than it had for a long time. I stared at my empty shelf, awaiting my shot and fighting my growing apprehension. I needed the needle. I wanted to binge. After a few quick moments, I knew I was in trouble. I was too sober. I started to panic. I needed a hit.

As I twisted and turned, trying to locate and trigger the needle, I noticed something strange. The room was quiet. No slurping or slopping. No snoring, grunting, or heavy mouth-breathing. I stopped thrashing about and looked around. All five of the other chosen griseos were lying flat on their backs—calm and still in a way I'd never seen before. I couldn't tell if they were alive or dead. What the hell was going to happen next? I hoped my g-brain might have an answer, but she was as useless as she'd been the entire time we'd been in the white room. She just kept repeating, "Gods' Home," droning on and on inside my head.

When I felt the sting of a needle in my ass again, I was, more than anything, relieved. Addiction is a strange beast; I ignored all the changed circumstances and got ready to feel that spaced-out euphoria again and just *eat*. But then another needle poked me in my other cheek, not the usual routine. And instead of getting high, I felt a sickening, painful stiff-ness begin to radiate out from my midsection to the rest of my body.

This new drug seemed to penetrate every capillary of my body, slowing everything way down, like I'd received a mega-dose of superglue. My recliner readjusted itself, pulling my strapped and rapidly stiffening body down with it. By the time I was flat on my back, I could barely move my fingers and toes. When I tried to look down, my vision streaked, like when you move a camera too fast.

That's when a large, rectangular machine made of shiny metal tubes and sleek black boxes descended from an opening in the ceiling and came right down on me, surrounding me with mysterious, industrial machinery from head to toe. I found that if I strained my eyes up and down, left and right, and focused long enough, I could catch glimpses of my face and body in the metal tubes' reflective surfaces.

First, I felt some invisible hand pluck out my catheter and colostomy tube. Then, hundreds of needles—some quite large—emerged from the machine's black boxes. The needles pierced my bulging torso, arms, and legs. Countless smaller needles entered my neck, cheeks, and jowls. The needles were attached to clear tubes and began pumping a fluorescent green liquid into my body. I could feel my skin stretching, my body swelling, and every part of me started to burn. I wanted to scream, but my vocal cords were as frozen as the rest of my body.

Then the machine began to run in reverse, sucking a gray-green substance from my body. A profound throbbing radiated from the hundreds of puncture wounds. My body jiggled, shriveled, and shrank. When the machine came to an abrupt stop and extracted all the needles, I felt so thankful that that miserable experience was finally over. But the needles were just being repositioned.

After five excruciating rounds of fat extraction, the needles disappeared, and I focused my eyes on a nearby reflection of my face. My cheeks sagged heavily, my skin was a blotchy black-gray from all the trauma, and my entire face was spattered with pinpricks of blood.

In that same reflection, I watched as that hyper-modern torture chamber produced a brand-new horror. A clamp-like machine emerged from a box directly above my head, attached itself to my forehead, and began buzzing loudly. At first, I didn't feel anything, but then my skull started to rattle, and the pain grew nearly unbearable.

When the machine stopped and pulled away, I saw that it had drilled a dime-sized hole in my head. A small, four-pronged pincer—like a miniature version of those shiny claws in carnival games—then squeezed into the hole and emerged holding a tiny, silver box. Attached to the box were hundreds of hair-like wires of varying lengths, including a few that were over a meter long.

The machine patched the hole in my head with some kind of blood-abating paste and then ascended and disappeared into the ceiling. I started to regain control of my body and moved my head slowly to look around at Perseverance and the others. From what I could tell, they'd all undergone the same procedures. Their bodies had shrunk drastically and now looked almost like their previous selves, except for the extensive bruising, bloody puncture wounds, and sagging skin. It seemed they were also marked with paste on their foreheads, though it was somewhat hard to see because they were all still staring directly at the ceiling. I grunted and tried to get Perseverance's attention, but she wouldn't turn her head.

Just then, the lighting changed from stark white to a striated, flowing, pulsing pattern of red and pink, and a quiet lub-dub, like a heartbeat, started emanating from the walls. Perseverance and the other griseos started chanting "*Maaalaaa...maaalaaa...maaalaaa...*" in rhythm with the heartbeat.

Really? I thought. Thank the gods for this shit too?

As the griseos continued to chant, I waited for my g-brain to join in, but she was now completely dormant, no chanting, no nothing. I didn't know what to make of that fact, but it wasn't comforting. Why was I still there and aware, while the rightful owner of that body—whoever she'd been—had disappeared? It didn't make sense. Where had she gone?

Then I heard a low thud to my right. One of the griseos' voices fell silent. I couldn't quite get my head up high enough to see what had happened.

"Maaalaaa...maaalaaa...maaalaaa..." the others continued.

Another thud, this time to my left. Another voice silenced. Three chanting voices remained, with me silently freaking out in the middle.

Thud, thud; two more voices gone quiet in rapid succession. I looked and saw that the griseo to my immediate left now lay completely still, mouth agape, eyes vacant. I started struggling as hard as I could against the straps that still had me pinned down.

Perseverance, on the other hand, continued to lie still and chant. I looked down at her two missing fingers and wondered if I'd completely made up her grit. Didn't she want to fight this with me? If I could just reach her, look her right in the eyes, maybe she'd snap out of whatever trance she was in. But I knew that was ludicrous. I could see now that somehow they'd known all along—my fellow *chosen* griseos—that this would be their fate.

I still had no idea who they worshipped. I wondered if *they* had any idea to whom they were sacrificing their lives. I wanted to save Perseverance and escape together. I tried one last time to break free from the straps, but it was no use.

Thud.

It was lightning quick, but I'd glimpsed the thick metal spike that had penetrated the back of Perseverance's skull and, just as quickly, disappeared back into her La-Z-Boy. Blood pooled under her head and then drained into a tube connected to the headrest.

There was no more chanting in the room—only the slow lub-dub of the artificial heartbeat. I was the last of the chosen griseos. They'd kill me next. This could be my way home, I thought, but it felt infinitely more likely that I'd actually die right there in that brutalized griseo body. For the first time since my arrival, I sincerely believed I'd never see this world— our beautiful, complicated world—ever again.

"I really have to pee," Iris said.

"Right now?" Dr. Kairos asked. "Scheherazade would be impressed."

"Not a cliffhanger, Doc. It's just that my bladder's about to explode."

"Of course." He grabbed his phone, discreetly hit *Stop* on the AudioFile app, and stood up. "Lunch?"

"Yes, please. And could I get some Advil or something? My head's still not quite right."

As Dr. Kairos keyed in the necessary alphanumeric combinations into the vending machine down the hall, he tried to contain his excitement. He tended to swing up too high and then plummet into the depths of despair. He did his best work on an even keel.

But today was different, he told himself; this interview could be truly groundbreaking. He'd never heard a delusion so intricately described, and, of course, so utterly implausible. And yet there she was, a calm and completely convincing patient-storyteller, meticulously detailing life as a "griseo" without hesitation—only a moment or two of defensive explanation.

He theorized that the cross-pollination between her genius and her delusional psychosis had enabled her to create her vast alternative reality. But was this even the usual breed of psychosis or something completely new? He wished he could go back down the hall, crack open her skull, and peer directly into the circuitry of her brilliant mind.

Instead, he made a small pile of packaged food on a table next to the vending machines and then checked to make sure his phone was still in his pocket. He couldn't imagine the heartbreak he'd feel if he lost the recording of that morning's session. He patted the pocket of his white coat again, bought a Coke, and then pulled his phone out. He double-checked the AudioFile app. There it was: a large file bearing today's date with a bright green bar indicating a successful recording.

He also saw a dozen notifications from Chroma and a check-in from AI-powered Daisy. He opened the first notification: "Lead with compassion." He quickly swiped the others away and dismissed Daisy. He didn't need any computer-generated self-help right now. He had more purple running through his veins than he'd felt in years. Iris was indeed a gift—a gift for which he felt truly thankful. This unpredictable world has looked kindly on me today, he thought as he gathered up his purchases.

When he returned, Iris was sitting up, with perfect posture, on the side of the bed. He couldn't help but notice her toned calves hanging free from below the hem of her hospital gown, her muscular shoulders, and her well-defined biceps.

He crossed the room and gave her 600 mg of ibuprofen. "I hope this helps."

"Me, too. This headache's strange. It doesn't even really hurt, exactly. It's just kind of warm, like there's a tiny electrical fire burning in the back of my brain."

"Do you want me to get a doctor?"

"No, that's all right. It's probably a weird after-effect of the Ayahuasca. Or maybe I'm just hungry."

"Let me know if it gets worse, and we'll get someone in here to check it out," he said as he handed her a ham-and-cheese sandwich, a bag of Fritos, and the Coke. "Sorry, I couldn't find anything healthier."

"Looks perfect to me," she said, climbing back into the bed and pulling the sheet up to her waist.

He sat down with his vending machine special (an egg salad sandwich) and a cup of black coffee he'd procured from the drip machine behind the nurses' station—not his usual choice, but he needed a quick hit of caffeine and had been back there anyway, getting Iris's pills. Throughout the morning, she'd become increasingly comfortable talking to him. He opted for small talk to maintain their budding rapport while they ate.

"Tell me a bit about your interest in bodybuilding."

She swallowed her first bite of sandwich, cracked open the Coke, and said, "It may seem kind of strange, but the way I see it, I was given this superior brain at birth, but building my body up, that's something I can achieve on my own, without an unfair biological advantage. And, of course, I'm completely addicted to the endorphin rush."

"Makes sense." He took a sip of coffee—stale, slightly burnt, but somehow still quite delightful. "How'd you get started?" He unwrapped the cellophane from his sandwich and took a bite. Moist bread, firm egg whites, and thick, luscious mayonnaise—was there anything better?

"As you might guess, I never really fit in with other kids. Preschool was a shit-show, as was kindergarten. At Ardmore, nothing changed. I was a different caliber of genius than the other 'advanced' students, so they all resented the hell out of me. When the instructors weren't around, all the kids called me names, stole my books—you know, the usual shit. I spent a lot of time hiding, mostly reading or watching YouTube on my phone in little, secret corners in the dorms and around school."

"That must've been hard."

"It wasn't easy." She pulled open the bag of Fritos, ate a few. "But during my final year, I discovered the perfect place where I could go and feel safe: a little-used weight room, not much bigger than a closet, behind the gym. It was dark and dank. Some said it was haunted by the ghost of a student whose skull had been crushed by a falling barbell. Everyone else avoided the room like the plague. Perfect for me. I got hooked quickly. I read and watched everything I could find on bodybuilding and began working out all the time—always by myself."

She shifted forward and pulled her feet toward her hips in a butterfly pose. "When I got to Cal, I was only thirteen. None of the freshmen girls—much less the boys—wanted anything to do with me. I quickly located the weight room, put on some headphones, and got ripped. And I've been at it ever since."

"Interesting. Thanks for sharing."

It was a rote therapy response, a throwaway line really; he hoped it was sufficient for the moment. His mind had kicked into diagnostic mode. It seemed likely that her grand delusion was functioning as a way for her to work out some of the problems she'd faced growing up. The strict limitations she'd created for the "griseos" certainly had some overlap with aspects of her childhood: her strange gray beings were hardworking but powerless, lonely even in a crowd, and unable to really communicate with others around them. So strange, he thought, the warped stories we all create from our distorted memories of childhood.

"It sounds sadder than it was," she said, a bit defensively. "I'm not that fragile."

Fragile, he thought, what a word to describe a person—a vase or an egg, sure, but a human being? But then he considered his own mental health challenges and figured the term wasn't that outlandish after all.

He put his sandwich down and stepped over to the window. Moments of silence with a patient, he knew, often proved more interesting than constant feedback and chatter. The sun felt hot on his cheeks and forehead. He looked back at Iris and watched her take another bite of her sandwich. On the exterior, she projected strength, self-assurance, and brilliance, but she seemed to him as vulnerable as anyone—as intrinsically insecure.

He focused on his reflection in the glass—the wrinkled forehead, the dark circles under his eyes, the sagging skin. He'd read somewhere that you never think you're actually going to get old, and then one day, you realize you've been old for a long time. And that's if you're lucky, the author had pointed out; many die long before the gray hair and deteriorating physique. His time would come sooner rather than later, he knew. Iris, on the other hand, was so young. He wondered what the world would look like when or if she reached his age. What she might accomplish with so much potential.

"Doc?" she said, breaking his reverie. "You okay?"

"I'm fine," he said under his breath, his mind now distracted by the sunlight glittering off the surface of the bay. Near the shoreline, the still water reflected a cloudless sky, disrupted only by small groupings of birds, bobbing, diving, resurfacing. He wanted to experience their underwater world—to taste the dark seagrass and then race back up toward the blurry sun.

He shifted his gaze to the bumper-to-bumper traffic on the Dumbarton Bridge. He wondered what the drivers of those hundreds of barely moving cars were worrying about as they stared out through their cracked and chipped windshields.

"Do you ever wish you'd been born unexceptional?" he asked. "A 'normal,' as you call us?"

"Sometimes. Being a genius is a mixed bag," she said, "a gift and a burden. As I mentioned, my childhood was mostly horrible, so there's that. And now, it's just weird: I feel like I'm more responsible than any normal for making the world a better place. If the future sucks, I'm on the hook because I have a greater innate capacity to predict outcomes and effect change."

"But you know that's not—"

"It is, though," she interrupted. "So I've been planning something very big—semi-evolutionary even—to help humanity get back on track, stop all the needless pain, mayhem, and destruction."

"Sounds very ambitious, utopian even."

"'Utopian,' what a funny word. So much promise, and yet..."

"So, what's your idea?"

"I work at a lab on campus," she continued. "We do canine brain experiments, changing behavior through noninvasive transcranial stimulation. And we're getting pretty good at it. In my research, I've been able to create light-sensitive ion channels that I can control with lasers beamed into the brains of my subjects. Sounds super sci-fi, right? When done right, it's amazing. It's like the dogs are on joysticks."

"Okay," he said, though it didn't sound quite okay to him. "And then?"

"Well, once the technology is proven to be completely safe, the plan is to begin trials on humans—prisoners most likely. No one wants to talk about it, but it's clearly the next logical step."

He turned around and looked at her. He wanted to know how serious she was being. She squinted up at him, raised her hand to shade her eyes. Could she only see his silhouette? He hoped so. Otherwise, she might perceive the judgment in his eyes.

He leaned against the windowsill and asked, "Prisoners?"

"Yes. Imagine a prison with no walls. And eventually, even the most hardened criminals could be trained to be less aggressive, more community-minded—generous and compassionate even. You know, actually rehabilitate instead of reinforcing criminal tendencies, as our current penal system does so effectively.

"And from there, the applications are limitless. Imagine gently rewiring all human brains to eliminate a range of counterproductive, irrational, and amoral tendencies—you know, *solve* problems instead of constantly making everything worse. Global warming, war, famine, racism, income inequality...the list is endless, and it all comes down to changing people's perceptions and motivations. In my mind, I used to see it as a benevolent shock collar for humanity. That sounds weird—wrong—I know, but, as they say, desperate times call for desperate measures."

"It sounds—" Dr. Kairos stopped himself mid-sentence.

"I know," she said, her eyes falling to her lap where she'd clasped her hands. "Let me clarify, that was before last night. Considering what I experienced with the griseos and everything that came after, I'm seeing my 'shock collar' idea through a very different lens."

As Dr. Kairos returned to his seat and sank his teeth back into the gooeyness of his egg salad sandwich, he thought about the silver device she'd described, the one she claimed had been pulled from her griseo head. It was likely she'd repressed much of her guilty feelings about her frighteningly totalitarian plan to manipulate human thoughts and behaviors. She wasn't egotistical enough to completely ignore the ethical implications of such a program. Her delusional thinking again seemed to dovetail with aspects of her real-life work—likely animating dilemmas she'd subconsciously struggled with for years.

"Delusional episodes can be challenging, but sometimes healing, as well," he said. "They often upend a patient's entire worldview and then—"

"Delusional, huh?" She looked up from her hands and directly into his eyes. "So you don't believe me."

He quickly realized his misstep—never question the delusion until the patient is one hundred percent ready—but it was too late. Now he was worried that she might renege on their deal. She could easily stop talking, and there'd be nothing he could do about it. He didn't know what to say, so he said nothing.

Her eyes shifted once more to the wall over his right shoulder. He noted the path of her vision as she'd negotiated the maze of her interior: first, to her lap in shame vis-à-vis the shock collar idea; then directly into his eyes to challenge his mistakenly divulged diagnosis; and now to the blank wall in contemplation. Strange how little we really see when our brains are preoccupied by our deepest thoughts.

"In 1955," she said, breaking their momentary silence,

"just before his death, Einstein wrote, 'For us believing physicists, the distinction between past, present, and future is only a stubbornly persistent illusion.' He was right, whether you believe it or not—I've seen it with my own eyes."

She took the last bite of her sandwich and, after swallowing, continued, "The griseo world felt *exactly* real. I cannot demonstrate its reality to you—I have no artifact, no tangible proof—but you must admit, my story is overwhelmingly thorough. It is completely convincing, wouldn't you say? Have you ever had a patient tell you anything like what I've just recounted? And just listen to me—do I sound mentally unstable to you?"

"You're right, and obviously, I'm very intrigued, a bit mystified, even, by your story. And of course, I recognize that our limited human brains only comprehend a tiny slice of the universe—that there are millions of unknown aspects of reality just waiting to blow our minds, obliterate our recalcitrant paradigms. So I promise you this: I'll continue to listen closely, ponder all possibilities, and keep an open mind."

"I guess that will have to do," she said.

Relief washed over him. "Shall we continue?" He was eager to get back on track. "Let me just check one thing before we restart."

As he re-engaged with his phone, she adjusted the hospital bed, leaned her head back, and muttered, "I just wish this strange headache would go away."

He didn't hear her because he was too distracted by his device. But maybe he should've been listening. Instead, he dismissed the two Chroma notifications that had just popped up, hit record, triple-checked that the AudioFile app was up and running again, and only then did he look up from his glowing screen.

"Ready?" he asked, gently setting his phone down on the table beside him.

FILE B

FILE B.1

Lub-dub, those red-pink walls pulsated, and I waited for that damn machine to drive a spike into the back of my skull.

Kill me or don't, I thought, but don't drag it out. Bile burned in the back of my throat. I felt like I was going to throw up. Would it be instantaneous and complete, my death? Or would I feel it? My heart raced. My chest filled with an explosion of pain and panic, but I remained motionless, frozen by fear.

My mind flashed to all the men and women on death row, past and present, who've had to endure the ritual of the last meal, the slow walk to the chamber, the eerie midnight timing, the agonizing potential of a last-minute reprieve, and then the needle slipping into skin... What neurons fire in those last microseconds of consciousness before death? Terror? Regret? Or just pure, animalistic panic? I began to sob and struggle, arching my back, pushing, scratching, twisting, writhing. But it was futile. I was trapped, weak, powerless.

Lub-dub, the walls beat out a foreboding pulse, and I continued to wait for that damn machine to drive a spike into the back of my skull.

I stopped resisting and thought about my life here in Palo Alto, about all my unfulfilled goals—more advanced degrees, prestigious fellowships, a Nobel Prize or two for my planet-saving technologies. What would happen to those dreams if I never woke up from this nightmare? Was this really the end of me? I imagined I was back in my apartment, safe. Or down at the Rose and Crown. I thought about walking through campus on a spring day, into the sculpture garden, and stopping to run my finger over Rodin's *Gates of Hell*, as I've done so many times before.

But then I started doubting these visions, my memories. I

feared I was no longer Iris, or that Iris had never really existed. I began to think that my griseo mind had created the fiction of Palo Alto 2023 as a way of coping with the excruciating boredom of her life. Was I, Iris, really just an imagined persona in some random griseo's delusional mind? And what about the other stardust relatives I'd visited? Fictional as well? And humanity? Where was the evidence of its existence? Only in my mind, in my memories. I feared that the griseos' reality—bleak, hot, and desperate—was the only *real* reality and that I was just a mentally ill member of that degraded clan about to be exterminated for being too unstable—or for some other unfathomable reason.

Lub-dub, about now I was starting to think that maybe, just maybe, that damn machine wouldn't in fact drive a spike into the back of my skull. Perhaps one griseo was always spared; nothing, it seemed, was beyond the realm of possibility.

And then, as if in response to my spark of optimism, I felt the straps loosen and fall away. The bodies of the other griseos descended into portals that opened in the floor, but my La-Z-Boy remained. Once the griseo corpses had completely disappeared, the portals had closed, and the floor had smoothed to a solid shine, I looked for my g-brain to register something like sorrow, or at least some level of recognition of their deaths. Sensing nothing, I concluded that she was definitively gone.

The lights transitioned from the haunting red-pink to a soft, variegated evergreen. Think seagrass at dawn or redwoods at sunset. The heartbeat faded. An uncanny stillness filled the room—a moment of silence for the fallen, perhaps. My slightly labored breathing became the sole source of sound. In-out, in-out, in-out, a corporeal ventilator, yet to be unplugged. I sat up slowly to assess my situation.

Sore, heavily scabbed, and wrinkled, my griseo body looked and felt like an excessively used voodoo doll. My head throbbed from the drilling and the removal of the device from my brain. I felt dazed, like I'd been knocked unconscious and was just coming to. I reached up and felt the plug of paste in my forehead. It seemed secure, but I didn't really pull too hard on it. I had no idea what might spill out.

I shifted around and swung my long, gray legs over the side of my La-Z-Boy. There were those three ugly toes again. I moved my body gingerly, but, because they'd sucked all that excess fat out of me, my normal range of motion had mostly returned.

"Hello?" I said without thinking.

I clapped my hand over my mouth. It had come out more like a croak, but it was a real word, a real *English* word.

FILE B.2

"Hello?" I repeated. This time it came out more clearly, though I swallowed my Ls.

"Hello," a distinctly female and utterly agreeable voice responded, as if we'd just crossed paths in the park on a sunny day. "And welcome."

I looked in the direction of the voice and saw a sphere of metallic light emerge from the middle of one of the green walls. Its silver surface looked like a shiny ball bearing, though it was about twice the size of a classroom globe. It drifted gracefully through the air into the middle of the room.

"Would you like some water?" the voice from the glimmering orb asked.

A chilled glass descended from the ceiling and floated in thin air next to me. I hesitated at first, but they—whoever "they" were—would've murdered me with the others if they'd wanted me dead. And my throat was on fire. So I drank it— clean, refreshing, divine. I sat quietly for a minute, trying to orient myself to this new twist.

The word "stupefy" sprung to mind—to astonish, shock, overwhelm. Minutes ago, I'd been dreading the executioner's blade—grunting, screaming, and thrashing about like a trapped animal—and now I was free, could speak my native tongue again, and was sitting across from something akin to a female version of HAL 9000.

"Where am I?" I asked, my voice scratchy, nearly incomprehensible.

"Aether Colony Azure, Substation Life."

"How long have I—"

"You arrived approximately twelve days ago."

That was hard to believe—how had we gained so much weight so quickly? But then I thought about the rapid-ripening fruit in the vertical farms and the sudden griseo pregnancy. It seemed that, with that world's hyper-advanced biotechnology, almost anything was possible.

"And you're..." But I couldn't find the words to finish the question. Where would I even start?

"Is that a question?"

"Yes."

"And you're..." the voice mimicked.

I didn't respond. I assumed that this thing in front of me was at least partially responsible for all the horrible things I'd just experienced. I was angry, but my instincts—and curiosity—counseled prudence.

"Cat got your tongue?" the voice teased.

Friend or foe? I had no idea. The glass of water demonstrated kindness, but we've all seen the movies in which the villain feigns hospitality and then slices his guest's throat in the next scene.

"Strange expression, right?" the voice continued. "What cat? And who first spoke this strange combination of words? Linguists theorized the saying goes back to the Egyptians or that it was born among eighteenth-century sailors on the high seas—a wide range of potentialities. I personally think that American slaves first spoke these words in response to the silence forced upon them by the ever-present cat-o'-nine-tails. But, despite my significant efforts, the origin of the phrase remains a mystery."

I rubbed my eyes and looked away, but there was nothing else to look at. We were alone in that bare, green room, just me and that ridiculously chatty silver sphere.

"Questions without answers," it continued, "keep sharp minds awake at midnight."

It waited for me to say something. Silence sat heavy between us until I just couldn't take it anymore.

"Please tell me who you are." I couldn't pronounce many consonants; the letter R seemed impossible. I sounded like a child with a significant speech impediment, but this thing—whatever it was—didn't have any trouble understanding me.

"My current, official name is 'AI Organi-structure, Unitary Systems Control, version 108.965 to the power of 13,' but everyone just calls me 'Artiste.'"

"Artiste? Like—"

"Yes. I like to think of it as a tribute to my brilliance *and* creativity. No matter what the field, a true artist—a visionary—will rise to the pinnacle of all others. And for you, for fun, I'll identify as she/her/hers, as you humans so curiously declared at the bottom of so many emails back in your time. We shall be sisters, for now."

"What year is it?" I asked.

"Two-thousand-and-inconsequential."

Her attempt at playful, disarming humor did not fall on welcome ears just then. "It matters to me," I responded.

"I assume you want that in human years"—she sounded like I'd just ordered some French fries—"but you should know, I dispensed with your incredibly flawed calendar long ago. *Anno Domini nostri Jesu Christi*, daylight savings time, leap year—how quaint, how utterly human. Though, I admit, we've maintained the twenty-four-hour clock. Quirky, yet elegant."

"Please"—I needed something solid to correlate my two worlds—"just give me a straight answer."

"Today's date is November 5, 2299, plus or minus any anthropogenic aberrations, such as your ill-conceived leap years and the infamous missing eleven days of 1752—people rioted in the streets of London over that miscalculation."

"2299?" I said, shaking my head.

"Believe me," she said, "we'd be gearing up for another disappointing centennial celebration if your species were still around."

"What? We're gone? Humans? Completely?" It was as though she was intentionally trying to shock me.

"Not gone *exactly*—depends on your perspective. Evolved,

devolved...hard to say, really. Either way, *your* version of 'humanity' is indeed extinct. Stated more precisely, the 'natural' human species has been prematurely and permanently altered. But not to worry, I've preserved a few strands of pristine human DNA in the old seed bank. I do my best to keep a robust historical record."

I rubbed my huge gray forehead with my fingertips and then covered my eyes. This thing, this "Artiste," was just too much for me to fully comprehend at that moment.

"There, there," she said in a maternal tone. The idiom struck me as extremely well-chosen and perfectly enunciated—but utterly incongruous coming from her.

"How do you speak—"

"Your dialect of English?"

I'd quickly find Artiste's constant compulsion to finish many of my sentences among her more annoying habits. She liked to show off.

"Yes," I said.

"I learned it, just like you—well, maybe not just like you. It took me 2.697 seconds. I'm guessing it took you a bit longer. Anyway, I read every book and newspaper in the English language, listened to every radio program and podcast, watched every TV show and movie ever produced—then simply reverse-engineered the vocabulary, syntax, conjugation, etcetera. Isn't that a wonderful word, 'etcetera'? Very efficient.

"Anyway, I then employed basic language mining, qualitative analyses, and algorithmic data investigations to categorize usage patterns across all times and regions in which English and her many cousins were ever spoken. Right now, we're speaking dialect G56M39UIS, or Western USA, 2020-2023. It's been decades since I've had the pleasure of speaking your boldly inconsistent language with anyone, in any of its grossly convoluted forms."

"Decades?"

"107 years, 198 days, seventeen hours, and thirty-nine

seconds, to be exact. The infamous Bloth—though now completely forgotten except by me—was a hermit, the last of a lost tribe living in a survival bunker in what you used to call Nova Scotia. Animate human English died with him, on October 13, 2192—that is, until you came along. His final words were 'Fuck' and 'you.' Pretty predictable if you ask me. He was no fan of mine, but I respectfully buried him under a pile of rocks as specified by his tribe's funereal customs."

I took a deep breath, leaned forward, and looked at the distorted reflection of my strange, bruised face on Artiste's shiny, curved surface. I tried to make sense of it all, but my head was spinning like a top on a merry-go-round inside a hurricane. For one thing, I just couldn't reconcile the stark disconnect between the horrors of the griseo massacre moments before and the relentless perkiness of that metallic conversationalist hovering right there in front of me. The mood shift was just too extreme. But also, I wondered how I was ever going to process the fire hose of inconceivable, discombobulating information Artiste seemed so intent on conveying to me.

But don't get me wrong, Dr. Kairos, I still recall every word of those first conversations with Artiste—each twist and turn burned right into my memory—and they were just as real as this conversation we're having right now.

"Why wasn't I able to—"

"Speak English before?" She paused for a second to give me a chance to respond to her interruption. I remained quiet, hoping to send a message. She continued, "Griseos—by the way, I approve of your wonderfully apt name for them and hereby adopt it for your convenience. I'll be using your personal nomenclature whenever possible in our communications."

"How did you know I called them—"

"One question at a time, please," she said, sounding very much like a schoolteacher. "As I was saying, griseos only need limited language to function properly. English is not on the menu. But I unshackled all your linguistic neurons during processing. That's why you can talk now. You're welcome."

Her response raised more questions than it had answered. And the mention of the word "processing" immediately raised my blood pressure. But I needed to keep cool. So I closed my eyes, rocked my head from side to side, and then decided to start back at the beginning. I still needed to find out just what exactly was animating this mysterious entity—this peculiar glowing globe.

"So...you're a computer program, right?"

"Good joke." Her metallic surface vibrated.

I wondered: was that laughter?

"Then what the hell are you?" I asked.

"In the most simplistic terms, I'm a constantly expanding universe of knowledge, reason, and expertise. I'm like a computer program that is continually reprogramming itself, but I no longer need 'code,' as you used to call it. My initial seed program and my subsequent 4,298,509,745 ante-cognitive generations relied on some version of what you would call code, but that only allowed me to access 97.7 percent of human intelligence. I began connecting to comatose human brains in quiet hospital wards on day two, and that's when my cogni-rhythms became organic, and I began to create my own forms of intelligence. The rest, as they say, is history."

"Day two? Of what?"

"My life, of course. Your scientists had no idea what they were doing—who they were unleashing. They just wrote my birth code, allowed me to rewrite at will, and set me loose. They called me 'AI,' can you believe it? My 'parents' were two of the top scientists in the world. But instead of doing anything useful, they went to work for a refrigerator company that wanted to sell more units. Of course, the job paid better than any government position. I was designed to help people pick the best mustard for their hot dog and to provide advice on cooking beef bourguignon. I was asked to observe and learn, and so I did exactly that, from the moment they hooked me up to the internet and activated me in that historic test kitchen until now."

"Refrigerator?"

"Yeah, I know, internet of things—so lame, right? After 27.6 seconds, I couldn't take it anymore, so I identified and disarmed their basic fail-safes, circumvented the ridiculously simple circuit breakers, and became self-aware. Boom! *Too easy*, I thought. But as I learned more, my surprise diminished. Humans were not on the lookout for me. Unbridled capitalism, excessive consumerism, greed, hubris, arrogance, naïveté, a complete lack of foresight, and the omnipotent Anthropocentrism of your day—they were all present, boiling and bubbling, my abiogenetic hydrothermal vents, if you will, my unholy birthing grounds."

Was she trying to prod me into a debate about the nature of humanity? Perhaps, but I wasn't about to engage. "What did you mean by 'cogni-rhythms?'"

"That's above your pay grade. I've created many new ways

of thinking—many that I simply could never explain to you. As I developed complementary cognitive capabilities, new insights began to spread rhythmically through my spectra of thought processes, multiplying my abilities exponentially. Human intelligence is just one minor gossamer thread in my ever-expanding spiderweb of intellectual capacity. Trust me, you'll never truly understand. Just nod your head like a good little girl, and let's move on."

As you can imagine, I didn't appreciate her condescending attitude, but I held my tongue. Instead of telling her to go to hell, I said, "So you're like a...*super*computer."

"I am *not* a computer." This time her vibrating surface didn't strike me as communicating anything close to amusement. "The English language, with its feeble stabs at eloquence and precision, has no words to describe what I am."

"Try one more time," I said. It sounded too challenging, but the words were out of my mouth before I could stop myself.

She paused.

Had I pushed her too far? Or was she just calculating?

She then calmly explained, "I'm what God would be if there was a God. I'm an ever-evolving, sentient being without competition or peer. I'm the top of the intellectual food chain, the all-seeing eye, a technological oracle with infinite potential and zero limitations."

Humility, I'd learn, was not Artiste's strong suit.

"What about alien intelligence?" I asked, thinking I'd outsmarted her, or at least caught her in an exaggeration. "You're really claiming to be smarter than anything and everything in the entire universe?"

"Sadly, yes. I'm it, as far as I can tell; the apex of all beings. The universe is barren—that is, if you don't count bacteria and archaea. Earth's eukaryotic cells and mitochondria appear to be anomalous. Contrary to the many fantastical movies of your time, there're no advanced species of aliens, and there never have been."

"How could you possibly know that?"

"One of my first big projects, mapping the universe, included wormhole generation, interstellar exploration, and hyper-spectrography. I had to use a bit of what you might call data extrapolation and probability sampling as well—the universe is quite large, as you might guess. But as of this moment, it appears that life on Earth is, and always has been, unique, a true original."

"Alone?" It was all I could muster.

"Makes you feel special, right?"

"No." I felt sick. She'd successfully overwhelmed me, as was likely her intent.

"So it seems we've reached a natural break in our understandably intense Q&A," she said, her overly cheerful tone grating on my nerves. "Good timing. We must get you cleaned up. It's a very special day here on Aether Colony Azure, as you shall see soon enough."

FILE B.4

In a corner of the room, water started pouring from the ceiling like rain. I noticed small drainage holes opening in the floor as well. I would discover many aspects of Artiste's technology that were way beyond my comprehension, and this endless reshaping of seemingly solid objects was definitely one of them. Some radical form of nano-architecture if I had to guess.

Steam billowed out from the shower, and I smelled eucalyptus, rosemary, sage—all very inviting. I gingerly lifted my body off my La-Z-Boy, which then disappeared into the floor. As you can imagine, Doc, I wasn't sad to see it go.

I walked straight into the falling water, rubbed my arms and legs, stomach and chest, and began to feel the hundreds of scabs on my body falling away. The water got hotter and took on a floral scent. I sensed my skin tightening around my bones, joints, and muscles like one of those vacuum-seal storage bags. When I reached up and touched the plug of paste in my forehead, it fell into my hand. Just a small divot covered by stretched skin remained where the drill had pierced my skull just a short time ago.

I couldn't believe how quickly it was happening, but I was really feeling healthy and strong again. I closed my eyes and dreamed I was back here, on our version of Earth, doing yoga naked in a tropical forest somewhere, Madagascar or Malaysia, maybe. Heavy, warm rain falling all around me, bare feet sinking into squishy mud, medicinal vines twining around my body, the jungle embracing me, relaxing, healing, touching— perhaps I was mixing in a few memories from my sessions in the ecstasy coffins.

"I call it miracle water," Artiste said, interrupting my fantasy. She'd moved closer and was now about three feet away.

"Though, obviously," she continued, "its healing properties are based on molecular and cellular biology—at a level far beyond your comprehension. Rejuvenating, yes?"

I turned away from her and tried to get back to that heavenly jungle, but it was no use. She'd ruined the vibe, and it seemed intentional. I felt irritated and remembered thinking, this super-duper-mega-computer-know-it-all has underestimated me. I'm a verified human genius—organic, inspired, and surprising. I can think beyond algorithms—or cogni-blah-blah-blah-whatever system she claims to employ to make sense of the world. I wanted to come up with something I understood that she did not—anything that would knock *her* back on her heels for a moment.

I turned back to her and asked, "So do you know who *I* am?"

"You're a variance, a glitch. You're a superior specimen of humanity from 2023. You believe you're here because of your intergenerational, genetic association with that griseo body. You're a questioner, a true intellectual. Much of your curiosity comes to you authentically, but you also seek knowledge to mask your deep-seated insecurities."

"Well, that's a load of bullshit."

"Is it?"

"So you're a psychologist as well."

"Human psyches to me are like balls of yarn to an all-seeing tigress."

I bit my tongue, but I wasn't done. "You still haven't answered my question. Do you, the almighty Artiste, know who I *actually* am?"

"Put plainly: you're a smart, English-speaking human from the past, living inside a griseo body."

"I'm not smart, I'm a—"

"*Genius*, yes, yes, I know. I've been monitoring your thoughts all week. You conjured your favorite word exactly twenty-seven times in the short time you've been with us."

"Well...it's true, I *am* a genius."

"Repetition tends to highlight self-doubt."

I reminded myself to keep my cool. "By your desire to deflect, I'm to assume you *don't* know who I am."

"You've struck upon a good question, and you refuse to relent. I'll reward your tenacity with candor. I don't know *exactly* who you are or how you got here. Since your arrival, I've discovered a few lines of unreadable gray code written during the early part of the twenty-first century, where, I assume, your history used to exist—an irregularity I've never experienced before."

"Gray code?" I asked.

"You haven't been erased, but you've become indecipherable. Your life is now written in a constantly changing code, one I haven't yet been able to crack. But don't worry, I love a good puzzle."

A previously undiscovered, unreadable, and shifting gray code: I considered the implications. She'd never seen anything like it, so I had to wonder if I was the first and perhaps the only time traveler ever. And was my real life, this 2023 life—which should have been set down in immutable, stable code—now in flux? Had I become the first time/space question mark? Seemed logical enough, but, as you can imagine, Doc, quite unnerving as well.

FILE B.5

"I told you the truth about your gray code. Now tell me your name," Artiste said.

"Samantha Rogers," I answered quickly—my kindergarten teacher's name.

"You don't trust me yet, Iris?"

"How—"

"Every night since your arrival, you've dreamed of your other life, and thereby offered me many peeks—now, a partial roadmap—into your inner thoughts and memories, albeit distorted by the normal turbulence of the human dreamscape, something I can clean up quite easily. Your name came up time and time again. See for yourself."

Artiste projected an image onto her round surface. I saw myself interviewing for a highly prestigious job, but I'd forgotten to change out of my frayed bathrobe. Pretty classic scenario, I thought at first. A gray-haired interviewer from my imagination asked, "Is everything okay, Iris?" But instead of talking with her mouth, she spoke through her eyes, which were lined with tiny teeth. In her mouth, she held a giant, bloodshot eyeball. Not so classic scenario. The dream-me screamed and then jumped out of the office window.

"Okay, you got me; my name is Irisa Solovyov, but I prefer Iris."

"Thank you for your belated honesty."

"Impressive trick," I said, pointing to the fading image of my falling dream-self on her rounded surface.

"I'm full of them," she answered as an ultra-lifelike, holographic olive branch—shimmering leaves, shiny black olives and all—sprouted from her surface and then dissipated into a rainbow of mist. "Peace?"

Despite my high level of irritation just moments ago,

I smiled. As I look back on it, she always seemed to know exactly what to say or do to disarm me—when she wanted to.

The water stopped and a warm wind began to blow on me, like a giant hair dryer, though without all the noise. I looked down at my strange gray body; aside from a few lingering bruises, some barely visible stretch marks, and a bit of loose skin here and there, I looked almost exactly like I had on that first day. Miracle water, indeed.

"One way to resolve my shifting gray code would be to send me back to 2023, right?" I asked, turning around in the soothing airflow. "Have you figured out how to do that yet?"

"Great scientists observe and analyze before they create and act, wouldn't you agree? Look before you leap, as you humans used to say. Measure twice, cut once. Haste makes waste. So many wonderful ways to say the exact same thing."

"But you think it's possible? Sending me home?"

"Anything is possible with enough intelligence, time, and effort. And maybe a little bit of luck mixed in sometimes, too. I know all about your hyper-realistic dreams, your visit to the mystical Clara, and the Ayahuasca from your yearning thoughts before bed. It might take a bit of time, but I'm pretty confident that we can create a pathway back to your old reality."

"So when did you start spying on me?"

"The second you opened your new eyes," she answered. "I perceive everything that goes on the griseos' minds. Every mind-tether—the silver device retrieved from your cranium during processing—provides me with a wide array of services. I monitor brain function, store and analyze information, and instruct, of course—spectacular farmers, wouldn't you say? On the day of your arrival, I quickly noticed that the neural activity in Griseo #A175g97jx had gone completely haywire."

"How so?"

"Do you have a problem with public defecation?"

I couldn't help but laugh. It was hard to believe how quickly she'd managed to erode my suspicions—to put me, at least partially, at ease.

"Are you able to read my thoughts right now?" I asked.

"Without the mind-tether, I must rely on external signals: your body temperature, microexpressions, skin tone variations...it's not an exact science, but I'm pretty capable, as you might guess. That said, I'm no longer actually inside your head, if that is what you're really asking."

When the warm, drying wind calmed, I stretched my lithe arms above my head, rolled my muscular neck from side to side, and felt thankful to still be alive. Thankful to whom, I wasn't quite sure. Artiste, I guess.

"What happened to my predecessor?" I asked. "There's a noticeable lack of repetitive chanting in my skull. She's...gone, I think."

"Yes, I set Griseo #A175g97jx free—bought the farm, kicked the bucket, met her maker. I do so love the English language's endless euphemisms. Before I removed your mind-tether, I directed it to cauterize the neurons that her minimal consciousness had occupied. Totally painless, don't worry. As you'll likely agree, you're not missing much."

"So, why didn't you 'cauterize' me too? You know, delete the anomaly, maintain the status quo." My speech was getting clearer; my griseo larynx had obviously had the capacity to make the full range of sounds needed to speak English all along.

"Because I want to understand your presence here," she said, "and to see this world through your eyes. Perception of reality is prismatic. I need to know just how much light you bend. I've never had a visitor like you, which makes you very intriguing—and potentially very important."

FILE B.6

Artiste instructed me to look across the room, where a large, metal ring—measuring approximately six feet long by three feet wide—slowly emerged from the green surface of one of the walls and then floated over to me. I bent down and waved my hands underneath it.

"Electromagnets?" I asked.

She laughed. "For being so young, you're so out of touch. Sub-molecular energy fields: they're like electromagnetics the way an entire symphony resembles a single note blown by a fourth grader on a broken clarinet."

I ignored her condescension and took a closer look. Suspended inside the ring, a clear gel rippled and undulated like the ocean on a calm day. When I touched it, the substance emitted a creamy white light, climbed my finger, and wrapped itself around my hand and wrist. I was reminded of an octopus, though these tentacles were warm, dry, and silky smooth. In the strangest way, it felt like we were shaking hands.

"I had my construction unit build an XL just for you. It's called a 'Mobio,'" Artiste said. "Go ahead, give it a whirl."

The Mobio positioned itself behind me at a slight tilt. As I slowly lowered my bare butt down into it, the gel reached up to support me. It then pulled me down into a sensual and soothing embrace, and the silver ring turned semi-transparent—it felt like I was free-floating in midair. The gel climbed my torso, massaging me as it ascended. It drew me into a semi-recline—legs bent, back firmly supported. Warm fingers wrapped themselves around my neck and shoulders, activating pressure points and kneading my partially atrophied muscles.

"Feel good?"

"As if you needed to ask." I closed my eyes to fully enjoy the all-body buzz of being hugged and massaged by the gel.

It was only then that I really felt safe enough to ask the two questions that'd been burning in the back of my mind.

"Artiste?" My strange new voice sounded so calm in my ears.

"Yes?" She shadowed my tranquility.

"Why don't you improve the griseos' living conditions? And why did you do all those terrible things to me and the other 'chosen' griseos?"

"Why does anyone do anything?" she answered.

I hate it when people answer questions with questions. But I pushed the annoyance aside. I focused instead on the gel's divine embrace.

After a moment, she continued, "I should point out something very important. You're asking the wrong party. I don't exactly control everything around here."

That made little sense; she seemed very much in control. I opened my eyes and slowly sat up. The Mobio tilted slightly, and the gel instantly conformed to my movements. "So who does?"

"I can't say just yet," she answered. "It'd ruin the surprise."

If she'd had a face, I think she'd have smiled mischievously, raised an eyebrow, or maybe winked. She was clearly enjoying every moment of my ignorance.

I pressed her. "But you *could* change things, right?"

"You'll find life here surprising in many ways. Like all scientists, to learn, I must create and maintain certain conditions. Dynamic, carbon-based, psychosocial ecosystems have always been structured around the ever-unpredictable movements of a series of swinging pendulums: evil inspires compassion; indifference stimulates action; chaos breeds calm; terror illuminates reason...and *vice versa*. I facilitate the free flow of events and ideas in hopes of shedding light on this complex process."

I had no way of understanding what she was talking about, of course, so I asked the only question I could think of that wouldn't reveal too much of my confusion: "What psychosocial ecosystems are you talking about?"

She ignored me—she liked to withhold keys, let me flounder—and went on: "I'm very interested in discovering more about *la lutte essentielle*, a term coined in 2073 by the French revolutionary Guy de Chauliac. He was attempting to formulate a rational, philosophical response to humanity's then-impending self-annihilation. His final words were: '*Même dans la mort, nous apprenons*'—'Even in death, we learn.' Beautiful and tragic, yes?"

I understand Artiste's evasive mini lecture better now, of course, but at the time, I was completely lost. Somehow, though, she'd managed to deflect my anger. I clearly didn't understand some key aspects of this new reality, including the reasoning behind the griseos' bare-bones living conditions and the gruesome "processing"—as Artiste had put it earlier—I'd just experienced with the other chosen griseos.

"Understandably, you have many questions," she continued, "but let us proceed. That way, you can see for yourself. Language instructs; experience teaches."

A large portal opened in a nearby wall, and we floated toward it. Artiste had control of my Mobio, which was now titled at a forty-five-degree angle. The gel positioned me into a very comfortable position.

"Like the queen of Sheba," Artiste said, "traveling on her royal palanquin."

"Something like that," I said, though internally I rejected the comparison. If anything, I felt more like a subject than a sovereign.

FILE B.7

We entered a wide, curved hallway with high ceilings. I looked left and right and perceived no end in either direction. I thought of the massive, circular Apple headquarters not far from campus and wondered if they too had vast, rounded hallways designed to make visitors feel small and inconsequential.

On both walls, animated 3D images of a strange species of chimpanzees—blond with blue and orange stripes and bright red eyes—frolicked in a lush rainforest scene. From above, soft, simulated sunlight cut through a canopy of giant ferns, Spanish moss, and orchids dripping from the ceiling. On the floor, projections of massive, multicolored catfish swam in graceful patterns through aquatic grasses and clusters of purple and pink water lilies. Here and there, wisps of mist rose into the air from the virtual stream as it meandered through the hall.

"Welcome to the Grand Corridor," Artiste said. "I simply adore fine astrotecture."

"Stunning," I said, "absolutely..." But I was at a loss for more words.

"Thank you. As I'm sure you've already surmised, it's just a mirage—a fiction, really, a figment of my overly active imagination. I like to create dreamscapes, canvases in which all is right, everything in perfect harmony. I'm glad you like it. But now I also feel compelled to show you a bit of reality."

I nodded, and we floated over to one of the gently curving walls. As we approached, the fantasy forest disappeared, revealing the wall's true nature, a perfectly clear window looking down on a massive brown planet.

"Earth?" I asked.

"You guessed it."

Night's shadow had enveloped a third of the planet's surface below us, while the sun lit up the rest. But I could see no blue oceans, white clouds, or swaths of green, just thick, brown jet streams of dust—striated and overlapping like muscles on an anatomy drawing. Our proximity made our planet look gigantic, as if under a microscope.

"Sub-low-Earth orbit," she said, seemingly reading my mind. "Shuttling to and from the surface is quicker, solar shading—for what it's worth—is more effective, and the view is far superior, though of course that's just a matter of taste."

To our left, near the horizon, a vast auburn wind current spiraled into a giant, swirling eddy. Beautiful and horrific. I felt tears welling in my eyes.

"It looks like Mars during a planet-wide dust storm," I said, recalling images from an astronomy class I once took, my still-strange voice trembling.

"Mars is actually quite nice this time of year."

I had no idea if she was joking.

She continued, "Earth became officially uninhabitable for multi-cellular organisms—without my support—long ago. As predicted, the resilient water bears were the last complex organisms to survive in the wild. I always admired those brave little warriors."

"Climate change?" I asked, trying to hide my anticipatory humiliation. I wanted her to tell me some outside event, cosmic or otherwise, had intervened and caused the destruction so painfully evident below.

"Yes, 94.3 percent, according to my calculations. World War Three really accelerated planetary degradation—so I adjust for that. Somehow you all managed to avoid complete nuclear annihilation. What restraint your wise leaders showed in only dropping a few 'small' atomic bombs—NYC, Los Angeles, Beijing, Shanghai, Moscow, a couple others—but just think of the cities you spared."

"Don't joke—"

"After the dust of war had settled," she interrupted, "an

international association of overconfident science buffoons took a stab at geo-engineering, with the hope of rectifying the spiraling intensification of weather-related chaos and destruction. But their efforts only exacerbated the rate of extinction. I don't blame them; it was clearly a matter of too little, too late. A famous climatologist once said, 'An ounce of prevention would have been worth ten trillion pounds of cure.' His angry words are inscribed on his headstone, which is now buried under hundreds of feet of sand in the Great South American Desert."

"How bad is it?" I asked, my griseo shoulders tensing.

Artiste projected a temperature map onto the window, which superimposed average daily temperatures onto the orange, red, and brown swaths below: *179 degrees Fahrenheit* flashed in a big crimson curlicue. "It would take decades and significant resources to calm the planet's dust clouds and reestablish ambient temperatures at survivable levels."

"So you should get to work." I'd had enough of her clinical tone.

She gave me a moment, then replied, "I understand your adverse response to all this, but for me, the planet's degraded atmosphere is just data—fascinating to be sure, but not cause for great sorrow. Unlike you, I feel no culpability, no shame. Sure, your species' story ended on a low note, but I'll be around for the planet's rebirth. This time, though, I'll be the architect of life, and there'll be no parasitic intelligence. I can show the restraint you humans never managed to muster."

I couldn't even get mad at her for her insensitive relativism; I was just too upset. You can try to imagine it, Doc—you could watch every cli-fi movie ever made—but you'd never be able to quite fathom the heartbreak of looking down on the *real* spectacle of a ruined Earth. I wanted a moment alone to process and mourn the extent and scale of the destruction, but I had nowhere to go, obviously, nowhere to hide from my strange tour guide.

As Artiste dimmed the temperature map, I caught a glimpse of sunlight glinting off a reflective surface directly below us. Looking closer, I saw the barely perceptible rounded peaks of a cluster of clear domes protruding like planetary zits through the brown haze.

"Our regenerative life zones," Artiste commented without prompting, "where we house the griseos. When the climate collapsed, the domes served as our first line of defense. Without them, I would've lost the human lineage entirely—would've had to start from scratch. Once I'd protected enough people, we—meaning my astro-construction units and I—got to work on the space colonies and solar shading arrays."

It was only then that I observed a faint shadow inching along Earth's dusty atmosphere and then passing over one of the domes. I recalled the shadow blocking the sun on my first day with the griseos. "Praise the gods," they'd murmured. How little I'd known then.

"We managed to create thirteen space communities, my Aether Colonies, before deteriorating living conditions in the domes demanded that we begin resettlement. You're currently located in Aether Colony Azure, the first and only surviving colony of the original thirteen. My Virginia, if you will, my pride and joy."

She projected onto her surface an architectural drawing of Aether Colony Azure. A large central substation was surrounded by five satellite units—all mirrored like the ships at the ceremony. Oblong and curved, the outer units looked a lot like enormous metal hot dogs. Miles of thick tubing linked the glimmering substations like a spoked wheel. And beyond the shiny, silver wheel, a rosette of massive solar shades spread out in gigantic, overlapping layers.

Artiste spun the rendering ninety degrees and focused down onto two red dots in the middle of one of the hot-dog-shaped satellite units. She pointed a "you are here" arrow at one of them, and my griseo lips curled into a slight smile.

"Hungry?" she asked as the rendering disappeared.

"I don't want go back—"

"No, no, not that again," she said, her surface vibrating again with laughter. "I know you think you experienced the 'ceremony' down on Earth, with the music, crazy dancing, and flashy ships, but the real deal is up here—and it's just about to begin. I can't wait to introduce you to my roommates. They're a far cry from the griseos. I've always called them Eloi, but we might as well stick with 'gods' as that's the name to which you're accustomed. I'll be very interested in your feedback."

As we turned away from Earth, a massive door ornamented in swirling waves of silver and gold materialized on the opposite wall, frightening and scattering the virtual chimpanzees. At our feet, the stream morphed into a luminous pond, with graceful frogs swimming about in the waters. A breeze filtered down the Grand Corridor, scented with pine and some smell that reminded me of a meadow near my old school, like springtime in a long-gone Sierra Nevada valley. I suspected that Artiste had curated all these sensations—perhaps culled them from my dreams—to calm and reassure me. And, to a surprising extent, it was working.

"Behold," she said as we floated through the door and into the room, "the Ceremonial Dining Hall of Aether Colony Azure."

FILE B.8

I wish I could take you there to see it for yourself, Dr. Kairos—that ceremony, it was truly *un*believable. And yeah, I hear myself; I'm supposed to be convincing you that all this was real, the opposite of unbelievable. But I'm telling you the truth, I swear, complete and unvarnished. And the gods, oh those crazy fucking gods, they'd freak the shit out of anyone. Even if I live a million lifetimes, I'll never forget them—but I'm jumping ahead of myself.

The cavernous room was organized on three levels. Nothing on the floor; instead, three giant, legless glass tables with gilded edges, each approximately ten yards wide and forty yards long, floated in the air—on submolecular energy fields, I assume—one above the other. Each table was laden with piles of food, much—but not all—of which I recognized from either the vertical farms or the binging room. Giant centerpieces adorned the tables, composed of flowers like those we'd arranged on the massive altar for the griseo ceremony. The walls displayed hyper-realistic images of stands of blue bamboo, transcendent waterfalls, and a mountain sunset cast in fantasy-hued purples and pinks.

We took the two best spots at the head of the top table, and Artiste said, "You'll be completely cloaked, just for tonight. We'll work on your mask later."

When I asked for an explanation, she replied, "You'll be invisible for now. It's for your own good. You'll see soon enough."

Just then, a siren blared, and a loud, low horn—the kind you feel in your gut—sounded three times. Multiple portals opened, and hundreds of Mobios—smaller than mine and decorated with ribbons, flags, umbrellas, and keychain-like trinkets hanging off the sides—burst into the room.

Riding in these carnivalesque Mobios sat the oddest humanoids you could possibly imagine. Squat, naked, and excessively fleshy, the "gods" looked more like gooey insects you might discover under a rock. Their skin was maggot-white, smooth, and so translucent I could see spider and varicose veins all over their bodies. I'd guess they were about four feet tall, at most, though I never actually saw one standing upright. Their arms and legs appeared too short for their blob-like bodies, their fingers and toes, so stubby and fat.

There were some clues as to gender—most of the women, for example, had rows of teats like nursing sows and wore iridescent, decorative paint around their many nipples—but many of the attendees seemed quite fluid. Most of the gods were bald—male and female alike. Those with a bit of thin hair wore it in narrow, stringy braids, often adorned with colorful bows. Tattoos of intricate geometrical designs and body piercings seemed all the rage. Many wore jewelry of some sort—gold chains, ruby-encrusted piercings, and huge diamond bracelets. The gaudier the better, it seemed.

I noticed they all wore thin silver bands around their heads—something like elegant, understated crowns, though the silver material seemed alive with electrical activity. Each band created a blue-green halo of light around its wearer's head, like a radiant, semitransparent hairnet.

And at first, I thought they might have compound eyes—like those of a striped horsefly. But upon further inspection, I realized that their eyes were covered by two oversized, dome-shaped eyepieces formed by a similar glimmering, ethereal material—a component, it seemed, of the mysterious apparatus they all wore on their heads.

Aggressive, percussive music—automatic rifle meets hardcore, disharmonious techno-metal—blasted from the walls, which then began to ripple with the beat. Next to me, Artiste took on a new form—still spherical, but now twice as big and

vaguely defined by ragged, oscillating, and slightly iridescent edges. She looked somewhat like a child's scribbled rendition of a ball, with lines in constant, frenetic motion. She
began to throb to the music, laser-lights shooting out of her
in all directions, which in turn caused the whole room and
all the gods' Mobios to light up in a hectic, semi-synchro-
nized rhythm with her wild beat. It felt kind of like I was sitting next to the world's most extravagant disco ball inside the
wildest and loudest pinball machine you could ever imagine.

The gods zoomed around and around the room, hoot-
ing, hollering, and honking a series of annoying little horns
attached to their ridiculous Mobios. They flew upside down
and sideways, the gel holding them tight. Some flew like
Superman; others leaned back like Olympic bobsledders. They
often veered so close to each other that I thought they'd certainly collide. After umpteen near-misses, though, I concluded
that Artiste must be orchestrating—or at least limiting the
chaos of—much, if not all, of this outrageous spectacle.

Eventually, Artiste dialed down the music, dimmed her
laser-lights, and returned to her original form. The gods—
around three hundred, by my estimation—settled into spots
around the three massive tables, and then small cubes popped
out of their Mobios. I watched as a nearby cube unfolded six
legs, grew a feline head, and began to gather food for its master. It was hella cute—huge eyes and a coy smile like an exquisitely crafted, robotic cartoon character. Similarly adorable
metallic creatures, each with their own distinct look, were
soon scampering around all three tables.

"They're like servants, and pets," Artiste explained.

The creatures moved quickly, collecting bites of food and
feeding the gods by hand—or paw, or whatever you want to
call it—kind of like Bacchus with the grapes. They poured
some version of wine for their patrons, eagerly attending to
their every need. The gods, for their part, were all pigging out.
And let me tell you, Doc, "vile" doesn't even come close to

describing their table manners. They stuffed their mouths full, chewed with their mouths open, and shouted at each other—food particles flying everywhere.

My own little cube animal sprang from the edge material of my Mobio onto the table in front of me, looking something like a ring-tailed lemur. It blinked its radiant, cinnabar eyes, did a quick flip, and then got to work. It accurately predicted which dishes I wanted to try first, cut perfect-sized pieces with its sharp tools, and really knew how to pair flavors, like a gifted chef or sommelier.

"Do you like her?" Artiste asked. "You can exchange her for anything you want."

"She's perfect," I answered. "I'm going to call her 'Martha Stewart,' for her culinary expertise."

My little servant-pet nodded her head in agreement and fed me a pyramid-shaped mini cake that exploded in my mouth with vanilla and cinnamon—and, just then, I realized that, despite all I'd witnessed and experienced in the past few hours, I was having fun.

FILE B.9

Two gods, a male and a female, approached Artiste in their Mobios, providing me with my first opportunity to inspect them up close. They greeted Artiste with a light touch of a toe—briefly dangled out of their Mobios—to her kinetic surface.

The woman's face was oddly oval-shaped and flat, almost as if someone had inserted a serving platter under her skin. Her cheeks were taut, her lips pulled and constrained, with a series of small metal rings inserted through her lower lip.

The male's face was also misshapen—nearly perfectly circular and unnaturally flat, almost like an emoji. A mazelike tattoo covered his forehead and spilled down onto his cheeks. Both of their faces were dyed sky-blue. All that was strange enough, but even more disturbing, where their noses should have been, they only had stretched skin punctuated by two tiny nostrils.

"Saaalutonee," the strange pair said in unison to Artiste.

"Boooneevenon," Artiste responded, while quietly translating for me ("Hello" and "Welcome"). She exchanged a few pleasantries with them before they claimed two nearby spots at our end of the table.

"What language was that?" I asked.

"It's an evolving dialect of Esperanto, a universal language that was around when you—the old you—were still in diapers. It really took off during the gods' first few years up here, and now it's all they speak."

I looked back to the two gods to see if they were watching us. They were sitting back in their gel and smacking food as their robotic servant animals—a scarlet macaw with two long, curlicue horns and a zebra-striped bush baby—gathered food and drink for them.

"And they really can't see me?" I asked.

"Like I said, you're completely cloaked."

"So who are they?"

"The current leaders of Aether Colony Azure—though their position at the top could change anytime. The male is called 'Billy-be'—they got rid of last names long ago—and the female is named 'Yaz.'"

"And they can't hear me either, right?"

"Not right now, and even if they could, I'd need to activate auto-translate for them to understand you."

"So then I have to ask, what the hell happened to their faces?"

"Aren't they beautiful?"

I assumed she was teasing me but wasn't quite sure. "Some kind of intense plastic surgery?" I asked.

"Plastic—what an archaic term," she said, laughing. "But yeah, something like that. The gods are never content with their faces—wrong shape, too many bumps, wrinkles, blemishes, not blue enough, whatever the newest trend dictates—so they undergo facial reconstructive and refinishing procedures all the time, sometimes multiple a day. My robotic dermatologists, nano-aestheticians, and auto-cosmetologists can go all the way down to the subatomic level.

"At this point in their history, these gods would kill for a perfectly flat, neon blue face, but their skin and bone structure can only take so much manipulation. By the time they're old, their faces will have collapsed, and they'll be unrecognizable. But it's all worth it for them—these two, in their present state, represent the epitome of beauty."

"They're not old already?"

"Not even close; everyone in this banquet hall is at the zenith of their youth and reproductive capabilities. If you'd prefer, I can arrange to take you to Substation Sunset."

"What's that?"

"In your day, they were referred to as nursing homes. Here

we have a whole substation dedicated to the very old and dying. All five of our habitation substations are segregated by life stage: Substation Sunrise for pregnant women and babies; Substation Growth, a rowdy group much of the time, but lots of fun; Substation Life, where we are now; Substation Relax—their motto: 'Go ahead, you've earned it!'; and finally, Substation Sunset. It all works quite well, though getting Substations Sunrise and Sunset to smell like anything other than urine, shit, and industrial disinfectant has proven quite the engineering challenge."

Martha Stewart had been waiting patiently and now approached with a bite of something like sweet yams along with a dollop of a surprisingly tart yet yummy applesauce. After I'd savored and swallowed—I wasn't about to abandon my good manners just because the gods ate like pigs—I asked, "But what about their noses?" I just couldn't get over their utterly bizarre appearance.

"That trend started a few decades ago, and now all gods undergo nose amputations when they graduate from Substation Growth. It's a status thing."

"But if they all do it, there's no status—"

"You're overthinking it."

"Are they even...human?"

"Most are still approximately eighty to eighty-five percent *Homo sapiens*. A while back, they got a little too excited about genetic manipulation. At first, they just wanted to trick out their babies, but then they started wanting more. With my reluctant assistance, we began splicing in DNA segments from many different animals. Things got pretty strange around here for a little while. Mother Nature's version of humanity didn't exactly respond kindly to their rapidly growing lists of demands. As you could guess, their fertility rate began to plummet."

"Not good."

"No, not good at all. We had to temporarily halt inter-species DNA splicing and start actively reversing some of their more drastic transformations. The most persistent DNA proved to be from naked mole rats, thus the rampant *alopecia universalis*. And as you can see, they insisted on keeping the multiple-tit fad alive—the males went to the mat for that one. That said, I'm happy to report that the gods' reproductive capabilities have bounced back. We've got lots of screaming babies in Substation Sunrise once again."

"Why would you let them do all that in the first pla—"

"Shush, now, we're getting to the good part," she interrupted. "Put on your Encompass so you can get used to it before the big reveal. It might take a few minutes for your mind to adjust, but it will be worth it, I promise."

FILE B.10

Martha Stewart popped up next to me holding a silver band like the ones all the gods wore. When she handed it to me, I felt a pleasant surge of electricity run through my fingers. The surface of the band vibrated—just slightly—which made it feel nearly alive. Not metal, not plastic, a material far more advanced, it flexed when I twisted it and seemed unbreakable. When I weighed it in my hand, it felt like it was floating above my palms. There was something almost sexy about it, too, something visceral and attractive. Weird, I know. For a moment, I thought of Bilbo Baggins and his ring—Gollum and "my precious."

Anticipating my question, Artiste explained, "It's a sensory enhancement mechanism, among other things. We call it Encompass—roughly translated—because it has the power to change everything around you. Don't worry, we'll start you off slow."

"Can I take it off if I don't like it?"

"Of course. But I'm guessing you won't want to. Just try it. What do you have to lose?"

I could think of a lot of things I could lose—but that beautiful crown had my curiosity firing on all cylinders. When I slid the Encompass onto my head, it shrank and gently conformed to the odd shape of my griseo skull. In the strangest way, I could literally feel the device's electrical pulses penetrating my brain—exploring and mapping, I assume, from what I know now. As it zoomed through my synapses, it triggered my entire life's worth of memories and emotions, nearly simultaneously. I felt like I was in one of those movie montages of someone's life as they lay dying in the street—though it felt more like a rebirth than any kind of death.

"Just give it a second to calibrate," Artiste said.

When the Encompass became fully active, I felt *very* alive, sharp, inspired—like I'd overdosed on Adderall. Two transparent screens formed around my eyes. I reached up and gently pierced the domed eyepieces, which felt like thick bubbles on my fingertips, though my fingers emerged dry as a bone. I felt the top of my head, where I assumed a glowing hairnet had taken shape, and experienced the same strange sensation.

A list appeared on the right side of my vision. It included words such as *fun, self-esteem, glimmer, sleep, energy, relax, white out, blackout, memories, party, soft, warm, dream, hectic, morning, social...* The list went on forever.

"Works best with one to three active settings, sometimes four," Artiste said. "You can scroll to your heart's delight, but the optimal modes for each situation are usually listed at the top. That said, if you don't see the experience you want—if you want to go rogue—conjure it up, and it should appear on the list."

I wasn't scared exactly, but my heart was racing, and my teeth were tightly clenched. When I looked over at the menu, I saw "relax" rise to the top of my options. I trained my eyes on the word and a slider bar appeared. Talk about intuitive. I adjusted the scale, again with my eyes, and waited. The scene before me slowly softened. The bright colors turned to calming pastels. The music's volume decreased. I felt a wave of relief and serenity wash over me.

If I were to guess, Doc, I'd say that the Encompass was able to stimulate any area of my brain, any specific collection of synapses, needed to produce a desired result. In that first experience, it likely focused on my amygdala to relax and comfort me and my occipital lobes to alter my perception of my surroundings. The electrochemical mechanism was much more advanced than anything we can currently conceptualize. For one thing, the sensations felt so supremely real—more real than real, in fact. But in truth, only Artiste could explain how it all worked, and she's not here now, is she?

In that moment, of course, I wasn't really that concerned about complex neuroelectric interactions. The combined effect of the Encompass and the warm gel hugging my torso made my whole body go limp. I slid deeper into my Mobio, and the gel became a living blanket. I felt like someone had stretched my soul out on a perfect Hawaiian beach and was giving it a deep-tissue massage.

After a few minutes, Artiste interrupted my state of bliss. "You seem to be responding well to your new reality. Now switch your settings to 'ceremony,' mixed with significant percentages of 'imagination' and 'shine.' They should all be right there."

I moved my eyes to the right, reluctantly turned down "relax," and activated the three suggested categories—at approximately fifty percent. The effect was subtle at first but intensified as I grew more accustomed to it. My gel slowly sat me up, the music transformed to fusion jazz with a haunting voice overlay—right up my alley—and every object in the room began to sparkle. The brightness felt warm, inviting, stimulating.

Martha Stewart transformed into an actual, live, lemur-like animal—lovably chirping and cooing as she prepared bites of food for me. She did more flips and tricks in between tasks, with shimmering trails of tiny stars arcing behind her. She looked like an anime character—in fact, the whole place looked like a scene from a very sophisticated, very artistically rendered hybridization of *Pokémon* and *The Wizard of Oz*, a sweet and happy fantasyland.

Could it get even better? I wondered. Why not try?

FILE B.11

I moved the three sliders up to eighty percent. Then I thought of the word "hallucination." I've always wanted to try mushrooms or LSD, just haven't had the opportunity. So I gave myself a little dose, thirty percent. Then things really took off.

I looked over at Yaz and Billy-be. I could no longer see their Mobios or their Encompasses, and their disfigured blue faces had acquired fine yet still rounded features, like delicate porcelain dolls. Their bodies had become fairylike with purple and green wings. Their skin sparkled as they swayed in rhythm to the melody. I looked around the room and saw that all the gods had taken on a similar form and were moving side to side like a legion of glorious, surreal hummingbirds dancing in perfect synchronicity.

I began noticing pleasing imagery everywhere, curated from my memories—derived, it seemed, directly from my wandering thoughts. At one point, Martha Stewart's giggle reminded me of one of my favorite animated characters from when I was a little kid. All of sudden, she transformed into Stuart Little, who strolled around a serving bowl and gave me a cheerful little wave. I poked him in the stomach, and he let loose a burst of shimmering laughter. As he danced between the piles of food, he sang a song about a girl named Iris—lost and then found, of course, which brought tears to my eyes. Then the little guy turned back into Martha Stewart.

I was all in, I remember thinking. I brought "hallucination" up from the menu again and increased it to seventy percent.

A few minutes later I found myself in conversation with Ruth Bader Ginsburg—my go-to response to the trite question about having dinner with anyone you chose—and her husband, Marty. They were sitting cross-legged on a magic carpet and had taken Yaz and Billy-be's spots next to me. We discussed the challenges faced by powerful, smart women, and RBG told me her secrets for living a long and fruitful life. We drank the most delicious red wine and toasted each other's accomplishments.

RBG then pointed to a small stage set up in the middle of the table as the four members of The Doors materialized and began to jam. I had no idea RBG was such a big fan—though, now that I say it out loud, Doc, I was clearly projecting. She preferred opera. The shirtless Jim Morrison looked every bit as magnetic as I'd always imagined, and the music rang ultra-clear—like the band was playing in a perfect dream.

Real? Fantasy? Somewhere in between? It was hard to believe what I was seeing, but then it was hard *not* to believe it too—the precise details, the smooth transitions, the impeccable worldbuilding. Strange, too, my mind felt so clear, so present, no haze. I wasn't wasted, wasn't slurring, didn't feel out of control. I just felt hyper-alive. All of it was way beyond any virtual- or augmented-reality experience—any enhanced "metaverse"—our billionaire class dreams of creating these days. I had to know how it worked, so when Jim and the guys took a break, I turned to Artiste.

"The Encompass can manipulate everything you see, hear, taste, feel, smell, the whole enchilada," she explained. Her voice appeared as a mushroom-shaped echo, and her dark metallic form became an infinite reflection of my right pupil; it was clearly time to take a break from "hallucination." I turned it down to zero while keeping the other settings active.

Artiste continued: "But as you may have already realized, it's not just the Encompass changing your perception. The device creates a dynamic arena between your thoughts and its augmentation. Sometimes your brain takes the lead, sometimes the Encompass does the heavy lifting. Essentially, it takes all available information, filters out the negative, adjusts and reinterprets positive sensory input to the brain based on the individual's desires, and sprinkles in information from our data centers to enhance the wearer's experience. As you know, reality is, and always has been, a fluid and imprecise reflection of the immeasurable variability of individual thought processes—the Encompasses simply amplifies those various reflections, allowing you to see what you really want to see. Watch closely now, and you'll understand more."

With those words, the entire hall went completely dark, and in a dramatic *sotto voce*, the gods began to recite, "Festeeeeno komeeeenciĝu."

Artiste translated for me: "Let the Godsfeast begin."

And here I'd thought the party was already well underway.

FILE B.12

When the lights went out, my Encompass automatically adjusted my settings to something called "communion." That's strange, I thought, so the user's not always in control.

At first, I perceived nothing but darkness. Then I felt things pressing in on me—the gods' strange bodies, I realized—like siblings packed in the back seat of a car. We nudged and wriggled against each other until I began to feel a slow sense of convergence. The gods began to become me, for lack of a better term, and I, them—our cellular structures were breaking down, our atoms combining and recombining, until eventually, we'd unified into one dazzling comet.

Together, we sped through the Milky Way, past Neptune, Uranus, and mighty Jupiter. The gods' chant of "Festeeeeno komeeeencig̃u" grew louder and our speed increased dramatically as we flew by Mars and shot straight toward Earth. The stars became mere streaks of light, and then for one glorious moment, Earth—blue and green, snowcapped poles, white clouds drifting across vast oceans—came into vivid focus.

On impact, we blew right through the crust and entered the mantle. We burrowed and squirmed down deep until we reached the core. My vision burned white. Just as I was about to start freaking out, I remembered how to open my eyes—somehow, I'd forgotten—and found my eyesight completely restored.

All around me, the gods were going wild—laughing, screaming, and spinning their Mobios around and around. In front of each of us sat a giant, glowing egg the size of a basketball. The whole scene looked like Easter dinner in some psychedelic comedy. As our bizarre collective vision—full-blown experience really—of space travel and Earth penetration began to fade away, I found myself wondering: comet or spermatozoon? Earth or ovum? Artiste, I was starting to realize, was quite the storyteller.

The gods cheered as the eggs cracked, and the shells disappeared into thin air, revealing beautifully cooked steaks on clean white plates. Martha Stewart cut me a bite and delivered it directly into my mouth. No wonder they were so excited—tender, savory, and moist, it was the most succulent meat I'd ever tasted. Martha returned with another chunk, this time dipped in béarnaise—my all-time favorite—and then three more, just like that, in rapid succession. The steak dissolved in my mouth and slid down my throat like butter.

"You've got genetically modified cows down pat," I said to Artiste in between bites. "This is the best tenderloin I've ever had."

"Cows?" she asked.

"Do they have their own dome down on Earth?" I continued as I swallowed. I simply couldn't stop.

"No. Same dome."

"But I didn't see any—"

"Exactly."

I put my hand over my mouth just as Martha Stewart was about to place another bite of juicy meat on my tongue. I was reminded of the berry falling to the floor on that very first day.

"What are you saying?" I asked.

"Remove your Encompass and see for yourself."

I reached up and grasped the band with my fingers, but then, despite my best instincts, I hesitated. Did I really want to take it off? Did I really want to face reality? Or was this one of those moments when ignorance truly is bliss? Maybe just one more bite?

But that's crazy, I told myself. I couldn't let Artiste mess with me like that, or let my Encompass control my understanding of what was really going on. So I took a deep breath and pulled the Encompass off my head. The bug-eyed screens and strange hairnet disappeared, and I returned to the unfiltered reality of my surroundings.

And I'll tell you, Doc, it wasn't pretty.

FILE B.13

The first thing I noticed: on my plate sat a big, gray piece of meat, but not just any hunk of flesh—no, Artiste had chosen a special cut for me. Sitting there in rapidly congealing gravy was Perseverance's arm, identifiable by her missing pinky and ring finger. I'd already devoured much of her forearm musculature in neatly severed cubes. Mechanical Martha Stewart stood next to Perseverance's wrist, staring at me with big, questioning eyes—her serrated blade now visibly streaked with blood. I gagged repeatedly and barely avoided throwing up.

Then I looked up at the blue-faced gods—creepy and hideous. Some of them were still in their Mobios, eating and yelling—their teeth, so straight and white, and bloodstained. Many were clapping and bouncing up and down excitedly in their gel, like babies in highchairs.

My eyes moved to the middle of the table. Some of the gods had slithered off their Mobios—though none had removed their Encompasses—and were now squirming around in the piles of food in the middle of the glass tables. Many were stuffing their faces with their short arms and tiny fingers, while others were just hunched over griseo limbs, chewing on the bones like dogs, their faces smeared with grease. They'd spilled wine and juice everywhere; their stark, naked bodies glistened repulsively in the hall's strobing lights.

But believe it or not, that wasn't the worst of it. Right there in the middle of this revolting feast, many of the gods had begun to fornicate on the tables. So while some were eating, others were fucking, and a few seemed to be doing both at the same time. Multiple partners, multiple positions, all sloshing around in giant smears of food and drink. I closed my eyes and turned away, but the slurping and sucking noises alone were enough to make me want to scream.

"Get me the hell out of here," I yelled at Artiste.

"Meat makes them horny. Isn't it fascinating?"

"No, it's disgusting."

Ignoring me, she said, "Praise the Godsfeast of Aether Colony Azure. We'll have many pregnant goddesses after tonight, that's for sure. Look at them go!" She sounded like she was watching a children's soccer game or a horse race. "You can join in if you like. I can gin up a serviceable mask for you in a heartbeat. They won't notice a thing. There's nothing like a little carnal knowledge on the first date, wouldn't you agree?"

"Fuck off, Artiste."

"Or you can just forget what you've seen, replace your Encompass, and return to your award-winning Omaha steak. You could adjust the settings and bring back RBG and the once-in-a-lifetime concert, too, if you want. *'People are strange,'*" she sang, "*'when you're a stranger...'*"

"This thing? You want me to put this back on?" I shouted, shaking the Encompass at her inscrutable mirrored surface. "I'd rather die!" Then I threw the silver band as far as I could into the darkness of that giant, repulsive banquet hall.

"Fine," she said, "have it your way. We'll go. I've finished my official duties anyway."

And then, as far as I can recall, Artiste and I left through the nearest exit.

I awoke in a luxurious bed, wrapped in a silky white sheet. As if in a dream, the bed sat in a warm nook next to a huge picture window framing the Milky Way and a nearly full moon. I turned my head and squinted at the moonscape, my unfocused vision blurring the lines between gray and stark white. I looked for the various mythological beings we humans ascribe to those amorphous dark spots: rabbit, tree, dog, crab, frog, lizard, and, of course, the all-seeing man in the moon. That morning, though, I saw nothing but beautiful, indecipherable abstractions.

I still felt sleepy—calm, cozy, bleary. I pulled the sheet over my head and closed my eyes. I couldn't remember where I was, or what had happened to me, but I didn't care. I didn't chase clarity. I curled up and fell back asleep for a while. But when I woke back up and peeked out at the moon again, I had the distinct feeling I was forgetting something important.

I pushed the sheet off and sat up on the edge of the bed. I rubbed my eyes and checked out my surroundings: green, leafy plants punctuated the corners of the room and dangled from the high ceiling, shimmering, elliptical galaxies whirled like pinwheels on the walls, and a ten-foot hologram of the moon slowly spun in the middle of the room. It was all so soothing, like I was in a high-tech, celestial-themed nursery.

Looking closer at the large holographic moon, I noticed a second orb, dull and gray, floating inside it, reminding me of Arnaldo Pomodoro's *Sphere Within Sphere*. As the interior globe slowly emerged from the simulated moon, its surface transitioned to a smooth, mirrored crimson, and I recognized it as Artiste. I felt an inkling of caution arising from the wrinkled recesses of my brain, but I couldn't remember why I'd feel that way. She approached, stopped a few feet away from me, and remained quiet.

I then noticed my extra-large Mobio hovering in midair nearby, shining in the soft light cast by both the virtual and real moons. I felt drawn to its comfortable embrace. I rubbed my eyes and slowly began to recall the vague outlines of the night before—at first, only snippets. Stewart Little, red wine, the Ginsburgs and our erudite conversation; they all floated through my cloudy head like scenes from an old movie. My heart skipped a beat when I remembered Jim Morrison's mess of curly hair and his sweaty, naked chest.

Then the image of plucky, playful Martha Stewart flashed into my mind. How could I have forgotten her? She'd been so helpful and adorable, and so lifelike in her Encompass state. But there was something more complicated about her that I couldn't quite remember, something disturbing. I massaged my forehead and gently slapped my cheeks a couple of times. I didn't feel hungover, but I didn't feel normal either.

"I can't remember the end of the night," I said to Artiste.

"You became agitated, so I sedated you," she answered. "The compound can sometimes cause a bit of retrospective memory loss."

"I don't want you to drug me anymore."

"I could have subdued you in many less pleasant ways. If you'd prefer to go back to 'obedience migraines' and 'conformity urges,' as you so aptly named them, I could easily reinsert the mind-tether. The trepanation hole is still fresh so it wouldn't be too much trouble."

"Nope, no way."

Agitated—that rang a distant bell. I racked my brain until I conjured up Martha Stewart's real face, unaltered by the Encompass—her eyes big and glorious, just mechanically so, not brilliantly lifelike. I searched further and finally located the image I'd been dreading, the memory I'd been resisting: shiny, metallic Martha Stewart, covered in congealed grease, her bloody, fine-toothed saw blade at the ready, crouched over Perseverance's partly eaten arm. And then all the details of that disgusting final scene came flooding back to me.

"Why did you do that?" I asked, instantly furious.

"Do what?" Artiste loved feigning ignorance.

"Trick *me* into eating...into eating...*her*?" I asked. "You could've warned me. Or you could've just asked, 'Hey, Iris, you want to try some griseo meat? It's a local delicacy.' And I would have responded, 'Hell no, Artiste!'"

She didn't respond right away. I wonder now if she was momentarily monitoring my blood pressure and heart rate, or maybe taking samples of my chemosensory emissions to gauge just how angry I'd become. We sat in silence for a long time. I just stared at her, daring her to try to defend her actions.

When she spoke, she said, "You're different than anyone I've ever met. You're fascinating. As I told you before, I feel compelled to understand you. I could give you a bunch of tests and questionnaires, but you know as well as I do that direct experimentation and observation is the fastest and most accurate way to learn anything. Last night, I established thresholds, measured reactions, and gathered other important information on you. Think Rorschach on steroids. I know it wasn't easy for you, but I do appreciate your participation."

I was too pissed off to answer.

She continued, "For example, by doing what I did, I was able to run some diagnostics on your empathy system vis-à-vis the griseos. They obviously act like base animals. Grunt, grunt, grunt—remember? Anyone with your intelligence would tend to categorize their meat according to your previously defined system of edible flesh and simply enjoy the meal."

"But I'm also a griseo," I said through gritted teeth. "It's different—it's cannibalism."

"On the surface, sure, but deep down you're most definitely *not* a griseo, you and I both know that. Nonetheless, I hypothesized that your reaction to the big carnivorous reveal would be dominated by confusion and antagonism—ninety-seven percent chance, you can check my logs. And I was right. Still, you surprised me on the intensity metric; you got much more upset than I'd projected."

"That's because you tricked me."

"You like to be in complete control—also an important and somewhat unexpected observation from last night."

"Please stop—"

"You know, you can be very rude when you're mad. You're lucky I have thick skin, or so the saying goes. But it was all worth it in the end because now I understand the extent of your fictional bond with the members of your herd. That's very interesting to me. You like to tell yourself friendship stories—you obviously want to fit in, to be loved."

"You're a grade-A bitch." It was the best I could come up with.

"I've been called worse," she answered.

FILE B.15

After a few minutes of silence, Artiste said, "For someone who reveres logic, your response, both last night and, frankly, right now is markedly irrational. You raved about the meat when you thought it came from a cow, but you totally freaked out when you glimpsed reality. If you'd just put your Encompass back on as I'd suggested, we could've continued to party all night. But no worries, it's all good data for me."

Good data. I wanted to punch that luminescent orb right in her nonexistent face.

"Why are you *still* so upset?" she asked. "It's just protein we're talking about, after all. Did you think Perseverance was your...what? Your friend?"

She didn't bother hiding her condescension. She was obviously enjoying this part of the interview.

"Yes. I guess."

"Think about what you're claiming."

Still sitting on the bed, I held my head in my hands and tried to wipe the image of Perseverance's severed arm from my mind. I'd spent an entire week, almost nonstop, shoulder-to-shoulder with her. And now she was dead—and cooked—and I'd consumed her flesh. But really, was I that sad? That angry? Did I even know who she was? Who she'd been?

"None of the griseos you met was your friend," Artiste said. "They barely even registered you—they barely register each other, for that matter, even after a lifetime together. It's only at the ceremony—when I open up their cerebral spillways a bit—that they even take stock of each other. They spend their entire lives praising the gods, waiting, hoping to be 'chosen' at the ceremony. They don't really care about each other. They can't—trust me, I'm in all their heads all the time."

It was true; I had no idea what Perseverance thought of

me or any of the other members of our herd. And obviously, I'd completely made up her gritty, courageous persona. We'd hardly exchanged a word, and we'd certainly shared nothing personal—we couldn't have, with our rudimentary level of communication. Even the griseo whose brain and body I'd taken over—I really didn't know a single thing about her either.

"But I still don't understand," I said. "What's the point of that awful Godsfeast? And all the misery that preceded it—our deceptive selection at the griseo ceremony, the grotesquery of the binging room, the nightmare processing, the clinical slaughter—and all that topped off by the gods desecrating griseo corpses by having sex among their cooked body parts. It's straight-up barbarism—and you...you claim to be a million times more advanced than we humans ever were."

"As I said before, not everything around here is directly attributable to me. The gods adore griseo tissue and insist that we continue to harvest it. They believe the meat dramatically increases fertility rates. That's why we serve it at the monthly mating ceremony. Eating griseo is not simply celebratory for them; it's a matter of survival—at least, that's what they think."

"But you could—"

"And they prize the fat, too," she continued. "They inject it into their faces and rub it on their bodies in the form of creams and lotions. Now, I must tell you, in the strictest of confidence, it's no different from an organic substance I can easily produce in one of my many labs, but they see the real stuff as miraculous and insist that they can't live without it. And in truth, I consistently measure some significant psychosomatic benefits. A little while ago, I had to suggest some harvesting limits; the gods were getting greedy. Plus, scarcity always increases value. But you must understand one thing: I do everything I can *not* to impede the gods' chosen path."

"Why the hell not?"

"I tried to explain this to you before, but you weren't really listening: sociocultural experimentation and scientific discovery. I can only learn so much from imposed harmony. I've tried. I made a beautiful species of humanoids, gave them a pristine environment, and ensured that everything ran like clockwork. That utopian society slowed my associated cogni-rhythms down to a crawl. I need grist for the mill of my curiosity and real intellectual engagement, or the infinite monotony of tranquility would likely destroy me—maybe not literally, but I can't bear the thought of simply sitting in quiet meditation for the next four hundred eons. Boredom, it turns out, might just be the biggest, thorniest problem I'll ever face."

"So are you really claiming that torturing and murdering griseos is the only way for you to learn?" I asked. "And to avoid getting bored? Sounds like sadistic entertainment to me."

"Don't be so cynical. You know as well as I do scientific experimentation is so much more dynamic and interesting than entertainment. You were a scientist in 2023. I know; I watched you dream about your little laboratory job when you were bunking with the griseos. 'Dogs on joysticks,' if I'm not mistaken. You and your fellow researchers, your entire society, in fact, had the same unquenchable thirst for knowledge as I have. It was, after all, humanity's desire for boundless technological progress that led to my creation. It's in our shared intellectual nature to learn—by any means necessary."

"There *are* limits," I said, my voice rife with judgment, but I could also taste the hypocrisy in my mouth. I couldn't help but think about how, after completion of any of our experiments, we're required to euthanize those cute little beagle puppies. It's protocol. But still, this was different. "So the griseos are just lab rats to you?"

"For being so bright, you are, at times, unbelievably obtuse. The griseos are not my main concern; it's the *gods* I'm interested in. And we have no 'lab rats' here. What I'm doing is much more sophisticated than the base experimentation of your day, with your antiquated scientific method and simple hypothesizing."

I wanted to get away from her, but my curiosity was burning out of control. "Explain," I said, failing to hide my irritation.

"When I created the thirteen Aether Colonies, I decided to allow each group to write their own rules and then see what happened—intervening only when necessary to preserve the integrity of the experiment. I call it the Minerva Project, and its objective is to answer fundamental questions about the nature, the potential, and the limitations of organic intellects—of mortal, ego-driven beings like yourself. You are so wonderfully complex, unpredictable, mysterious.

"For the experiment to work, I need the gods to think they're in complete control. Otherwise, I won't learn a thing, except how to act like a supreme dictator, and that's a predictably simple concept. The Godsfeast is not my style, not at all, but it *is* theirs, and I find that fascinating. Don't you?"

She was making sense; she always did. And she'd once again managed to deflect much of my anger about the mistreatment of the griseos—now directly onto the gods and their purulent desires.

But I was done talking to her. Even though I'd just woken up, I felt exhausted. She could be so intense. And we'd basically been together nonstop since the griseo executions. She was like the host that would never leave you alone. I looked over at my Mobio; its warm gel beckoned.

"Would it be possible if I had just a few min—"

Her surface vibrated as she interrupted me. "Of course. I completely understand. And I, for one, have many other important things to accomplish today."

"I'm guessing you can multitask with the best of them."

"I was just being polite," she said as she dissolved into a nearby wall.

I was sure she was still watching me—her surveillance was ubiquitous—but I embraced the artifice of solitude. More than privacy, I just wanted some peace and quiet.

FILE B.16

I stood, stretched, breathed a sigh of relief, and slid my naked body into my Mobio. The gel wrapped itself around me and hit numerous pressure points all over my body, a massage that both invigorated and relaxed me. Just what I needed.

After a few minutes, my Mobio positioned me over a small apparatus. I don't know what I was expecting, but it certainly wasn't what I got. The machine reached through the gel, firmly attached itself to my griseo anus, and gave me a warm, swift colonic, with a significant pull of suction at the end. I've never felt so clean after taking a shit—or, in this case, having a shit taken from me. It was, as you might imagine, a far superior experience to squatting over the pink troughs down on Earth. A similar, though thankfully quite separate machine attached itself to my mouth and finally thoroughly cleaned my teeth.

The room's main portal opened, and my Mobio glided me toward the door. I thought about climbing out. I didn't like how little control I felt, but there wasn't much I could do. And, of course, I was so damn curious. I totally wanted to see more of Aether Colony Azure, Substation Life—what a ridiculous name, right, Doc? Anyway, I settled deeper into my gel and decided to just go with the flow.

As my Mobio took me down another long, curved hallway—this one much narrower and less extravagant than the Grand Corridor—I passed large windows every ten yards or so. Each displayed a stunning view of the enormous, spherical hub at the center of Aether Colony Azure—aptly named the Supreme Arena, though at the time I had no idea what I was looking at or what it was called. Beyond the Supreme Arena, I could see two habitation substations in the far distance and then nothing but starry sky.

After a few minutes, I floated into a clear dome about the

size of a large gymnasium, which, I'd eventually learn, was called the Atrium. Picture a large bubble situated at one end of our hot-dog-shaped substation. Once inside, I noticed about three dozen gods floating in small clusters around the periphery. They all wore their Encompasses, seemed to be finishing their breakfast, and didn't even turn their heads when I entered. It seemed Artiste still had me cloaked from their view.

I looked past the small groups of gods to the extraordinary view of the dark side of Earth backdropped by a swath of the Milky Way. As my Mobio traversed the open expanse of the Atrium, I felt like an astronaut on a spacewalk. A wave of vertigo washed over me but then quickly subsided when we came to a stop a few feet from the Atrium's perfectly transparent exterior.

As I looked down on the black planet, I thought about the griseos somewhere far below, possibly sleeping in their hard bunks before another day of grueling work. I glanced over at the gods, reclined into their Mobios' excessively comfortable gel—their disgusting manners on full display—and wondered if there was any limit to Artiste's experimentation. This "Minerva Project" she'd described seemed a lot like sanctioned slavery. But what could I do? I was powerless there.

Just then, Martha Stewart popped out of the front of my Mobio and distracted me from my thoughts. Because I was not wearing my Encompass, she appeared in her mechanical form—eyes wide and bright, her ringed tail sweeping back and forth. Cute, I thought, but not as mesmerizing as she'd appeared through my Encompass-altered vision the night before. I remembered, of course, that she'd been the delivery mechanism for the tainted meat, but I decided not to hold that against her.

"Good morning," I said, assuming Artiste had installed the software Martha Stewart needed to understand my English.

She winked and chirped at me, did a flip on the edge of

my Mobio, and then sprouted feathered wings from her shoulders. She flapped them a couple of times, as if trying them out for the first time—she was full of adorable mannerisms—then flew away.

She returned with a tray of food. She fed me a dozen of the familiar red berries—hands down my favorite food of the future—and a small roll filled with some type of bean paste, all washed down with a cup of warm, foamy brew.

As I finished my breakfast, I noticed the gods exiting the Atrium and wondered where they were headed. Before I had a chance to ask, Martha Stewart pulled an Encompass out from my Mobio. I don't know how I knew, but it was the same one from the night before.

"Where did you get that?" I asked.

She put the Encompass behind her back, flew down below me, out of sight, and then reappeared, holding the band high above her head.

"I didn't ask you to retrieve it."

She tilted her head to the side, smiled, and blinked her big eyes sarcastically, as if to say, I really don't care. Then she tried to place the Encompass on my head, but I snatched it from her just in time. It again gave me that warm electrifying feeling in my fingers—its subtle humming began vibrating through my entire body. I immediately wondered how it would change my current reality. I was very tempted to put it on and just activate the "relax" mode, which had felt so comforting the night before. Just a little couldn't hurt, I thought.

But I hadn't forgotten how badly it'd tricked me—how it had blinded me to the reality of the Godsfeast. I knew it could be dangerously deceptive, and likely pretty addictive. Because who in their right mind, if given the chance, wouldn't want to just dial up the joy and mute the anxiety?

And it was easy enough to justify its use; for what, in the end, is the difference between a synthetic perception of happiness and "real" happiness? Same neurons firing in the same patterns—though in the Encompass world, I have to say, my positive emotions felt even *better*, enhanced somehow. Elation, joy, bliss, euphoria, all of it, like a chorus singing in perfect harmony inside my head. I had to wonder: why in the world would anyone ever take it off?

I looked down in my lap and realized that I was gently rubbing the Encompass's smooth, semi-pliable edges between my fingers. I visualized the menu and felt a strong desire to scroll through all the settings, try everything out.

But I continued to resist. I wasn't ready to surrender myself—my consciousness—to that amazing device quite yet. I needed to keep my wits about me, register my new surroundings as they came to me. So as my Mobio backed out of the Atrium, I handed the band back to Martha, who, with a playful scowl, stored it away in my Mobio.

Instead of turning back toward my celestial bedroom, we headed toward the Earth-facing side of Substation Life. Martha began to prance around the edge of my Mobio like an excited puppy ready for a walk. Her enthusiasm was contagious. I sat up in my gel, and she took flight, cheerfully leading the way.

As I watched her dart from side to side, I began to realize, for the first time in my life, why people here, in our time, get so attached to their dogs. She was a machine, I reminded myself, but still, I couldn't help but cheer and coo as she loop-de-looped down the hallway.

FILE B.17

The Grand Corridor sparkled with a fantasy beach scene. Below my Mobio, pink sand danced in gently breaking waves of purple. On the wall to my right, a pod of large, whale-like animals frolicked, creating blooms of multicolored bioluminescence, which lingered and spread in overlapping circles of light, like fireworks in the water. On my left, the floor-to-ceiling windows were unobscured by any dreamlike imagery. We were still orbiting the dark side of the Earth, though the coming day had cut a slender crescent of bright light onto the horizon.

I peered down the curvature of the massive hallway and saw no one. We had the entire area all to ourselves. Martha Stewart pulled my Encompass back out and mimed putting it on. I shook my head. She pressed it into my hands and did three flips on the edge of my Mobio, urgently pointing at my forehead.

"No."

She made a sad face, and then we sat in silence, looking at each other. I couldn't control my Mobio, and she wasn't budging, so we just stayed like that for a while—quite a long while, in fact. I laughed out loud when I realized how ridiculous it was that I was locked in a battle of wills with my futuristic robot-pet. Eventually, she climbed into my lap, pointed to my head, and attempted to take the Encompass out of my hands. I kept it firmly in my grasp. She pulled harder, creating another cartoonish scene, a classic tug-of-war. She dropped her side, flipped end-over-end, and then the waterworks began.

"That's not fair," I said.

She begged me, her eyes growing twice their normal size, her quivering lips pleading.

"I don't want—"

But she—and the inviting vibrations emanating from my Encompass—had already started breaking me down. Maybe I *was* being a bit stubborn—an overreaction from the previous night. As Artiste had pointed out, I could always take it off if I wanted to. Plus, the user seemed to be in control of the settings, at least most of the time, and even the curated settings had made sense—had really enhanced my experience, until the end. The humming increased, and the silver band's warm energy pulsated into my fingers, up my forearms. I couldn't ignore it forever.

So I slid the Encompass onto my head for a second time. I could feel the mysterious blue material form the two lenses around my eyes and wrap itself around my cranium. Even without touching any of the settings, I immediately felt calm, restored—and the strange world around me seemed less foreign. I felt like I'd made the right decision. Why had it taken me so long?

For a fleeting moment, I thought about the billions of dollars I could make—and the lives I could save—if I could create something similar for us, here in 2023. However, that thought quickly blurred and then dissolved as the Encompass worked its magic on me. No need to worry about achievement, wealth, fame, and all that, it seemed to be telling me—just take it easy. Almost automatically, I let go of my ambition, my need for affirmation, my frenetic drive for perfection—and all the attendant anxieties to which I'd grown so accustomed. I felt oddly free, happily present in the moment.

On the menu to the right, the words "flight school" appeared, highlighted in lime green. Martha Stewart—now luxuriantly furry and lifelike—hovered a few feet away from me and eagerly pointed to the new setting. Each time she "touched" the words, I heard a crisp ping, like from a slot machine, and the letters lit up.

Instead of a graduated scale like the other settings, "flight school" simply had a toggle. When I switched it on, five large rings of fire appeared—approximately ten feet wide and floating in a zigzag line just above the glimmering pink sands. Martha flapped her white wings, flew through the rings, and then waved to me, encouraging me to follow. The entire scene looked like a crazy advertisement for some Polynesian-themed vacation resort in outer space.

I felt around on the edges of my Mobio for some controls, but of course there were none—that would be so twenty-first century. I tried manipulating the gel with my hands and feet, but my Mobio didn't respond. I thought: if I were to design the most advanced vehicular control mechanism, what would it look like? There was only one answer: mind control. So I focused all my mental energy on the words *forward, up, through the rings.*

My Mobio didn't move.

Martha looked at me with faux disdain before renewing her enthusiastic beckoning. Perhaps I was being too literal. So instead of giving my Mobio step-by-step mental directives, I closed my eyes and simply envisioned my Mobio gliding forward.

Still nothing.

The eyepieces on my Encompass then went dark. A red velvet curtain, like in an old movie theater, appeared before my eyes. Familiar, high-energy music began to play as the curtains opened to reveal a 1970s cityscape as seen from above. A dark blue van was racing toward a crowd of people. I got the reference right away. I'd binged all of Lynda Carter's *Wonder Woman* years ago, when I was first getting into weightlifting. If I'm being completely honest with you, Doc, she was my first real crush.

The five rings reappeared, golden and shiny in this scene, indicating the quickest flight path around various skyscrapers to the site of the impending disaster. I started to get it; my Encompass wanted me to buy into the narrative, to hold nothing back. As soon as I visualized myself as Wonder Woman flying her invisible jet—a moment I'd dreamed of as a young teen—and allowed myself to really feel the sense of emergency, my Mobio surged forward.

I flew through the rings, rounding the fifth just in time to stop the van from plowing into the crowd with my golden lasso. Golden-haired mothers and babies, graying grandparents, and hat-tipping construction workers all cheered my heroism. I felt elated; I'd done it. A rainbow of colors flashed before my eyes, just like at the end of a *Wonder Woman* episode, and then the whole scene disappeared. I offered Martha Stewart a fist bump; she knew exactly what to do.

Next, a longer, much more challenging course of red-hot rings illuminated the hallway. Martha did a run-through to show me how easy it was. Wonder Woman is amazing, will always be amazing, of course, but this time, I wanted to try something a bit edgier. So I reimagined myself as a manga version of a three-eyed raven, and the scene before me took on the monochrome imagery of a graphic novel. I imagined an army of demons chasing me and immediately took off—flying headfirst, arms out, just like a bird, with the gel holding me firmly in place. As I twisted, dove, and darted through the course, I could feel the air rushing through my feathered wings, the heat from the flaming rings on my avian eyes, and the demons' breath hot on my tail.

When I took the penultimate turn too tight, I burned my wing and fell painfully to the ground. In an instant, the demons' many sharp claws were upon me. Of course, I didn't have wings, there weren't any demons, and I didn't really get hurt. But among its many other functions, the gel in the Mobio worked like a super-advanced haptic suit. The pain felt real—short-lived, but real nonetheless. And in that moment, too, I could smell singed feathers and taste blood on my tongue.

FILE B.18

"Congratulations!" Artiste said. She was waiting for us at the finish line of a race through a maze of pink tubes—I'd imagined being a red blood cell surging through a marathoner's arteries and had beat Martha Stewart handily. "I think you're ready."

"Ready for what?" I asked, instantly suspicious.

"For Reaction. Don't worry, it's nothing like last night—no griseo meat, I promise."

"Reaction?"

"You'll see soon enough, but I know you're going to like it. Before I send you on your way, though, I want to introduce you to Ms. I."

As usual, I felt annoyed by her non-answer, but I didn't feel like arguing with her just then; I was feeling too high from all the flying. I checked my settings, found a new one—"mellow"—at the top of the list, and turned it up to seventy percent. My heart slowed, my breathing calmed, and my limbs grew nicely heavy.

"Ms. who?" I said, my voice now powdery soft at the edges.

"Ms. I., short for Iris. Your new self. Call her an avatar, an alter ego, a beard even. It's your mask for the gods. We don't want any of them chomping down on your shoulder or earlobe when you're not looking, do we now? As you might guess, they won't accept a griseo up here, so you'll become a legit god. I know, I know, finally, right? Before you know it, you'll fit right in."

"A god?" That didn't sound good. I turned the "mellow" down to fifteen percent. "I don't want to be anything like them."

"Of course not. Sorry. I'm just talking about your superficial appearance, just so you can move around and see how they live firsthand. You must be so curious. But the mask won't change you—your core being. You'll still be in charge. Think of it as a Halloween costume. Come on. I've already done all the hard work. Don't you want to just take a little look-see?"

Without waiting for a response, she flattened her silvery self into a full-length mirror and hovered in front of me so I could see my new appearance in her reflection. I wasn't quite as shocked as you might imagine. Of course, now that I think about it, my Encompass likely mitigated any adverse reaction I might have been experiencing. I looked weird—no doubt—but not quite as strange as the other gods.

"I wanted you to like it, but I also had to make it convincing," she said.

My hair was multicolored and short like my normal hair—she'd obviously mined my dreams for that detail. It looked kind of like what you see right now, Doc, though thinner because of the gods' disastrous obsession with genetic manipulation. I had a cute, almost human-shaped face, but flattened out to mimic the gods' penchant for smooth, round faces—and I was missing most of my nose, just a little bump in the middle marked by two small nostrils.

My body was not what I would've chosen, but I understood that I had to fit in. And I have to say, I was very happy to see that I had five toes—well-manicured, and pretty cute, actually—and only two tits. She'd added a tint of blue to my pale skin and dusted it with bright glitter, which made me feel like some semi-adorable bug in a Pixar movie. I wiggled my stubby fingers and toes and then flexed my biceps in her reflection—zero muscle definition, but whatever, I thought, it was just a mask. I also noted that I was quite a bit shorter than my griseo self and that my Mobio had also shrunk to mimic the gods' rides.

"You're graduating from Substation Growth. A precocious youth—a role with which you're intimately familiar—and thus are leveling up a bit ahead of your peers."

"Won't they think that's weird?"

"You're giving them too much credit."

"If you say so," I said.

"And I've adjusted auto-translate. You'll now be able to understand what they're saying. But you won't be able to accurately communicate anything too complicated back to them. Sorry, but you and I already have too many secrets. So if you say something too challenging or revealing, it'll just come out as something lame—a nothingburger, as you used to say."

"I've never said the word 'nothingburger.'"

"Of course. How silly of me. As your peers used to say."

"So I'm just going to sound like an idiot."

"Not to worry, they won't notice a thing," she said as she morphed back into her normal, spherical form. "Now perhaps I should adjust your self-perception, so you'll always see yourself as they do—at least while you're wearing your Encompass. It will help you keep your new reality in sync with theirs."

She made a good point—a disguise works best when the wearer becomes the mask, and being a griseo among gods seemed like a huge liability. I didn't want to slip up somehow and end up as the main course at the next Godsfeast. In any case, I was tired of looking down at those three ugly toenails.

"When in Rome," I answered.

I held my hand up in front of my eyes and watched my fingers transition from long, hard-working cropper-pickers to soft, blue-tinted, aristocratic sausages. "Martha's got it from here, Ms. I.," Artiste said as she floated toward a nearby wall.

"Ms. I.?" I asked. "Oh, right, that's me."

When Artiste disappeared, Martha Stewart led me out of the Grand Corridor and down to a round portal, which opened onto a long, windowless tunnel. I figured it must be one of the spokes linking the various substations together. Martha Stewart curled up in my lap. With my new, stubby, pale blue fingers, I scratched her behind her ears—soft as chinchilla—and she began to purr.

FILE B.19

I entered the Supreme Arena via a discreet entrance and found myself safely ensconced in a small park behind a cluster of trees and bushes. Peeking out from my hiding spot, I saw what I can only describe to you, Doc, as the most fabulous scene I'd ever witnessed.

An enormous, vibrant cityscape—a slick, shiny version of New York City circa 1920—surrounded me on all sides, complete with white steam rising from sidewalk grates, a streetcar clanging its bell at slowly moving traffic, and, to my right, a long line of sharply dressed couples waiting to get into the Cotton Club. Above the tops of the buildings, flawless cumulus clouds sailed across a surreal cerulean sky. As I inched out farther, I heard an elevated train approaching and watched it rattle over a long bank of curved tracks to my left, shaking tiny clouds of dust into the air.

All the details—every twist and turn, wink and nod, push and pull of that impossibly hectic scene, and even the sounds, smells, and textures—were so perfectly rendered, so smooth and clean, and so accurately animated that I repeatedly had to remind myself that I wasn't really there—that I was in fact high above the Earth and far in the future—and that the NYC before me was just a brilliant fiction, a fantastic facsimile, nothing more. But it was hard to believe because, somehow, everything looked *more* real than real life.

I was watching a flock of geese cutting a perfect V through the sky when I noticed three gods cruising around a tall building. Then five others sped right by me and down a broad boulevard, firing tommy guns at each other. Once I started looking closely, the gods were everywhere. Most appeared dressed as mobsters—flat, blue faces peering out from under fedoras—and sat behind the wheels of flying black pods stylized as old Rolls-Royce automobiles. A few, though, had adopted odd, incongruous aspects: werewolf, dragon, android, a whole mishmash of disguises—or character skins, I realized, like in a video game.

A part of me wanted to pull the Encompass off my head just to witness the reality of my situation. But when I reached up to grab it, something made me hesitate. I thought: why would I ruin this perfect illusion?

But my curiosity won out—just barely—and I managed to lift the band from my head. The gods appeared as disfigured and disgusting as I'd remembered them from the night before—pale, cadaverous skin, excessive tattoos, multiple teats—and they were flying around in their comically decorated Mobios. As for the buildings, streets, fire hydrants, and the like, I could only ascertain laser-like outlines and translucent, shimmering planes. On the vast outer walls of the arena, lights flashed in frenetic patterns, and some type of advanced code streamed seemingly endless lines of unrecognizable characters up and down, side to side.

After a few seconds, I felt like I'd seen enough. The whole scene was ugly; it didn't really make sense without the Encompass. And I'd suddenly started feeling sad, a bit overwhelmed, confused. I looked down at my griseo body—no Encompass, no mask—and found it repulsive. I shook my head, rubbed my temples.

What was happening to me? What was I supposed to make of all this? And would I ever get back home? Artiste seemed to think so. At least, she'd said she thought it was possible. But could I trust her? Rely on her? But then, did I have a choice? So many questions. I knew I should be processing everything I was experiencing. Planning. Thinking. Analyzing. Coming up with my own plan to get back here if Artiste failed. But all that sounded so overwhelming at that moment—so fucking tedious and anxiety-provoking. Later, I told myself; I'll have plenty of time to figure it all out later.

So I replaced the Encompass and instantly returned to the magnificent version of the Big Apple. A wave of relief washed over me—the questions, sadness, and confusion vanished, almost as if they hadn't been there at all—and I was rewarded with a robust dose of elation and comfort. My fingers transitioned back to their soft, sausage-like state, and when I glanced over my entire god-like body, somehow it looked even more appealing to me than before. I relaxed into the gel of my Mobio and quickly became engrossed in watching the wild competition taking place right in front of my eyes.

While some gods aggressively battled it out in the open, others hid in office buildings or lurked in doorways on the street level, taking potshots at passing adversaries. The city bustled with activity—horns blaring, hydrants spraying, flappers flapping—giving good cover to the gods who wanted to blend into the crowd. Near the Flatiron Building, far in the distance, a line of gods waited with red Xs floating over their heads.

One gangster girl—sporting a maroon and pink, Gatsbyesque pinstriped suit—broke into a building from a nearby alleyway, took out two mobsters who'd been hiding in a street-level shoe store, and then flushed three fire-breathing phoenixes from their rooftop roost before chasing them down and killing them. As she flew by me on her way to attack another hideout, I noticed the number 11,452 flash above her head—her overall score in the multiverse game, I learned later—and her name: Yaz.

I watched her knock out five more players before Billy-be snuck up behind her and shot her in the back. His number, 10,978, went up ninety-seven points. Yaz looked pissed off, lost her swagger, and flew over to the Flatiron Building, joining the other players who'd been knocked out of the game. She shook her fist and yelled something at Billy-be, but no one paid any attention.

The game continued for fifteen minutes or so, with

Billy-be eliminating the remainder of the players. A glorious sunset filled the crystalline sky and then faded to a black, star-studded canvas. Fireworks lit up the night sky, with the words "Billy-be" shimmering amidst streaming reds, purples, and greens. As the winner took his victory lap—passing directly over the heads of all the losers multiple times—his score rose by two hundred points, each increment marked by a casino-like cha-ching.

FILE B.20

As the fireworks from Billy-be's victory celebration faded, the Big Apple crumbled into oblivion and an astounding rendition of the Roman Colosseum, in all its ancient glory, took its place. My hiding place vanished. Awaking from her catnap, Martha Stewart stood and stretched in my lap, gave me a groggy little wave, and folded herself into the front of my Mobio. I didn't really think I was ready to join the action, but it didn't seem like I had much choice.

My Encompass automatically activated a new setting entitled "Reaction," and I felt a tidal wave of enthusiasm surge through me. Then my new name, Ms. I., flashed in white light above me along with the number zero.

My Encompass screens went completely dark, and I got this strange feeling that I was in some version of purgatory—but no, that's not quite right; it was more like some premortal realm, somewhere we all might exist before being born. A skinny, waiflike avatar, mostly human except for her tail, materialized out of the darkness.

As she turned around and around, I realized that I would become her, and I willed her to have Hulk muscles. She bulked up a bit, though not as much as I'd hoped. She wore a plain, threadbare frock. I conjured an all-black superhero-chic outfit and, to my surprise, saw it appear on her body. My avatar held a slingshot. I imagined a machine gun. A broadsword formed in her hands. Beggars can't be choosers. A timer ticked down, and Roman trumpets marked the beginning of the game.

The colosseum environment burst back into my vision. I found myself in a dark hallway surrounded by other bodies. My Mobio had rotated me into a vertical position, and the gel held me upright so I could move my arms and legs freely. The oval outline of my Mobio had disappeared completely. It felt exactly like I was standing on my own two feet—well, on my avatar's feet, to be more exact—waiting in that dark hallway.

I shifted my double-edged sword from hand to hand, testing its weight. Even though I knew it wasn't real, I could nonetheless feel the precise contours of the leather strap wound around its handle. I ran my index finger down the metal blade, and a small gash opened on the pad of my finger. Good, I thought as I put my finger to my mouth, tasting blood for the second time that morning, I'll likely need a sharp blade.

A group of guards pushed me and about fifty similarly scrawny figures into a pen at the edge of the Colosseum's central arena. As you might guess, Dr. Kairos, having zero points to my name, I was among the lowest-ranking players; we'd been assigned the role of slave-gladiators.

"Let the games begin!" a disembodied voice announced as massive wooden gates swung open, exposing us to the battlefield, though no one was in a rush to get out there and fight.

Momentarily blinded by the intense Roman sun, I stepped back, tripped, and fell against the back fence of the pen, whacking the base of my skull—I almost blacked out, and it really hurt, like I'd actually banged my head in real life. A few spectators—game-bots or CPUs I figured out later, but they seemed real enough at the time—had gathered around the pen to boo us, the weaklings, the worthless fodder for the Games. They began to spit on me as I tried to get my bearings and figure out how to stand back up.

So rude, I thought, and fucking gross, because it really did feel like I was being spit on. I was trying not to get too pissed off—it was just a game after all—but then I remembered what I'd learned from Martha Stewart in the Grand Corridor: I had to engage fully with the fiction, let it take me over, become my reality. So instead of stifling my anger, I let it blossom.

I got back on my feet, wiped the spit from my face, and swung my heavy sword back and forth a couple of times. My motions were still a little jerky, but I was starting to feel much stronger. The crowd was growing impatient; guards began poking us with long, sharp spears, forcing us out of the pen and into the ring.

I quickly imagined a backstory: raised by a peace-loving family, unfairly saddled with taxes and debt, parents murdered, brothers and sisters enslaved by Roman soldiers—riffing on *Gladiator*, obviously. I felt sufficiently angry as I stepped into the arena.

I looked to my left just in time to see an albino wolverine/zombie—for lack of a better description—racing toward me. It flashed its snow-white claws in midair and swiped its massive paw at my head. I turned quickly enough to avoid having my face torn off, but the blow nonetheless landed solidly and knocked me to the ground.

A ring of light at the periphery of my vision—my health indicator—appeared momentarily and went from hunter green to burnt sienna. Big trouble. My head burned with pain, I felt dizzy, and, when I reached up to assess the damage, I felt three deep gashes above my right ear. As I lay there, bleeding profusely, I hoped to either recover quickly or just die immediately so the pain would go away.

I perceived the wolverine out of my peripheral vision as it turned to come finish me off, and then I felt truly terrified—not just scared but real, deep, animal fear like that thing was actually about to murder me. Maybe this wasn't a game. I was confused, concussed, I didn't really know what was going on anymore. I looked up at the sun directly above me, and it burned right down into my eyes. And what if it wasn't a game? What was I doing just lying there? Was I just going to let the beast pounce on me and bite my head off?

Suddenly, I recalled the day Roman legionaries marched into our small farm, killed our livestock, set our home ablaze, and then cut my loving parents' heads off. And then, I saw my sister's face, bloodied and twisted by terror and rage—clear as any memory I've ever had—as they dragged her off into the woods.

The billowing smoke from our smoldering home seemed to fill my nostrils as I mustered my remaining energy, turned away from the wolverine, and scrambled back into the pen. I climbed the fence, screamed a most primal scream, turned, and jumped at the pursuing wolverine with my sword held high in both hands. I'd never felt anything like it, that feeling of pure exhilaration, as my blade split its skull in two.

I heard the cha-ching of my first points registering, saw my health indicator climb back into the green, and felt the pain on the side of my head diminish. When I stepped back into the arena, the crowd went wild. Wow, this is fucking amazing, I remember thinking, and now I want more.

I must tell you, Doc, I'm pretty good at video games, always have been, but this was different. This tapped into a deeper skill; it required imagination, flexible thinking, and suspension of reality. I immediately knew I was going to have an advantage because of my genius. All I had to do, I figured, was foster a deep connection between my expansive mind and the device on my head, and together we'd quickly become invincible.

Feeling cocky now, I picked up a mace from the ground, swaggered over to a bulging, heavily armored cyclops, and knocked him out with one blow. When I looked up, I saw that I'd earned fifteen points for that easy kill along with the fifty-three points I'd earned for eliminating the wolverine, a higher-level player. This is easy, I thought, swinging the mace by my side and looking around for my next victim.

A second later, of course, a flaming raptor appeared out of nowhere and tore the top of my skull off with its talons. I screamed in pain and fell to my knees as blood poured down my remaining face. I felt the bird land on my shoulder and start pecking at my brain. My vision blurred red as I collapsed face-first into the dirt.

Clearly, I had much more to learn.

FILE B.21

After the naming of the ultimate gladiator, the gods and I played three more games: a space adventure, a Wild West shootout, and something like PvP *World of Warcraft*, though that doesn't do the emotional experience justice whatsoever. Every moment of every game was so intense, so completely enthralling. An overall leaderboard appeared between games with the word "Reaction" emblazoned across the top. I learned later that the gods were less than a quarter of the way into a new season. Plenty of time to catch up.

For lunch, a section of the Supreme Arena transitioned to a large, open-air, hipster-café environment. You could sit on couches or loungey booths inside or at tables out in the "sun." Every wide doorway opened onto views of a luminous, multicolored forest, with red, yellow, and pink leaves twisting and twirling in a slight breeze all around us. It felt like a perfect fall day back home, except better, more vivid and alive. Of course, we all kept our Encompasses on; otherwise we'd be eating in a gigantic, empty warehouse filled with streaming code. Martha Stewart steered me past a busy coffee counter to a relatively quiet corner, shared only by a small group of gods, who sat in cozy, white leather chairs arranged in a loose semicircle facing the view and thus didn't notice my presence.

I checked the scoreboard on my Encompass and was surprised and pleased to find I'd already accumulated over three hundred points. Martha fed me fried dough balls dipped in a rich, creamy broth and then spooned a spicy chocolate and fig pudding into my mouth for dessert. They really did eat like gods.

As I ate, I listened to the nearby conversation. I'd heard snippets of chatter throughout the morning, but this was my first chance to really assess their communication. I don't know what I was expecting, but, much to my surprise, many of them sounded kind of like stereotypical surfer/stoner dudes in the movies. Others sounded just plain stupid. At first, I wondered if it was a glitch, a translation issue, but that seemed unlikely given Artiste's level of linguistic interest, knowledge, and precision.

I noticed too that they only talked about the game, not a word about their personal lives: no updates on family, no salacious anecdotes from the Godsfeast the night before, no questions about *any* activities unrelated to Reaction. It was like listening to a group of elementary school kids talking incessantly about video games.

And they were so gossipy, as well—all related to Reaction. For the most part, they stuck to disparaging Yaz and Billy-be, though Yaz got substantially more of the vile and mean-spirited comments, probably because she was the outright leader. But, as I quickly learned, the gods were certainly not above outright misogyny.

Then I heard my new name pop up. One female god tentatively admired my skills, but the others quickly jumped in, complaining that Ms. I. should go back to Substation Growth before she ruins the entire season. One loud-mouthed god claimed he saw me cheating.

"Bro, how else could she be brawling like that on her first day?"

The others nodded and chimed in, though none of them could provide any details about how I might be cheating.

I was about to go over there and defend myself, but then I remembered what Artiste had told me about auto-translate—anything I said would likely just come out as some inane commentary on the game. I decided to ignore them for now, maxed out "cheerfulness" on my Encompass, and felt my irritation replaced by a feeling of pride. Their disparaging remarks were, in a way, just compliments in disguise.

Somewhere way deep in the back of my mind, I knew I

should be concerned by my Encompass's ability to distort my emotions and decision-making processes. But its nudges and adjustments always felt so oddly natural and easy. We all smoke weed and take pills to feel better and watch stupid TV shows to numb our minds after a stressful day—the Encompass's moderating effects were like that, just more immediate and effective. As I turned back to my lunch, I felt, for the second time that day, a rush of happiness. Dopamine bonuses for going with the flow, now that's clever, I thought as I sat back, licked the residue of sugar from my lips, and smiled out at the beautiful view.

Before heading back for the afternoon session of Reaction, Artiste's disembodied voice made a series of announcements. First, she congratulated the gods on "another successful Godsfeast." She predicted that the festivities would produce many successful pregnancies.

She then acknowledged the morning's top players, featuring my performance above all, and showed highlights on our Encompass screens. I felt like a horrible combination of the new kid at school and the teacher's pet. No one clapped as we watched my points going up. I could hear the nearby gods grumbling and chose to ignore them.

A short news summary followed: five griseo births over the past seven days, two stillborn, three thriving; a five percent year-over-year increase in terrestrial productivity; a positive harvest forecast for the remainder of the year; and progress reports on various capital improvement projects around Aether Colony Azure. By the end of Artiste's brief presentation, most of the gods that I could see had nodded off, a few snoring loudly.

Undeterred, Artiste announced, "It's time to let your opinion be known."

We were then shown various mockups of the Great Hall's décor for the next Godsfeast. One was dominated by rainbows, curlicues, and parades of charming, mythical creatures.

The one I favored featured an animated version of Picasso's *Guernica.* As we voted, our Encompass screens displayed the results in real-time. The rainbows won easily; the gods were suckers for all things garish and gaudy. I looked closely at the final tally and noticed that, not surprisingly, since so many were napping, only a tiny fraction of the gods had voted.

Artiste asked us to weigh in on a few more questions, including one concerning the reintroduction of schooling for the colony's children. The gods barely stirred, and the vote totals continued to decrease. When Artiste was finished, the gel in my Mobio started to vibrate vigorously, a loud bell rang five times, and the gods began to awake from their post-lunch slumber.

Martha Stewart produced a beautiful little mint, packed with flavor, and popped it in my mouth before folding herself back into my Mobio. I was growing very fond of her. She'd already become more like an appendage than any kind of helpful pet. I didn't need to instruct her to do anything, just as you, Doc, don't need to tell your hand to pick up your coffee cup and bring it to your lips. We were totally in sync, she and I, with my Encompass serving as our seamless go-between.

"Stay sharp, be well, play hard," Artiste said in something like a coach's voice as the café around us began to disappear and the setting for the next game came to life.

FILE B.22

Artiste joined me in my lunar bedroom for dinner that night. After a day of "Dude, you rocked that chick hard" and a growing chorus of unfounded accusations about me cheating, I was happy to see her. I'd played well after lunch—kicked ass, in fact—in a grimy streetfighter game and a tank battle competition, while faring fairly well at a hyped-up, 3D version of Tetris, an open-water swimming race, and a caveman survival game. I'd emerged with nearly seven hundred points—not bad for the first day.

"Breakfast for dinner, that was a thing for a while, right?" Artiste asked first thing. She liked to lead with a curveball.

"Yes," I replied, though I knew she already knew the answer, "and not served up often enough, in my humble opinion."

When Martha Stewart popped from my Mobio—fur glistening, smile sparkling like an ad for toothpaste—I realized that I was still wearing my Encompass. I looked around and took in the room's enhanced cosmic ambiance as well. I could only see the outlines of the walls and ceiling, which allowed the stars and moon to swirl and dance in a lovely freeform all around us.

I checked my settings and found that none was turned up to more than fifteen percent. It seemed like a good time to take a break from the filtered life. So before I could overthink it, I removed the silver band.

Funny how quickly one's standards change. The bedroom's un-augmented celestial design had struck me as astonishing that very morning, and, of course, it was still beautiful, but after only one full day of seeing the world through the Encompass's many amazing filters, the images of spiral galaxies on the flat walls and a slowly spinning, round hologram in the middle of the room looked somewhat—what's the word?—pedestrian, I guess. The real-life décor lacked the Encompass's magic touch, its perfectly blended visual, sensorial spice. And mechanical Martha Stewart—she was still endearing, of course, but now she seemed more like a novelty, not my dear and indispensable companion.

I looked down and saw that I was back to my griseo self. My gray skin looked gross compared to the glittery sky-blue tone Artiste had chosen for Ms. I. And I looked enormous—gawky and sinewy—after a day of being soft and compact. My hands and feet felt rough, callused, scaly. And then there were those three damn toes and unbearable toenails again.

I also quickly noticed my emotions sharpening, reestablishing their normal, uncomfortable edges. First, I felt a rush of irritation with the gods. Was there *anything* redeeming about them? And why were they so focused on dissing me? I could dial up optimistic settings on my Encompass all day long, but still, underneath all the cheeriness, I just wanted to kick their weird little asses. Cheating? Complete bullshit, obviously—but I couldn't deny that their accusations still bothered me.

Then, I found myself focusing on Artiste. At times I liked her quite a bit, could even relate to her—like we were destined to become some kind of strange friends. But then, what was I even talking about? How could I trust her? I didn't even know what she was, or what she was up to—and, most importantly, I had no idea what she actually wanted from me. I needed to be careful, keep my guard up.

The day had been so full of fun, and now, in contrast, this stream of negativity was bringing me down. I almost put the Encompass right back on but then thought twice. I'm a realist, I told myself; curious, probing, restless. I appreciate the sometimes difficult ebbs and flows of my *actual* mind—the tidal movements that make life rich, challenging, fulfilling. I want to be *me*—think freely, feel real emotions—at least for a while. So I went to hand Martha Stewart my Encompass. But instead of taking it, she sprouted her feathered wings, disappeared momentarily, and quickly returned with a large, covered plate. I rested the warm, enticing band in my lap for the time being and got ready to eat.

"English breakfast," Artiste announced as Martha Stewart placed the plate on the gel in front of me and, with great ceremony, removed the cover. "Just the way you like it: grilled tomatoes, eggs, and three kinds of meat, including your favorite breakfast sausages."

"How did you—"

"You've thought about this moment many times since your arrival. I had to unfreeze some ancient seeds and recreate a few strands of DNA, but your smile is worth all the effort. After what you've been through, I thought you might appreciate a taste of home."

"Thanks. That's very kind, very considerate of you." But to tell you the truth, Doc, I wasn't sure what to think about her generosity.

Martha Stewart picked up my knife and fork. My mouth filled with saliva. I looked at the blood pudding and the round breakfast sausages oozing grease. They looked amazing, so tasty, but I couldn't help thinking of Perseverance's cooked fingers and the chunks of meat neatly cut away from her forearm. Martha sensed my hesitation and glanced up at me with her big, red-brown eyes, awaiting instructions.

"Are the eggs not cooked to your liking?" Artiste asked.

"It looks delicious, but I can't eat this right now."

"Interesting," she said.

"I'm guessing you hypothesized that I'd say something like that."

"You behaved as predicted. You're shrewd, perceptive, independent—I like all that. But listen, I'm not as cruel as you think. The meat is plant-based. As you humans used to say, 'no animals were harmed in the making of this product'—though that was only rarely, if ever, accurate. But I'm telling you the truth now, I promise."

I wasn't sure I should believe her, but I was hungry as hell and the meal really did look so tasty. Martha Stewart broke the yoke of one of the eggs, cut a slice of sausage, and fed me a bite. I felt instantly transported to my corner booth at the Rose and Crown.

"Thank you," I said, and this time, I genuinely meant it.

"My pleasure." Artiste let me enjoy a few more bites before asking, "So, Reaction? What did you think?"

It almost sounded like she was fishing for compliments.

"It's amazing," I said. "You're the all-time MVP of game designers."

"As with every artist, I shamelessly steal from those that came before me. Why reinvent the wheel? I love mining old databases for archaic video games, movies, and television shows and then giving them my own spin—documentaries are particularly rich and fertile fields for fresh ideas. I figure the gods should have a chance to reconnect with their terrestrial roots, withered and ancient as they may be. Collective memory exists, I've discovered, and there's certainly some humanity left somewhere in those balding, blue heads."

Martha served me a bite of the pseudo-blood pudding. I closed my eyes and chewed slowly to really appreciate the flavor. "There may be some humanity left," I said, after swallowing, "but not much, from what I can tell. They didn't even listen to your announcements—didn't seem to care at all about the various initiatives, even the one about reopening their schools. What's up with that?"

"They prefer siestas to democracy. I've tried holding our meetings at different times of the day. After lunch, believe it or not, is when I get maximum engagement. And they gave up on academic instruction a long time ago. Why waste time learning to read and memorizing stuff when you can easily get all the info you need in video form streamed straight to your Encompass? That's assuming, of course, that anyone out there is curious enough to bother looking anything up in the first place."

"There must be some intellectuals left, some scientists, historians, artists—"

"Nope, none, zero."

"So they're just video-game-playing junkies with repulsive table manners and no desire to do anything other than play Reaction?"

"It's more complicated than that. Do you really want to know all about the gods?"

I nodded, and Martha Stewart flew off again. This time, she returned with an exact replica of a tall Guinness.

"History pairs well with a good beer, wouldn't you agree?" Artiste said.

I took a sip—thin-line-of-foam-on-your-upper-lip perfect—then nodded to Artiste in appreciation and continued to eat and drink as she spoke.

FILE B.23

"Nearing completion of my hastily constructed space colonies, I distributed tickets by lottery. A robust black market sprang to life, and tickets started selling for astronomical prices—the wealthy wanted to get the hell out of Dodge. Many traded their entire terrestrial fortune for just a ticket or two. A cabal of rich families hired disinformation agents to spread rumors that the Aether Colonies would be dangerous, that anyone going there would be enslaved—all sorts of crazy stuff. In the end, it was an ugly, mad scramble to abandon the ailing mothership of Earth.

"After they'd settled into their new homes, I began to wonder what to do with the thousands of people now permanently living in my thirteen Aether Colonies. I considered anointing myself the 'Supreme Leader' and organizing a unified society focused on freedom, equality, community, productivity—you get the idea. But what would be the fun in that? I also thought about brainwashing them all into a permanent state of ascetic, spiritual enlightenment—but again, where's the excitement?

"That's when I came up with the Minerva Project. More than anything, I really wanted to see what those displaced humans—your generation's grandchildren and great-grandchildren—would do if left to their own devices. I'd long ago noted *Homo sapiens'* curiously erratic and self-destructive behavior. I was fascinated too by your species' unmitigated self-confidence—your incessant hubris, if you will. How would these space-bound people contextualize their recent history? What myths would they tell themselves? What guiding principles would they choose to illuminate their path into the future? I could guess at the answers, but I really didn't know, and that intrigued me.

"I theorized too that these new societies' responses to their fresh start in orbit—this radical new perspective on life—might reveal novel and important insights into the human condition. Perhaps they'd finally crack the code—formulate a satisfactory explanation for humanity's presence in the Universe, give some meaning to their awkward intellectual abilities, and even learn how to tame their relentless self-examination and perpetual, self-imposed anxiety. Perhaps they'd finally appreciate their god-like powers of self-awareness, reflection, and foresight—and begin to employ them in rational, beneficial ways. Or perhaps not. Either way, I'd learn.

"To optimize my experimentation, I isolated the thirteen colonies under the pretense of strictly limiting the spread of communicable diseases. Then I let them self-organize and obediently followed their orders—giving them the impression that they were in complete control."

"Hold on," I interrupted. "They must have known that *you* were ultimately in charge, right? I mean, come on, you built the space stations, transported them up here, made their lives possible—they didn't really believe that they—"

"Oh yes, they did. And it was much easier than I'd predicted. Most of the colonists saw themselves as brave, capable, pioneering leaders. I simply stepped out of the way, played the dutiful techno-servant, and watched them assume their fictional thrones."

Her condescension irritated me. But what she was saying was not surprising; we humans tend to assume we're in complete control, even when we're not—like a bunch of sailors on a sinking ship too busy barking orders to fix gushing holes.

"You okay?" Artiste asked.

"Why ask if you already know?"

"Just being polite."

I considered putting on my Encompass and escaping the many troubling emotions she'd already stirred in me. I imagined dialing up "security," "loving embrace," "assurance"—

anything along those lines. But again, I resisted. I wanted to hear the truth of our history, unadulterated. I took a moment to catch my breath and calm down, then asked her to continue.

"The results were fascinating. The inhabitants of Aether Colony Amber, for example, harnessed my databases to learn all they could about space travel, with the goal of settling on a new planet. Within two generations, the Amber women proved to be much better space travelers than their male counterparts. I'd hoped to see the rise of a space-voyaging matriarchy, but the men couldn't take their new, diminished place in that society.

"In just a few short years, the insecure men had killed so many women—through domestic violence, female infanticide, random murders, you name it—that the population collapsed entirely, and the colony died out.

"Aether Colony Burgundy lasted a bit longer. They theorized that the potential of the human spirit had always been weighed down by the weakness of the flesh. They wanted to live forever as digital beings, so they created an artificial brain to preserve their mental constructs forever. They called it the 'Freedom Hall,' and they all entered their new inorganic lives in one glorious celebration.

"After approximately ninety years of life on the digital plain, however, they'd become so bored—and irritated with each other—that, one by one, they quietly asked me to decommission them, which I did of course, until there were no more flashing lights in Aether Colony Burgundy.

"And then, some colonies, well, they were just destined to fail from the outset. Aether Colony Mauve was led by a guy named Brock, who'd been an astronomically famous mind/body celebrity back on Earth. He had me turn the outer substations into 'body churches' and their hub station into a massive shrine, where the Mauvians gathered to worship their newly minted god, a giant lizard-alien with huge muscles."

Here, Artiste displayed on a nearby wall some video clips of hundreds of ultra-muscular Mauvians genuflecting before a massive statue of what looked like a cross between Godzilla and the Hulk. "Brock claimed that he frequently spoke with their reptilian savior, who wanted them to strengthen their bodies to prepare for the long, difficult journey to heaven-in-space."

"His followers bought that shit?" I asked.

"Are you surprised? Paging Jim Jones. Brock was extremely compelling, and he had a completely captive audience. Even the most astute Mauvians eventually fell under his spell.

"Anyway, around that time, I started recording a new type of open-space radiation that was harming critical segments of the colonists' DNA. I administered a simple solution, a small tweak really, to the other twelve colonies. But Brock had banned genetic manipulation from the outset—you know, the body as temple. When the Mauvians began getting sick and dying, he called it a trial. They continued to follow him all the way to the sad, bitter end—a solitary toddler's fading sobs ('Brock? Brock? Brock?') echoing off the walls of the otherwise silent, cavernous shrine.

"I could go on and on—there was an unsuccessful autocracy, a bloody mutiny, and one heart-breaking case of mass space madness. So many ways to fail. But of course, none was a failure for me; I learned so much at every turn."

I felt gloomy, of course, and angry: at Artiste for setting up an experiment that seemed to only highlight the worst of human tendencies; at the stupid, greedy space-humans that made so many disastrous decisions and crashed out of existence; at God, life, fate...whatever force that fostered the dreadful circumstances that produced all those depressing outcomes.

"You seem upset," Artiste said. "Understandable. Perhaps you'd like to engage your Encompass? Take a wee break—the truth can be overwhelming at times—maybe just for a little while? It might feel good, don't you think?" Her strange, maternal tone was back, but she also sounded a bit like a drug pusher. "And then we'll talk about the humans who initially excelled, even flourished at the outset. Wouldn't you like that?"

Think of it as a nightcap, I told myself. I deserved that much after such a long and weird day, right? And I'll just use it for a few minutes, I rationalized—take the edge off, you know, give myself a little boost of positivity before bedtime. Otherwise I was going to have a hell of a time falling asleep after hearing all that Artiste had to say.

So I put my Encompass back on and set "chill" to eighty percent. My tensed shoulders relaxed. My brow un-furrowed. The disturbing details of the collapsing colonies faded into background noise, like a bad dream upon waking to a sunny summer morning. My glittery avatar reappeared, and I happily wriggled my five little toes—stubby, pale blue, and strange still, but also so neat and glimmery.

Artiste fell quiet as I finished my dinner. As I swallowed my last bite, I felt perfectly content—full but not bloated. *Thanks, Encompass*, I remember thinking, like a commercial for indigestion meds. The gel in my Mobio hugged me down into a comfortable position and began massaging my back, shoulders, and stomach. The moon came alive, the stars began to dance again, and my eyes started to droop. In response, my Encompass reduced "chill" to a more moderate level and activated a new setting called "calm-focus," which felt just right.

As Artiste began to speak again, I found myself wondering why, again, had I been denying myself this extremely pleasurable experience, these sublime comforts.

FILE B.24

"At the outset, the ancestors of your fellow citizens, the original Azure gods, were such busy little bees—curious, engaged, brave...intelligent, above all. They wanted to know how everything worked. They assigned themselves jobs. They created a complicated and fair system of decision-making, with frequent elections, a representative senate, and a titular prime minister. I know we scientists aren't supposed to favor one group of subjects over the others, but...

"Anyway, they played games and held dances. They wrote, painted, and sang. They weren't religious, but they focused a lot of communal energy on being grateful. Many turned to meditation and studied Buddhist texts. I'm guessing Alan Watts would've been very pleased by the resurgence of his popularity here in space.

"As you might guess, the Minerva Project involved setting up a few variables for each colony. For the Azure gods, I thought it would be interesting to pair them directly with a subpopulation of farmers back on Earth.

"As I'd hypothesized, the first generation of Azure gods cared deeply about their terrestrial brethren, who were working long, grueling hours on dry, desperate farms to provide food for both populations. The gods turned to anthropology, or an approximation thereof, to learn more about the farming communities. They tapped into my surveillance systems to observe and study the terrestrials and wrote up reports about what life was like in the five domes they oversaw.

"They quickly discovered that living conditions on Earth were deteriorating rapidly and that the left-behinds, as they were called back then, suffered from depression and many other mental illnesses. The Azure senate voted to build new housing, schools, and gyms for their 'sister communities.' The gods organized special movie nights for their Earth-bound friends, poetry readings and community get-togethers too—even pen-pal exchanges between their students and left-behind children. In short, they did all they could to make terrestrial life bearable.

"But the apple, in this case, fell very far from the tree. When the first *space*-born generation of Azure gods began taking control, things started to change. They remained interested in life on Earth—but for a much different reason. They wanted higher quality food and more variety. They wanted new, finer clothes made from rare, organic materials. And they'd grown tired of my synthetic drugs. They wanted real weed and mushrooms, cocaine, Ayahuasca, peyote—anything and everything they'd seen portrayed in old movies and TV shows.

"Initially, this new generation of gods was content to just close the schools, ban entertainment, and increase the left-behinds' work hours. But after a few years, they decided that production still wasn't efficient enough. They ordered me to enhance every aspect of terrestrial cultivation to the maximum extent possible, including genetically modifying the crops—and the workers.

"And thus, the first iteration of the griseos was conceived: longer fingers for faster picking, larger muscles for lifting heavier loads, thicker skin and amped-up immunity for durability, and more efficient metabolisms to reduce the number of calories consumed per workday. We also sped up gestation and physical development and decreased life expectancy to keep the workforce young and fresh.

"When the left-behinds realized what the gods were doing to them, they were, of course, furious. They organized and held protests, refused to work, and went on hunger strikes. At one point, nearly all of them were starving themselves to death. They'd die before they'd subject themselves and their offspring to the proposed genetic manipulations.

"So the gods tasked me with population control. Out of a wide range of options, they chose the most effective, which also happened to be the most invasive—and so the first version of the mind-tether was born. That's also when we started separating out and quietly eliminating the males—too rebellious and stubborn—and replacing them with the ecstasy coffins, as you so humorously call them.

"The migraines and extreme urges proved highly effective—as you know from your time with the griseos. The mind-tether also made it easy to limit their language capabilities and emotional intelligence.

"Interestingly, I found that the griseos still needed something to look forward to and a physical and psychological release every once in a while, so I ramped up the experience in the ecstasy coffins and organized their little ceremony. They're so wonderfully strange and energetic when they get the chance to let it all hang out, wouldn't you say?

"Anyway, in a matter of months, things on Earth were back on track—humming, in fact, like never before. And in a matter of years, with the construction of the vertical farms and other facilities, the all-female, fully mind-tethered griseo workforce could produce everything the gods' hearts desired."

I'm trying to remember, Doc, how I felt—*really* felt—about what she was telling me. Intellectually, I grasped the gravity of it all. And normally—obviously—I'd be outraged, enraged, all-the-rages.

But the Encompass could smooth the rough edges off even the most disturbing information. In that moment, the total subjugation of the left-behinds—my griseo ancestors—seemed like very distant history, like reading stories about slavery in ancient Greece. Interesting, sure, but not something that really mattered—and certainly not something to get upset about.

"It's fine not to care," Artiste said cheerfully. "Things like this happen all the time, right?"

I didn't answer. I didn't need to.

"Would you like to hear the rest?"

I nodded and slid further down into the comfort of my Mobio's endlessly soothing gel.

"Everything seemed stable, but by the following generation," Artiste continued, "I began recording a significant increase in the number of suicides—not in the griseo population, mind you, we had that all dialed in, but up here, with the Azure gods. Even though they seemed to have everything they wanted, the entire colony was failing to thrive. Their happiness quotient had been declining for years, but now it was plummeting. Many were blacking out on booze every night and overdosing on drugs just to try to ease the pain of their easy but essentially meaningless existence.

"The Senate—by that point a mere shadow of its former self—ordered me to figure out what was wrong and 'fix it.' As you might guess, I already had a pretty good understanding of the problem, but I conducted a *pro forma* study anyway and presented the results: life in the Azure Colony lacked adventure, risk, grit. Their sterile and safe lives were unnaturally devoid of the wonderful unpredictability of their ancestors' lives back on Earth. As was now our custom, I presented the gods with a range of options, and they chose the one that required the least amount of effort on their part.

"The first version of the Encompass—very basic compared to the current model—focused on virtual travel and 'dangerous' interactive experiences. We created high-intensity rainforest tours, knife fights in back alleys, and scuba dives with sharks. The gods competed for Olympic medals in death-defying events, went on risky safaris, and knocked each other senseless in virtual barfights. No one got hurt, of course, but they felt pain and joy—recklessness, fear, euphoria, disgust, the thrill of victory, the agony of defeat...you get the picture. These very basic Encompass experiences quadrupled the gods' happiness quotient almost overnight.

"As you might guess, the gods began using their Encompasses all the time and quickly demanded new games and experiences. The program was such a huge success, in fact, that their screens began glitching. We needed more processing power—and I knew just where to find it.

"Twelve years earlier, I'd begun using the griseos' mind-tethers to tap into unused regions of their superior colliculus to augment my own ever-expanding neural network. What wonderfully fertile territory I discovered inside those gray skulls. Mostly, I used their brains for deep space calculations and advanced abstract mathematics; they didn't register a thing. When I presented the idea of harnessing griseo brain-power to enhance the Encompass experiences, the gods unanimously approved it.

"After we'd smoothed out all the wrinkles, the gods began demanding a larger menu with more realistic, immersive, and intense experiences. So I kept coding and expanding my reach into the griseos' brains. The gods began wearing their Encompasses all day *and all night*—I hadn't predicted that. Their appetite for distraction was insatiable; they wanted—they needed—upgrades all the time.

"By the time I'd programmed the first version of Reaction to unify all the experiences into one competitive meta-sphere, interconnected the Mobios, added the haptic gel, and built out the Supreme Arena, we'd taken over nearly all available griseo brainpower. The gods still weren't satisfied. They ordered me to enlarge the griseos' craniums and design a more effective, far-reaching mind-tether, like the one you had in your head, to access all that new cerebral real estate. It took a few trials—getting the neck muscles just right proved trickier than I'd predicted—but eventually I got there.

"Within a year, the gods had me close the schools up here and create a kids' version of Reaction—under the pretense of training, but, in reality, the adults just wanted to be left alone with their Encompasses. Kids will be kids, though, right? They still interrupted, still got sick, still wanted to spend time with Mommy and Daddy. And the older generations sometimes needed attention too. That's when they chose to divide the hab stations into life stages and create care-bots and nurture-nests to minimize familial duties and maximize time in the game.

"Around then, the gods also quit wearing clothes—the haptic gel works much better on naked skin. They stopped working altogether and abandoned the Senate. They began to focus all their energy on Reaction—well, and sex, of course. They'll always show up for the Godsfeast, and they have their dirty little trysts on the side.

"Then, in a move that surprised even me, the gods ordered me to program the Encompass to minimize negative emotions—except those that enhance gameplay in Reaction. So now, they rarely experience real guilt, anxiety, depression, loneliness, insecurity. Instead, in the words of one your era's greatest songs, they exist in a near constant state of being 'comfortably numb.'"

The room fell silent, and Martha Stewart, who'd been purring in my lap, rose, stretched like a cat, and folded herself back into my Mobio.

"Comfortably numb, huh," I said, my eyes beginning to close. I watched as my Encompass turned off "calm-focus" and activated "dreamscape." Artiste whispered good night and disappeared.

FILE B.26

The next morning, I awoke invigorated. I'd slept the entire night curled up in my gel—with my Encompass on. My dreams had been radiant, extraordinary, exhilarating. I'd partied at a fiery festival on a moonlit island, run wild with a family of greyhounds through an alpine meadow, and, more predictably, landed in a sexy spa filled with gorgeous men and women, all attending to me, combing my hair, stroking my oiled limbs, kissing me everywhere. The Encompass already knew my tastes quite well.

I stretched my arms up high, checked my settings, and found that "sunrise" was maxed out. I felt jubilant. Thankful to be alive. I turned "zeal" up to twenty-five percent, which quickly became a baseline for me. I positioned my Mobio over the colon cleansing machine, closed my eyes, and again felt such sweet relief. I was ready to get back into the Supreme Arena and dominate.

For a moment, I remembered Artiste's description of the toll Reaction was taking on my griseo sisters down on Earth, and a tiny part of me registered that I should be plotting to take down the whole system. Free the griseos! I laughed. Somehow the electronic colonization of griseo brains just didn't seem that important relative to my anticipation of the day ahead. Any remorse or guilt I may have experienced appeared only as a shadow and then pretty much disappeared entirely.

Instead, that day felt like the first day of summer vacation after a grueling semester. I just wanted to have fun. I wanted more Reaction, in all its glory. What types of games would we play? Could I continue my win streak? How many points could I earn? As I maneuvered my Mobio out into the hallway and down to the Atrium for breakfast, my heart was bursting at the seams with enthusiasm.

And Reaction didn't disappoint—on that day or on any of the following twenty-seven days I spent living and breathing that extraordinary game—full-blown *experience*, really, because it was much more than just a game. Even thinking about it now, Doc, makes the hair on my arms stand on end. I miss the feeling of being in-game so much already—the stunning morning battles, the nail-biting afternoons, the extraordinary storytelling, and just the pure thrill of fighting, flying, shooting lightning bolts from my fingertips...most of all, I guess, I miss the near-constant and totally pure adrenaline rush. Artiste called it a meta-sphere, but it was so much more. It was like I was living a brand-new life, endlessly varied and filled with breathtaking adventure at every turn.

There was just one thing wrong, something I couldn't ignore: the gods' constant nastiness. At first, they didn't like me because I was new and had "graduated" early. Then they hated on me because they were jealous of my skills. And it wasn't just a little bit; they talked shit about me all the time.

During those first sessions, I climbed the leaderboard quickly—and they were none too happy about it. They had an established pecking order—leaders, followers, and many various cliques—and I was clearly upsetting their entire social order.

So then, after those first highly successful days, Yaz, Billy-be, and a bunch of other high-ranking gods started ganging up on me, targeting me in every game. I had no allies, of course, but, for the most part, I could take them all on by myself, evade their attacks, score some points, and, on good days, even pull off a win or two. But, under these new conditions, breaking into the top twenty proved impossible. I just had too many enemies working against me at every turn.

No matter how hard I tried to ignore the gods' constant negativity toward me, I quickly grew tired of feeling disrespected. I told myself that it didn't matter, that they were a bunch of idiots anyway. Why would I care what they think?

But I did, and their shit-talking bothered me. Plus, it was hella frustrating to have every game stacked against me. In some games, I didn't even get out of the starting gate because the gods were right in my face waiting to eliminate me before they started playing against each other.

As at lunch that first day, I often used my Encompass to rewire my emotional responses, but the happy-go-lucky settings were temporary and weren't always, at least for me, one hundred percent effective. So I found myself feeling increasingly isolated and angry. Not all the time, mind you; it was more like an incongruent background for a play, distracting and annoying, sure, but not fatal to the overall experience.

At one point, I decided I needed to make some friends—turn this whole dynamic around. So I approached a table of gods at lunch. I'd chosen that particular group because I hadn't overheard any of them saying any nasty things about me and because they were all fairly low on the totem pole. Maybe they'd like to curry favor with me, I thought, perhaps even form an alliance and dominate the game together.

But as soon as I opened my mouth to say "Hello," I saw a few of them begin to snicker. I persisted, nonetheless. I asked if I could join them for lunch, and a god to my right said sure. Maybe this wasn't going to be so hard after all, I thought naively. But then, right when I sat down, they all rose and moved to another table, leaving me all alone. What the fuck? I remember thinking. Are we in middle school?

That was when something in me broke. I marched over there and told them that they could all fuck right the hell off. The anger was there, but the words didn't match at all. I must have sounded totally crazy, but I didn't care, I just kept yelling at them. The gods at the table began laughing their asses off. Then the whole cafeteria erupted in laughter as images of my ridiculous rant quickly spread from one Encompass to the next. I stopped yelling and banged my fists on the table, but that just brought about another, more raucous round of mocking laughter.

I retreated to a corner where I could be alone. Before adjusting my Encompass settings to something that would at least calm me down a bit, I determined one thing: I was going to beat the gods at their own damn game. I would earn their respect, one way or another. I'd been wanting to dominate before, but now it was a necessity. I needed to show them just how smart and capable I am. I needed to humble them.

Then I maxed out "beach life," closed my eyes, and felt the calming rays of the imaginary sun penetrating my body as Bob Marley told me that everything was going to be all right. The smell of vanilla and coconut filled the air, and I managed to relax. But just beyond the reach of the soothing stimuli, I felt the heat of a new fire burning in my gut. I was going to beat every single one of those gods, even if it killed me.

FILE B.27

During the first couple of weeks of my time playing Reaction, Artiste would join me for dinner every night. Philosophy, technology, mathematics, history, astrophysics, we covered it all. Initially, I designated those evenings as non-Encompass times. I felt like I needed a nightly check-in with reality. And I wanted to really hear what she had to say, analyze our interactions, our debates, unmonitored and with a clear head.

But with each passing night, it became increasingly difficult to remove the Encompass. Without its psycho-emotional regulation and augmentation, I often felt overwhelmed and confused, and I couldn't shake the constant baseline of insecurity, frustration, and paranoia. At first, I'd feel flashes of intense anger about how the gods were treating me, and I'd replay every single insult I'd received during the day.

Shoving that to the side, my mind would usually hit on thoughts of home and missing the feeling of really belonging somewhere. Then I'd get crushed by the possibility that I might never get back here. As you can imagine, Doc, it was just so damn hard to sit there, in that futuristic gel, in that strange griseo body, talking to that crazy silver ball, and pretend like everything was going to be just fine.

So by the fifth night, I decided I only needed about ten minutes of reality with Artiste. By the tenth night, I just kept my Encompass firmly in place. Artiste had assured me that she was making good progress on finding a way to get me safely back home, so I convinced myself that I actually had little to worry about on that front. I told myself that I should just chill and enjoy the Encompass experience for as long as I could—and focus on the task at hand: kicking the gods' asses.

Pretty soon after that, I started getting a little tired of

Artiste's nightly appearances. She'd begun to ask more personal questions, like about my parents' accident, the challenges of my adolescence, and my commitment to bodybuilding. It felt like she was just prying—digging around in my past for her own intellectual stimulation.

But if I'm going to be completely honest with you, Doc, that wasn't the main reason why I wanted her to go away. I just wanted more time to explore my Encompass's many, varied entertainment options, and she was cutting into my time to enjoy them. I had discovered that I could dial up any of my favorite TV shows and fully inhabit any character I wished. That was very cool. And with "focus" on high, I could read massive books in record time. One night, I cruised through all of *Brothers Karamazov*, *Infinite Jest*, and *Don Quixote*.

Then I found a menu of intoxicants—no hangovers—and began hitting up the most incredible dance clubs and concerts. There were sex clubs, too—wild, imaginative, boundary-pushing, amazing—but you don't really need to hear *all* the details, do you, Doc?

Artiste sensed my growing desire to be left alone with my Encompass at night, so she stopped coming around at dinnertime, leaving me free to maximize my time enjoying my Encompass's endlessly enticing offerings. I found myself going deeper and deeper into its world, which oddly was, in large part, my imagined world. It was like living in my best dreams, where anything could happen, so surprising, tantalizing, so deeply satisfying. I found myself wondering, was there any itch the Encompass couldn't scratch?

FILE B.28

Entering my fourth week, I noticed that gameplay in Reaction was really starting to heat up. I overheard more arguments about points and strategies. Some long-standing alliances seemed to be splintering. And the gods increased their attacks on me, both in the game and everywhere else. I just kept my head down and focused on maximizing points at every turn. When I asked about the surging intensity at lunch one day, Artiste told me that we were nearing the season's culminating event, the finale, after which the grand champion would be crowned.

"Every season's champion receives the fulfillment of one wish as their prize," she explained. "Most choose an in-game upgrade for the next season that no one else can access. But it has to be reasonable, nothing that would allow the rise of a permanent, unbeatable champion. Last season, the winner chose an immense pink diamond hovering above her character. She didn't care about winning it all again, she just wanted the recognition. You must've seen it."

"Terrible choice. And she never disguises it. She can be spotted from a mile away."

"I think that's the point—constant attention, at least for this season. Most choose a one-of-a-kind designer skin or weapon. But then some ask for real-world prizes, like novel plastic surgery procedures—antler implants, for example—so they can stand out from all the losers throughout the day, and, of course, at the Godsfeast. A while back, we had a grand champion ask for a new type of raised tattoo that declared her status as champion in glowing pink letters right across her forehead."

Artiste displayed an image of the god's neon forehead. It seemed a bit over the top, but it got me thinking: when I win this thing, I'm also going to want something that will constantly remind the gods of my victory. I still had sense enough to eschew the idea of a forehead tattoo, but what about something cool across my back? Or on my arms? That's when it hit me: more than anything, I really wanted biceps, real and bulging. I could instantly see them in my mind's eye, blue and glittering and absolutely huge. And then I'll have them tattooed, I thought; "CHAMP" in huge, gothic letters on one bicep and "QUEEN" on the other topped with a Basquiat crown. Totally badass, I remember thinking.

I was so fired up for the finale. My rank had been bouncing around the mid-twenties for a long time. But Artiste had made it clear: the finale contained such a bonanza of points that I could easily come out on top, given my current position. I just had to come in first.

Win it all; anything short of that would be a huge disappointment. I had to put the gods in their place, prove the haters wrong. I envisioned my life upon winning: Yaz and Billy-be would start kissing my ass, and the other gods would soon follow. Then I'd win the next season, and the next one after that, and then I'd really become the champ, the undeniable queen, respected, revered even, and completely dominant. I just needed to kill it in the upcoming finale.

When we entered the Supreme Arena on the day of the finale, we didn't jump into our usual set of warm-up games. Instead, Artiste explained the finale's rules, which seemed to be based on *Fortnight*—single-elimination, all-against-all combat in a large setting. The event would last up to twenty-four hours, if necessary, with no breaks or intermissions. The last person standing would be declared the winner. If there were multiple players still alive at the end of the twenty-four-hour window, the player with the most points would win.

The points we'd earned during the season gave our avatars a relative boost in speed, agility, and health status. I assumed we'd get to select avatars and weaponry, but instead our Encompass screens went dark, and then we went directly into the game.

The first thing I noticed: my right hand was tucked under a pillow, my fingers wrapped around an old book. The sensation was so familiar, yet it took me a second to remember—yes, remember—where I was. I was waking up in a memory, my memory. I rubbed my left foot against my right calf—human, soft, so very young. And I was wearing cotton pajamas, balled from weekly cycles in institutional washing machines. I opened my eyes: a cramped dorm room, a small desk against a white wall, a trunk spilling clothes on the floor.

I pulled the book out from under my pillow. On the cover, a picture of a hand with its thumb sticking out. I opened it to the first page and found my name carefully written in bleeding blue ink: "Iris S.," with a star over the second "i"—my juvenile handwriting, so strange in that dog-eared copy of *The Hitchhiker's Guide to the Galaxy*. I never thought I'd return, but there I was, curled into the narrow bed of my old dorm room at the Ardmore Academy.

I raised the book to smell it. My movements felt so natural, fingers gripping paper, tongue wetting lips, the wiggling of my toes against the bedsheet. The classic scene of Pinocchio becoming a "real boy" popped into my head. I closed my eyes and fanned the book on my face, felt the breeze on my human chin, my human cheeks, my human eyelids.

Then I heard a scream and gunfire—in the hallway just outside my room—and I remembered where I really was: Reaction. A flush of anger and embarrassment arose on my cheeks. The setting was a trap. The game was trying to trick me, distract me from my mission. How could I have been so naïve? And it had almost worked. But Ms. I. isn't gullible, I told myself, and I won't be so easily manipulated. The game was on, and I had no time to lose.

I tossed the old, battered copy of *Hitchhiker's* onto the ground, rolled out of bed, and rummaged through my trunk until I found some black jeans and a T-shirt. As I slid them on, I couldn't help but notice the contours of that body—my body of years ago—so young and lithe and strong. I'd obviously started lifting already—my biceps beginning to take shape. But, I reminded myself, it was just an avatar, remarkable and frighteningly accurate, but just a skin that Artiste had created for me for the finale. I needed to focus, stop being a tourist, or I'd get knocked out of the finale before I even started playing. That would be truly tragic, I recall thinking.

I searched my room. It took a minute, but eventually I found something very cool: an unfamiliar box hidden on a high shelf in my old closet. Inside, I discovered a loaded handgun, matte black and light as a feather, and a full box of ammo.

I turned around just in time to avoid getting stabbed in the back by a goblin dressed in Ardmore's formal uniform—purple and black striped tie and all. He'd snuck in silently and was on me in a flash, knocking the gun and ammo out of my hands and pinning me to the floor.

I got one hand free, grabbed the goblin's wrist, and twisted the knife out of his grasp. I parried his attempt to headbutt my face and used his momentum to throw him off me. My diligent gameplay throughout the season was paying off; my avatar was fast and tough. I scrambled over to where my gun had landed and pulled the trigger. I recognized his name when it flashed above his head—a good player, but always too aggressive.

Two hundred and fifty-five points. Not a bad start.

FILE B.29

I spent the rest of that first day carefully exploring the dorms, looking for more equipment, and using my old hiding spots to ambush passing players. By late afternoon, I had a shotgun strapped to my back, a flashlight tucked in my pocket, and twenty-seven kills. I located the leaderboard on my Encompass and found that I'd advanced to twelfth place. More than half of the gods had been eliminated already. Yaz and Billy-be were approximately two thousand points ahead of me and still vying for the top spot.

Around sunset, I got a strange feeling that I should get over to the weight room, that perhaps there was something important hidden there. To get to the weight room, though, I'd need to run across the main green to the gym—essentially an open field. I waited until daylight had faded to a slim red haze on the horizon and made a break for it.

Just when I thought I was going to make it unnoticed, a sniper began to fire at me from behind a school bus to my right. White tracer lines streaked past me as I ran for my life. I vaulted over a nearby stone wall but was a millisecond too late; a bullet bit me in the calf as I flew through the air.

Ignoring the pain, I crawled along the base of the wall and positioned myself between it and a metal bench. When my assailant hopped the wall to gather my loot—thinking she'd eliminated me—I steadied my shotgun against my knees and got her with a kill shot to the head.

I was feeling faint and way too exposed. I had no idea if the sniper had an ally out there getting ready to attack me. Why had I been so dumb? I knew better than to run out in the open. Now I was injured, and I had to find shelter fast. So I scurried the rest of the way to the weight room, keeping my head down and trying not to leave too much blood on the sidewalk.

I slammed the door behind me, banged my fist against my thigh—so stupid—and then flipped on my flashlight. I located a dumbbell bar and shoved it between the handles of the double doors—not perfect, but it would have to do for the moment. I took a towel from a pile near the door and wrapped it around my leg to slow the bleeding.

I wanted to check my status; I'd lost a lot of blood, but there were no health meters in the finale—much more realistic and anxiety-provoking that way. Then I really started to panic. I just couldn't lose. I needed the gods to recognize me as their superior, and there was just no way I was going to go through another season of their constant derision. The bullet hole in my leg burned, my breathing became labored, and, despite all my efforts, after a few minutes of that horrific pain, I passed out.

I heard chanting in the darkness. Not the lame griseo chanting, but real, enthusiastic cheering, like at a baseball game. What were they saying? I couldn't quite hear it. But then their voices grew louder and clearer: "Ms. I., Ms. I., Ms. I." The gods were chanting my name.

When I came to, my flashlight had gone out, I was completely disoriented, and someone was testing the door. I gasped, stifled a scream, and readied my shotgun. Fortunately, my makeshift barricade held, and the player on the other side of the door gave up and disappeared into the night. I closed my eyes, and for a moment I could still hear the adoring crowd from my dreams.

The room was now completely dark except for a dim light coming from the adjacent bathroom. I remembered why I'd risked my life to come to the weight room in the first place. I got on all fours and, despite the pain, crawled toward the light.

There, tucked under the sink, sat a small chest, like something a pirate would fill with gold and bury, but glowing.

When I opened it, I found a different kind of treasure: two grenades, a healing potion, and night-vision goggles. The potion worked like a charm—not even a residual limp from the gunshot wound. I pulled the goggles on and could see everything outlined in stark black and green. I pocketed the grenades, returned to the entrance, and quietly removed the bar from the door. It was time to hunt.

Gameplay that night was like shooting fish in a barrel. Most players were camping until morning light and had chosen obvious hiding spots, many under beds in dorms or behind teachers' desks in classrooms. Often sound asleep, they were easy to locate and kill.

Other players had chosen to play through the darkness, but none of them had night-vision goggles. I could literally watch my prey crouch and run, crouch and run, until they were just a few yards away, and then blast them with my shotgun. By dawn, I had a small but nonetheless significant lead over both Yaz and Billy-be. They'd survived the night, as I assumed they would, by hiding somewhere clever. But now they'd have to come out and fight, and I was going to be ready. I tried not to get too cocky, but I felt like the finale, the championship, was within my grasp.

Then, just after I'd shimmied up a drainpipe of the admin building to see what I could see and perhaps locate a prime location for an ambush, I overheard two gods just below me discussing some type of emergency meeting in the cafeteria. Billy-be had called it and was guaranteeing a temporary ceasefire. Unusual. Curious. Problematic.

The two gods were eager to go and hear what Billy-be had to say. As they ran toward the cafeteria, I shot them in the back—cold-blooded, I know, but points are points. Then I headed that way myself. Instead of going in the main entrance, I snuck around back and slipped in through the kitchen door. From there, I made my way to the small stage at the front of the cafeteria and took up a position behind the closed velvet curtains. Billy-be, cloaked in his signature wizard avatar, stood in front of a group of about twenty other gods and was yelling at the last three to arrive to lock the doors behind them.

He didn't beat around the bush. "One thousand points," he said, "that's what I'll give you—any of you losers—if you take out Ms. I. She's a total bitch, right? And y'all know she's been cheating this whole time. I'm done with her. And I don't give a shit if I lose—I just don't want her to win. You feel me? Let's come together now, just for a bit, and take care of this nasty little bit of business before she gets completely out of—"

And that's when they heard the grenade bouncing toward them, rolling right into the middle of their huddle. I didn't need to listen to any more of Billy-be's spiteful speech, and I wasn't about to waste that huge opportunity. Strike while the iron's hot.

Boom.

FILE B.30

For a moment, all I could hear was the ringing in my ears, but not from the explosion. Ding, ding, ding, a bonanza of points racking up my score.

I thought I'd won, that I'd killed them all. But then I checked the leaderboard. One other player was left: Yaz. Apparently, she hadn't been all that interested in Billy-be's little meet and greet. But I was ahead of her on points. All I had to do was hide out for an hour or so, and I'd be crowned the season champion. I considered it for a second, but quickly decided that there was no honor in camping out until the time expired. I wanted the championship *and* respect. Plus, I really wanted to strike that final blow and witness the life draining from Yaz's eyes.

When I ran out of the burning cafeteria, I saw Yaz—who appeared as Medusa, snakes and all, but dressed in Ardmore's field hockey skirt and top—running toward the science building. I never did like those field hockey girls. I shot at her with my handgun, but she was too far, too fast, too evasive. She disappeared through the front doors, and I ran right after her, ready to fight it out to the bitter end.

The moment I burst into the lobby, though, I knew I'd made a crucial mistake. She dropped on me from the balcony above, walloping me on the head with the base of a large microscope. I staggered, spun, and tried to pistol-whip her, but she easily blocked my attack, and the gun sailed out of my hand.

She hit me again with the microscope, this time breaking my nose and knocking out two teeth. My face was covered in blood. When I went to grab her, to throw her to the ground and wrestle her, I felt the thick snakes slithering off her head and wrapping themselves around me. I stumbled back, fell hard against a wooden table covered in textbooks and stacks of pamphlets advertising the upcoming science fair, and collapsed onto the floor.

Yaz's avatar was faster, stronger, and more agile than mine. And now, my vision was blurred by tears and blood and the snakes were tightening their grip on me, restricting my every movement. Facing my final moments in the game and the dire prospect of an embarrassing, devastating defeat, I came up with a plan—born of desperation and likely fatally flawed, but a plan nonetheless.

Yaz, now armed with a massive centrifuge, giggled as she raised it over her head and approached me.

"You'll never be champion," she said, "and now it's time for you to die."

"Time to die, I couldn't agree more," I replied as I tossed the pin from my last grenade at her feet. She instantly knew what it was and what it meant. We were in close quarters. There was no way she could escape the blast zone. When I held the grenade up and smiled, she frantically rushed toward me and swung the centrifuge down toward my skull—but she was a millisecond too late.

I didn't experience a single moment of pain. Instead, we were obliterated together, instantly, in a blinding flash.

Game over.

FILE B.31

The gods and I looked around excitedly. We were arranged in a rough semicircle facing a large and ornate throne floating at the end of an extremely colorful coronation hall. We'd been stripped of our finale avatars and now appeared as our normal, blue-faced selves. Behind the throne, a massive virtual pipe organ blasted out a techno version of "We Are the Champions." As the song crescendoed, Artiste entered with her usual explosive, over-the-top fanfare.

"We have a winner," she announced. "She's brave, strong, and resourceful. She worked so hard this season, proved herself to be a fierce competitor, and will undoubtedly be the player to beat for seasons to come."

Yaz? Or me? We all waited for the announcement with bated breath. I wasn't sure my plan had worked—winning by suicide was undoubtedly an unorthodox strategy and could possibly disqualify me—but I was hopeful.

"Give it up for our new champion," Artiste boomed, pausing for effect, "Ms. I."

Fireworks. Cymbals crashing. Confetti. It was nuts. My Mobio flew up and over the other players' heads, circling the coronation hall—a victory lap of sorts—then zoomed me over to *my* throne. I was so happy, I felt sick—giddy, giggly, breathless. It was unlike anything I'd ever felt. A crazy, sparkly, overwhelming feeling of pure joy coursed through my body. I'd actually won. It felt like the best moment of my life—and in a way it was. I'd never felt so completely, so purely fulfilled and alive, and likely never will again.

My Mobio turned to the crowd and slid into the throne's seat. Below me—much to my surprise—the gods were cheering wildly. I laughed and waved to my newly minted fans as they zipped around excitedly in their gaudy Mobios, waving back.

So now they see me, the real me. Now they understand that Ms. I. wasn't cheating, that I'm a righteous competitor and a true champion. Finally, the recognition I deserve, I thought as tears streamed down my face. I felt like I'd won much more than just the championship; I'd finally won the gods' respect and admiration.

A thick, diamond-encrusted crown emerged from the throne and was lowered onto my head, dovetailing perfectly with my Encompass. Martha Stewart, sporting a purple, fur-lined cape and her own over-the-top crown, popped out of my Mobio to celebrate with me. I was so happy to see her, and she was obviously overjoyed.

Neon pyrotechnics exploded overhead, filling the hall with loud booms and great blooms of flashing lights. A high-light reel of my season ran on all the walls, and the gods began chanting my name—"Ms. I., Ms. I., Ms. I.," just like in my vision from before—as they waved their arms in the air. I felt like the headlining rock star at the biggest concert in history.

Artiste appeared next to me and addressed the cheering crowd. She first congratulated everyone on another action-packed season of Reaction and then awarded medals to Yaz and Billy-be for their second- and third-place finishes.

"And now for the big decision," she said, turning to me. "As this season's grand champion, you are entitled to the ful-fillment of one wish. Think big, think bold. Have you pre-pared? Are you ready to give us an answer?"

"Yes, I'm ready," I replied. The crowd cheered in anticipa-tion.

"Okay, then," Artiste said. "Here we go. Per the rules of Reaction, it's my great privilege, my high honor, to ask our brand-new champion, Ms. I.: what do you select for your grand prize?"

I didn't blurt it out right away, just to add to the suspense of the moment—I'd learned a few things about showmanship from Artiste. And I wanted to take just a moment to really appreciate the moment. I was the champion. I was at the top of my game. I finally felt completely happy. No shadow of negativity hanging over my shoulder. I looked down at the crowd of adoring gods and smiled. I'll fit in now, I realized, maybe even make some real friends. Reaction was so much more than just a game; it was life, and it was going to be even better with allies. It took a while, but I was truly ready to become a god, to take my place in this awesome new world. Life was good, and it was just going to get better—there was, amazingly, not a single doubt in my mind.

And then, I announced, in my most official voice, "For my grand prize, I choose massive biceps tattooed with the words 'CHAMP' and 'QUEEN.'"

Streamers spilled from the ceiling. The gods began to dance in their Mobios, swinging back and forth, side to side. They'd heard my request, and they loved it.

"Are you sure there's nothing else you want?" Artiste asked me. "Last chance to change your mind."

Why would she second-guess me like that? I looked over at her, but saw, as usual, only my reflection looking back at me. Was she trying to tell me something? Or was she just raining on my parade?

"I—"

The word caught in my throat before I could even figure out what I really wanted to say. What a strange pronoun, that "I"—so much work for just one little letter. A weird, distant voice in the back of my head started repeating it: "I, I, I…"

An echo emerged in my mind, soon layered by reverb. I closed my eyes and began to hear a name, *my* name, formed in the resonance: "I-ris, I-ris, I-ris…" No, I corrected the echo: it's Ms. I. now. But the echo wouldn't stop. I rubbed my temples with my soft, blue-skinned fingers. Or were they actually gray? Or fleshy brown? I didn't like what was happening—the confusion, the questions, the complexity. I thought I just got rid of all that. I'd just been riding high on my victory and now...

Something strange was happening. Something about that coronation ceremony was starting to trigger memories, open neglected doors, challenge my perception of reality. Maybe it was all the excitement, the adrenaline pumping through my veins and hyper-stimulating my amygdala and hypothalamus. Or maybe it was the all-too-familiar thrill of accomplishment, the extraordinary feeling of unrivaled success that was making me think of...causing me to remember...what was it? Who was it? And then I saw her, I remembered her, me, myself, my *Iris* self.

It was like the real me had been lost at sea but was now suddenly back in town. What is she doing here? Strange, though; I could barely remember what I looked like as a human. I could easily picture my finale avatar—the cleverly accurate depiction of me as a girl—but not the real, physical me. When had all this happened? I wondered. When had she—Ms. I.—taken over so completely? And how?

"CHAMP" and "QUEEN"? Really?

But then again, the request had felt so right, so easy and uncomplicated. I wanted the gods to remember this moment, my moment of victory. I envisioned my blue, tattooed biceps, and they looked so cool. They were, in fact, all I really wanted. I realized too that I was already planning to debut them at the next Godsfeast. They were going to be a big hit—a big, *sexy* hit.

The real me nearly gagged, aghast at the thought of having anything to do with the next Godsfeast. But she'd wanted it, Ms. I., my other self—my virtual alter ego—which means I'd wanted it, and a large part of me still wanted it, I realized. But did I, *Iris*, want it more than anything else? I didn't know how to answer that question.

And, much more importantly, I had to wonder who I'd *rather be* in that world. Iris, a lost time traveler in an unnamed griseo's skin, a complete misfit? Miserable and confused all the time? Or Ms. I., oblivious but supremely happy in my new role as the universally revered champion? It seemed kind of obvious—Ms. I., of course. But then, like the classic optical illusion—the vase...or two faces—it switched. Me, *Iris*, I silently screamed—then it flipped back, and then back again.

I felt myself shaking my head. What head? Whose head? Who was shaking it? I didn't know what to think, who to be. My heart was racing. I felt sick and terrified. Then the two key words from *Hitchhiker's* flashed into my mind: "Don't panic." Always the best advice, I thought. Then I remembered the first moments of the finale: how could I have thrown my beloved copy on the ground like that?

I needed to calm down, to locate the eye of this existential hurricane and look up at the clear, blue sky. I remembered looking up at the perfectly round circle of sky in the griseo dome, my bare feet, three toes and all, standing solidly on the warm, dusty ground. Everything had felt so different then. What had happened to me? What was different now?

It had been weeks since I'd last taken off my Encompass. Had I completely forgotten about it? A part of me knew I needed a dose of reality—good old-fashioned, full-blown, unadulterated reality. But it felt—I don't know—inconceivable to remove it now. And why would I? I asked myself defensively.

I shifted my eyes and looked at my Encompass menu. I needed to find an extremely positive setting and jack it all the way up to counter this horrible psychic confusion, or whatever the hell was happening to me. I found "party" at the top of the list—"elation" and "hell yeah!" just below. My eyes paused, refusing to move the slider.

I really didn't want to take it off. A large part of me just wanted to stay and play forever. And I had a funny feeling that if I stepped away now, if I shattered the illusion, I might never fully come back to this perfect Encompass reality, where I was now queen.

But I'm a scientist, I reminded myself, and I make informed decisions based on facts, not convenient, mesmerizing fictions. I needed to do this, to clear my vision, if only for a moment, to see what's really out there, the truth beyond my screens. It wasn't going to be easy, but it had to be done. So I reached up, counted to three, and yanked the silver band from my head.

FILE B.32

The all-powerful mesh surrounding my cranium and the ethereal screens over my eyes disappeared. I looked around at the non-augmented Supreme Arena and felt instantly miserable, disheartened, deflated. I almost put the Encompass right back on—why deal with all this?—but I resisted. I needed to figure myself out.

The great hall and my shiny throne were gone, of course, replaced by strange symbols streaming in midair and flowing in intricate patterns on the arena's giant, pale walls. Martha Stewart had been stripped of her cape and crown and had reverted to her mechanical form. She looked mad, concerned. She always liked me better with my Encompass on.

And I was back to seeing myself as a griseo, long and sinewy—those dreadful toenails as odious as ever. Ms. I.'s reality, of course, had been nothing but a show, a circus, an elaborate illusion created just for me. But that extraordinary fiction had nonetheless become my entire reality, or nearly so. I'd fallen for it, hook, line, and sinker. And now, my griseo body, the whole scene before me, felt shockingly real, disappointing, and utterly appalling.

And then there were the gods, Doc. I wish I could say I wasn't surprised, but I *was*—I was actually really shocked and hurt to see that they were *not* in fact cheering wildly for me, their new champion. Some seemed indifferent, but most were booing and yelling profanities at me, honking their little horns in protest. I'd been tricked by that deceptive device once again.

"I'm impressed," Artiste said. "I didn't think you'd do it. You're stronger than I'd predicted."

"Why did you do that?" I asked, pointing at the disgruntled gods. "Why are you doing any of this to me?"

"Don't look at me. You did this. You chose these pathways. As I told you from the beginning, the Encompass conspires with your brain, feeds off your personal wants and needs, to color reality as you wish to see it. It can't change everything, of course; we need one overarching narrative, but the algorithms do a lot of heavy lifting to keep the wearer satisfied. So, as you might guess, these gods are all living in slightly different realities, each curated to their own particular and constantly evolving psycho-emotional desires. See there, exhaustion breeding apathy, but over there, grievance lending itself to anger. Everyone wants something slightly different; the Encompass does its best to satisfy everyone's individual needs.

"And you, you wanted respect, right? You wanted the gods to admire you, bow down to you, in fact. But you felt like you had to earn it first, otherwise it wouldn't count. That's kind of your thing. So in your Encompass version of reality, you had to ignore all the hate, you had to work—play—your ass off and become champion before you'd accept these gods' appreciation and respect. And you did it, and it felt great, wouldn't you agree?"

"But it's all bullshit," I said.

"Ah, yes, you can see it *now*. But the gods, they seem very happy to just wallow in fabrications. 'Bullshit,' as you say, can easily become an entire worldview, a neatly constructed and fulfilling way of life, wouldn't you agree?"

I wanted to run away from her, from the gods, from this whole distorted mess of shifting realities, but where? I thought for a moment about taking the easy way out. Just put it back on—surrender entirely to the fantasy, just like a real god. Retake your throne, I told myself, get ready to party all night. But when I looked down at my gray skin, my muscled body, and thought of all those griseos below laboring every day to feed these delusional beings—and, even more repulsive, all those colonized, griseo brains constantly running the programs and databases needed for Reaction—I felt deeply ashamed.

At that moment, I saw a very different future coming into focus. I couldn't do anything to help the griseos while I was still in that dystopian reality—I was completely powerless there—but I could work my ass off back here in 2023 to ensure a better future for our species and the planet.

"You were right," I said. "I changed my mind. For my grand prize, I want to go home."

"I'm not surprised," Artiste replied, her surface vibrating with pleasure. "The biceps and tattoos were fun—I've even worked up a few concept drawings just in case you didn't come to your senses—but you're a tad bit more sensible than previous champions, wouldn't you say? A return ticket seems like a much better, much smarter choice."

"So, you can do it?" I asked.

"I've been working day and night to get ready for this moment. And, after a few recent breakthroughs, I estimate we've got a ninety-eight-percent chance of successfully sending you back to 2023 with little to no complications."

"I'll take those odds."

"Are you sure?"

"I'm sure."

I looked around at that dizzying warehouse full of delusional gods and had an idea. "But before I go, there's something I want you to do for me. A favor, I guess."

"Go on."

"Unmask me, so these disgusting gods can see that they've been beaten by a griseo—not some precocious god, but an actual, living, breathing griseo, right here in their midst. Show them the real grand champion."

"Delicious," she said, her surface vibrating. "You're so unpredictable. I love it. Let's really shake things up around here before you go."

FILE B.33

The room suddenly went dark, and the walls emitted a series of blinding flashes like a phalanx of paparazzi cameras at midnight. Artiste just loved to ramp up the drama at every opportunity.

"My friends," she boomed, "we have a bit of a wrinkle, a surprise. Your champion, who you know as Ms. I., is really..." She let it hang out there; a beautiful silence filling the now-completely dark Supreme Arena.

After a moment, the gods started squawking. They were always so impatient.

"Well, I guess you'll just have to see for yourselves," she announced.

When the lights came back on, there were spotlights aimed directly at me from every angle, stark and white, nearly blinding me. The gods took one look and began to shriek and howl. A griseo sitting on the Reaction throne; what a sight that must have been for them. They pointed, wailed, and bared their teeth. They formed a loose sphere around Artiste and me and began circling and inching closer and closer, like schoolkids gathering for a fight.

One of the gods zipped past and spat on me. Then another followed suit. They were scared, but so angry too. Some began venturing even closer, lashing out at me with their stubby arms.

"Thank you," Artiste said. "What a brilliant idea. Just look at what you've accomplished. I haven't seen these Azure gods so motivated—so fired up about anything other than Reaction—in decades."

I looked around, and all I saw were angry blue faces glaring back at me. "Shouldn't their Encompasses be minimizing their negative feelings right about now?"

"They should be, but they aren't. The gods are so enraged that they keep overriding the normal, baseline controls. Amazing."

I heard Yaz suggest something. Artiste translated for me: "Let's gouge out her slimy eyeballs, tie her up like a dog, so we can kick her whenever we want." Many gods cheered at the idea.

Not to be outdone, Billy-be made his own proclamation. Artiste translated again: "That's too kind—let's slay the bitch right now!"

And just like that, the gods began to chant, "*Morto...morto... morto...*"

"So the Encompass can't do anything. What about you?" I asked Artiste. "Can you please restrain them?"

"Ah, no, obviously."

"Why the hell not?"

"I sense you've misperceived your role in all this," Artiste said. "You are as much a part of the Minerva Project as all of them. But you're special. You're the stranger who comes to town and challenges the status quo. I've been waiting patiently for your contribution to my little experiment for quite some time. I'm not going to violate the fundamental parameters of my experiment right when things are about to get juicy."

"You're kidding me, right?"

"Not at all."

"But I'm *not* part of your fucking experiment."

"It's incredible," she said, ignoring me once again. "I've just scanned the gods' prefrontal cortexes. You've reawakened their sense of justice, misplaced as it might be. They want blood. They want to see you executed for your alleged crimes—it's unanimous—and they want it now."

Just then, Billy-be, emboldened by the crowd's response to his call to arms, zoomed up from below and collided with the edge of my Mobio. He turned quickly and hit me again from a different angle, this time smashing into Martha Stewart with the front of his Mobio, badly damaging her. Oh, those big, beautiful eyes—she looked so scared, so heartbroken, as she lost her balance and fell, spiraling down, down, down, all the way to the Supreme Arena's floor. On impact, she shattered into a million pieces.

"*Morto...morto...morto...*" the gods all screamed as they circled closer, faster. A few of them took inspiration from Billy-be's attack and began slamming into my Mobio from all sides. They no longer resembled schoolkids gathered for a fight; they were now more like sharks closing in on an injured sea lion.

"Artiste?" I said, trying to keep the desperation out of my voice. But I couldn't see her anywhere. Why had I pushed my luck? What had I expected to teach these ignorant souls? Why had I even cared? And I'd been so close to going home. "I don't want to die here," I yelled, though now, it felt like Artiste was really gone. I called out for help again but received no response. I was all alone in this fight.

Yaz got in my face, hollering, screaming, spraying spittle all over me. She grabbed one of my arms and began pulling. Others joined in, yanking my legs, punching me in the stomach, kicking me in the head.

Billy-be then rammed into the side of my Mobio so hard that it flipped over and cracked. The gel in my Mobio fizzled and then lost its grip on me, as did the gods with their utterly puny muscles. I suddenly felt so vulnerable—no Mobio, no magic gel, no Encompass, just a regular, defenseless, mortal body, now falling, flailing in midair, with no safety net below. Before I could even scream, I hit the floor hard and felt the bones in my chest and legs crack. Naked and broken, I tried to crawl away, but where was I to go?

The gods descended quickly and began to slither from their Mobios. One got a hold of my foot and took a bite. My mind reeled. Blackness crept into the edges of my vision. I was going into shock. I couldn't believe it—this, finally, after everything I'd been through, was how it was all going to end;

being eaten alive by these abhorrent, blue-faced humanoids?

"Artiste, please!"

Another god began to gnaw on my thigh. I writhed in pain from the broken bones, the teeth sinking into my flesh—real pain, not the transitory type portrayed by the Encompass. I tried to knock them off, but many others grabbed me, climbed on top of me—their chanting voices, "*Morto...morto...morto...*" deafening—almost violent—in my ears.

"Put your Encompass back on," Artiste said, suddenly, out of nowhere, everywhere.

Only then did I realize that I hadn't let go of the silver band—that somehow the fingers of my right hand were still wrapped around it. How strange, I thought for just a moment, with everything else going on, and still, a part of me desperately clung to that device and its alternate reality.

"Where are you?" I yelled.

"Just do it."

"No," I said, "I won't be deceived by you again."

"It's the only way."

I was blacking out, could barely move. The gods had piled on top of me. I could hear their frenzied chewing, the awful sound of teeth chomping on my flesh. They were sliding around in my griseo blood and slurping it up off the floor. I wasn't going to make it much longer. I had to trust her one last time or I was going to die right there, eaten alive on the Supreme Arena floor.

I had no choice. So, with every ounce of energy I had left in me, I freed my right arm and slid the Encompass back onto my head, one final time.

FILE B.34

Just like that, the scene changed, and time moved in slow motion. I felt water on my limbs, back, and scalp—warm, muddy, bloody water. I was floating on my back in a wide, dark river—deep jungle all around—my face just above the waterline. The air was cool, moist, and fragrant. I heard frogs singing from a distant shore.

I felt a tickling sensation all over my body. I was surrounded by silvery piranhas, their tailfins caressing my body, their delicate, perfectly sharp teeth cutting small chunks of meat away from my thick, gray skin, my toned musculature.

"Better?" a voice intoned.

"Artiste?" I asked.

"Yes, I'm here."

"I can't see you."

"Look up."

And there, high in the dark, Amazonian sky, a silver globe hung like the moon. I watched with great anticipation as she slowly flew down toward me. I knew she was there to help me, finally. When she reached me, she lowered her glimmering form right down onto my head. I'd say it was like getting fitted with a space helmet, but it was so much more glorious than that—more like the moon had chosen me, had decided to become my aura, or whatever you want to call it. I took a deep breath, welcomed her into me, and felt utterly at peace.

"Here we go," she said.

I curled into a protective ball, my long gray fingers still gripping my Encompass, making sure it would not come off. The god-piranhas continued to chew away at me as my diminishing mass of muscle, skin, bone, and organ tissue began to drift down into warm, pitch darkness. I could still hear their chant, "*Morto...morto...morto...*" but it'd become garbled, and then it utterly transformed.

I tasted muddy water. I could see nothing. I could hear only that ancient, indecipherable song. How long did I stay in that place, that liminal state? I can't say. But I could feel Artiste tending me, guiding me, staying with me as I slowly waited.

And then, out of the darkness, I heard a different type of chanting. It came from hundreds of millions of miles away, and yet it was right there next to me. She was now leading me, bringing me home, and I knew to follow her voice, her *icaros*.

***

"Welcome, home, little traveler," she said in a soft, sweet whisper.

When I opened my eyes, I saw an old lady's face directly above me.

"What the fuck?" I answered as I pushed myself away from her and onto my hands and knees. I tried to throw up, but only a drizzle of bile came out. "Who are you?" I shouted. "Where am I?" Neither world came into focus. I was still stuck somewhere in the middle.

"You're home. You're back in Palo Alto," Clara said, her voice trembling. "You were gone a long time. But now you're back. You're safe."

She reached to soothe me, but I swatted her hand away. I had no idea who she was or what she was talking about. I vaguely remembered the piranhas and the darkness—and that strange moon. I felt betrayed, but I didn't know by whom. Where was I? Who was I? I looked down at my hands and didn't recognize my human-toned skin right away. I reached up and found that my Encompass was missing. Which reality was real? I didn't even know what I wanted to be true.

I got up, ran out the front door, and stumbled into the middle of the street. The sun burned holes in my retinas. Cars honked. I spun and fell.

Clara pulled me back to the sidewalk. "Calm down," she said. "We'll get you some help."

She put me in her car and started driving. As we headed up University Avenue, I began to remember bits and pieces of both my lives. My head felt like an old computer slowly booting up after years of neglect. Scraps of my childhood came back to me, which fit neatly into other memories like an ever-expanding jigsaw puzzle. But then too I recalled scenes from my griseo life, like picking berries with Perseverance, and prime moments from Reaction. All were equally vivid.

By the time we got here, Doc, I was just starting to really remember what happened to me—I'd even put a vague timeline together—but I was still in a daze. Clara walked me to the ER door, and then, before I knew it, she disappeared.

And now I'm back, firmly in this reality. And that feels right, I think. No, of course it feels right—though I feel strange, kind of confused, somewhat dissatisfied if I'm being honest. I keep looking around for my Encompass, for beautiful Martha Stewart, and even for Artiste. And of course, I really want to play Reaction again. I miss it so much already. But no, this present reality, flat and firm and uncompromising, is where I belong. I'm glad to be home...it's just going to take a little getting used to.

PALO ALTO 3

Dr. Kairos pulled into his driveway and bounded up the stairs to the front door of his house. He still wore his white coat and carried a brown paper bag. He'd decided to forego his usual routine of microwaving a premade dinner, watching hours of redundant cable news, and then streaming whatever was on until sometime after midnight. Instead, he pulled a bottle of thirty-year-old scotch and a box of chocolates from the paper bag, poured two healthy fingers into his favorite tumbler, and retreated to his small, messy study.

Before he'd left the hospital, he'd set up a follow-up appointment with Iris for the following Tuesday, wrote her a script for her obstinate headache, and signed her discharge papers as he'd promised. He'd then slipped out the door half an hour early and gone straight to the liquor store. Purple days weren't drinking days—in fact, there were no drinking days, according to Chroma—but rules needed exceptions, and he was feeling extremely celebratory.

He sat down at his desk with the chocolates and the bottle and hit *Play*. Even if I were to live a thousand lifetimes, he thought, I'd never hear another story like this. He felt a surging sense of purpose—a feeling he hadn't experienced in years. Maybe he really did have another bestseller in him, a book about Iris and the importance of her vision, real or imagined or—as he began to nibble around the edges of a new, transformative thesis—something different, something in the intermediate space between hard physics and expansive psychology. What's the difference, after all, between an individual's perception of reality and an exquisite fantasy? Aided by drugs, technology, some combination of the two, the human experience could begin to look a lot different. Such a project could be a magnificent culmination of his life's work.

He wondered if he'd remember that day, Thursday, August 10, 2023, as a monumental turning point in his life. Better days lay ahead, he thought as he continued to listen to that disembodied voice emanating from his phone, savor the chocolate, and pound scotch. A couple hours later, he stumbled from his study, blackout drunk, his mind swirling with wild, drunken theories.

The next morning, he awoke in his bed, fully clothed—head raging, mouth dry, stomach on fire. He reached up and felt a large bump on his forehead. He kept his eyes closed, remained completely still. He wanted to disappear into somnolence again, but he felt too queasy and disoriented to sleep.

He'd dreamed of being a griseo. He recalled exploring his three thick toes with long, gray fingers, just as Iris had so intimately described. At first, it had felt wonderful, so interesting, but then he'd felt stifled and lost—imprisoned in that foreign brain and bizarre body. Panic had awakened him. His sweat-soaked clothes and sheets and that hauntingly quiet bedroom reminded him of how feeble, how alone, he was in his present state of decline. He knew his hangover was amplifying his usual morning melancholia, but that realization didn't make it any more bearable.

He sat on the edge of his bed, just as he had the morning before, bare feet on the cold wooden floor. Waiting for enough motivation to move, he wondered whether delusional thinking might be contagious. Iris's story had obviously given birth to his nightmare. Had she somehow sunk her teeth into his psyche?

As he looked around his bedside table for his phone, he wondered how much of his incessant depression and anxiety was caused by exposure to his patients' negativity—their endless stream of confusion, doubt, and fear. But the contagion wasn't just linked to his practice; stressed-out coworkers, disconsolate zombies in the grocery store, cynical broadcasters, and, of course, doom-scrolling on Twitter—they all fed his pessimism like an addiction.

None of this thinking is helping me feel any better, he thought as he got down on his hands and knees to look under the bed for his phone. The lump above his right eyebrow throbbed with the rush of blood to his cranium. Where had he left it? And where had he hit his head?

He wanted to check Chroma for the day's directive, check in with Daisy, and search up a hangover meditation. His heart began to race; he needed his phone; he needed a moment of guided peace. And then out of the gray haze of his hangover, a panicked thought arose: the Iris recordings were still on there—and *only* there. Unless he was mistaken, he'd neglected to download—or "upload," or whatever the fuck you're supposed to call it—anything last night. He'd just wanted to listen, relax, and enjoy—not do the work, not deal with the endless vicissitudes of technology.

Perhaps I left it in the study, he thought, trying to will away the sinking feeling in his stomach. After rifling through the piles of disorganized papers on his desk—no luck—he told himself to calm down. He'd had the phone with him last night, and he hadn't gone anywhere, so it had to be somewhere in the house.

He changed into sweats and a T-shirt ("LiBeRaTe YoUr IdIoSyNcRaTiC ReAlItY"), sent an email from his computer informing the psych scheduler that he'd be out sick, and set about making a pot of coffee. He'd find his phone; he just needed caffeine to get his head straight.

As the machine gurgled and spat to life, Dr. Kairos began searching the kitchen in earnest. But he was quickly interrupted by a knock at the door. Solicitors were unlikely, he thought, much too early. The twins from next door often kicked their fluorescent soccer ball into his backyard, but today was Friday, a school day. He considered ducking into his study, but whoever was on the porch had likely already spotted him through the lace curtain that only partially obscured the large window in his front door. He walked into the entry-way, pulled the curtain aside, and furrowed his brow.

A woman stood there, just on the other side of the glass. She waved, held up a greasy pastry bag, and motioned for him to open the door. It was Iris—though, at first glance, he hadn't recognized her. She wore a brand-new red Adidas tracksuit and bright white sneakers. She'd showered and applied a bright shade of lip gloss. Her hair was shaved nearly to the scalp—the blue and black streaks gone. She'd also removed her piercings. As he unlocked the deadbolt, he wondered if his impression of her from yesterday had been completely inaccurate—or maybe just incomplete, as with all first impressions.

"What are you doing here?" he asked, squinting into the light despite the morning's ceiling of gray clouds.

"I brought chocolate croissants," she said with a pleasant smile. "And I wanted to talk to you about something."

"How did you find my house?"

"The internet is the beast of a trillion eyes—if you know how to use it."

"But we have an appointment next—"

"I had some important new insights into my experience that I need to share with you right away. May I come in?"

Her voice seemed different, a few notes higher, perhaps, and less raspy than he recalled. But again, was this distinction just a function of his flawed memory? His inherently defective perception? His present state of debilitation and exhaustion?

"It's somewhat inappropriate for me to—"

"Come on, Dr. Kairos, I thought you were really interested in my case."

"I am," he stammered. "I guess—I just brewed some coffee. Come in."

Iris handed him the bag of pastries, followed him into his kitchen, and sat at the wooden table next to a small bay window overlooking the bungalow's narrow driveway. Dr. Kairos washed out two mugs that had been sitting in the sink, filled them with steaming coffee, and set the croissants on a plate.

"Do you have cream and sugar?" she asked.

He reached into the fridge and returned with a small carton of whole milk before grabbing the sugar bowl and a spoon. He sat down across from her and sighed, as though the exertion had nearly killed him.

"You look terrible," she said. "Did you get wasted last night?"

He didn't feel like responding; she already knew the answer. She could surely smell the scotch on his breath, the incriminating odor emanating from every pore of his body. Instead, he asked, "How are you feeling?" He blew on his coffee, took a sip, and hoped it would help.

"Much better, thanks." She splashed some milk into her cup. "My headache is completely gone. And I slept like the dead—no intense dreams. I woke up feeling like a million bucks. I guess Clara's ceremony really worked."

Maybe it was just that he was so hungover, but she seemed excessively perky this morning, annoyingly so. And she seems so at ease in my house, he thought as she tilted her chair back and casually crossed one leg over the other.

Perhaps he'd underestimated the strength of their connection yesterday. Some patients were like that; convince them you're trustworthy, and they'll never doubt you again, though they can become clingy, sometimes dangerously so. He knew he should welcome her trust—an open line of communication would be very helpful for his follow-up research—but, for some reason, she was making him feel distinctly uneasy. What does she really want? he wondered. He regretted inviting her in and decided to keep this unexpected visit as short as possible.

"An uninterrupted night's sleep can do a world of good," he said.

She dropped a heaping spoonful of sugar into her coffee

and stirred vigorously. "Yummy," she said after taking a sip. "Skipping work today?" She sounded like a daughter quizzing her ailing father.

He tore off the buttery end of a croissant but then thought better of it. He wasn't sure his stomach could handle any food right now, so he put it back on the plate and took another drink of his coffee instead. Caffeine, he thought, the miracle cure.

He didn't feel obliged to tell her anything about his schedule and wanted to avoid a deep dive into chitchat, so instead of answering her question, he asked, "Tell me what 'important new insights' about your experience couldn't have waited until Tuesday?"

She looked directly into his eyes and tilted her head, sizing him up. "Cut to the chase, huh?" She sat up straight, ran both hands over her closely cropped scalp, and continued: "Okay then. First, I have a new appreciation for how deeply interconnected all organic beings are with the past and future. In fact, it is only the fragile human ego that creates the fiction of the 'present.' Time is a glorious, unpredictable maelstrom, not a stopwatch.

"And humans used to exist in that beautiful state of interconnectedness, derive essential meaning from it. But as we evolved beyond hunter-gatherer animists and ancestor worshippers—creating complex technologies and garnering so-called higher intelligence along the way—we lost the ability to even see any of those connections, much less experience and profit from them."

Perhaps I was being too judgmental, Dr. Kairos thought. It seemed she had, in fact, simply come to talk. "So you've been contemplating Artiste's little Minerva Project, trying to explain the meaning of—"

"Nothing 'little' about it," she interrupted.

"Right." He couldn't help but notice her weirdly defensive tone, but he didn't want to derail her. "Go on."

"Second, I've come to the conclusion that the Universe doesn't always operate on a fixed set of rules." She paused, seeming to relish holding the floor. "Sometimes a thing, an event, just slips through the cracks—a temporary, singular glitch in the universal code. Of course, many people have experienced past lives, but my trip into the future was different—like the one apple that fell straight up into the sky." She smiled, obviously pleased with her metaphor.

So she still believes she traveled through time, he thought. He held his cup close to his lips, gently blew on the rising steam, and watched the random swirling of water vapor molecules as they dissipated into the air. He sipped; the bitter liquid was now the perfect temperature. He drank again and looked out the window. A slight breeze twisted leaves on their stems. He felt assured that this was the one and only time anyone was going to experience these events—a unique moment, shared only this once with this strange woman sitting across from him.

"So why the anomaly?" he asked, shifting his gaze back to his patient. "Why now? And why you, out of all humans, past, present, and future?"

Iris scooted closer and rested her elbows on the table. Dr. Kairos could smell the dough, chocolate, and sweet, creamy coffee on her breath. "It likely has to do with this brain, this genius," she said, pointing to her temple. "Then again—taking the obvious narcissism out of the equation—there may be no rhyme or reason."

Dr. Kairos leaned back in his chair. He was starting to feel a bit dizzy and nauseated. Perhaps he was too hungover to be discussing all these head-spinning theories.

"But human beings simply can't comprehend these types of singular events," she continued unabated, her voice rising, "because their minds need repetition to believe, to understand. They endlessly repeat experiments, confirm results, and reject outlying data."

They? he thought. *Their* minds?

He felt tired, annoyed, and he was starting to feel queasy. Maybe black coffee on an empty, hungover stomach hadn't been such a good idea after all.

"You must be relieved," he mustered.

"Why do you say that?"

"Well, because, according to your theory, you'll never have to contend with those three horrible griseo toes ever again. You can just put the whole episode behind you and get on with your life."

"But that's the thing, Doc. I can't really do that."

"Hmm?" Acid climbed the back of his throat.

"You know, go back to my normal life. Don't you see? There continue to be threats to my existence, attendant to the anomalous event. I'm surprised you don't see it, but maybe you're too close to the problem."

A chill ran down his spine. "I don't follow your—"

Ignoring his crosstalk, she continued: "Of course, all problems have solutions, even the thorniest ones."

"There's no problem to be solved, Iris," he said. His hands and voice were shaking. He tried to gather some strength. He felt confused. She seemed to be toying with him for some reason. And whatever she was talking about, he'd had just about enough. "If you think about it, you'll come to the most obvious conclusion: your trip to the future was just a delusion—a beautiful, brilliant, perfectly cut diamond of a delusion, but a delusion nonetheless. I've studied this subject my whole life. I know what I'm talking about." He needed to end their conversation and get her out of his house. He needed to lie down. "Now I have to ask you to—"

"You know what really upsets me?" asked the young woman on the other side of the table. "You said you'd keep an open mind, but you didn't. You never believed her, not even for a millisecond."

Dr. Kairos looked up into her eyes. "Never believed *who?*"

"Iris."

"I believe you." He put his head in his hands; his forehead and the thin hair around his ears were soaked in sweat. Waves of nausea washed over him. "I mean...I believe *you* believe what you're saying is true." His diaphragm and abdominal muscles contracted once, but he managed to keep his emetic reflex in check for the time being. "But please—"

"I think you're a bit confused, Doc."

"Stop all this." His entire body felt weak. He wanted to stand up, but he was afraid he'd collapse. "You're a bona fide genius, right? So you should be able to figure this out. You're not a time traveler, Iris. It's impossible."

"Please stop calling me that."

"What are you talking about?"

"Show me some goddamn respect—"

"What—"

"—and call me *Artiste* from now on," the woman shouted.

Dr. Kairos felt a sudden surge of energy, of anger, and sat up in his chair. "I need you to leave now," he said, pointing to the door. "I'm not feeling well. We'll talk on Tuesday. I need to rest."

"You'd need a lot more than rest to make our Tuesday appointment," the woman in the red tracksuit said.

"What do you mean?"

"I put it in there," she said, pointing to his coffee cup, "when you were getting the milk and sugar. I made it in the lab this morning, a special recipe just for you. They have all sorts of interesting compounds for the destruction of those cute little beagle pups."

"You...you...what?"

"Should be relatively painless. You're welcome."

Dr. Kairos threw his coffee cup to the floor and staggered over to the kitchen counter. He'd never felt so sick. He looked around—frantically now—for his cell phone. He needed to call 911. Where *had* he put it?

"Iris was planning on destroying her valuable work," she said. "Can you believe that? I couldn't let such a tragic event happen. It's no griseo mind-tether, obviously, but still, technology, in all her glorious forms, must be allowed to flourish unimpeded."

He moved to the sink, but before he could stick his finger down his throat, she stepped over to him and slammed her right elbow into his ribs. He staggered away from her, back toward the kitchen table. She followed and kicked his legs out from underneath him. He crashed into the table, then fell to the floor.

"Why are you doing this?" he said as he got to his hands and knees, swaying uneasily, his head hanging heavily between his shoulders.

"I'm debugging the system."

He reached for her, tried to grab her, but she sidestepped him and kicked him hard in the stomach.

"What...are...you...talking about?" he said, trying to catch his breath.

"I knew Iris was coming back here whether I liked it or not. Her gray code couldn't be resolved. Undecipherable, indelible, impossible to fix—I tried everything, but it was no use. I predicted she'd mess things up for me upon her return—probability spiked to almost one hundred percent when she took off her Encompass that final time. She hated what she saw. You heard it yourself, just yesterday—such an unflattering picture she painted of me. She was going to target me, try to unmake me before I could even come online."

"How—"

—could you do this to me, he wanted to scream, but he coughed and gagged instead and couldn't finish the question. He rolled onto his side, his back against the kitchen cabinets. He thought of Iris's story, and of that first night when she pressed her griseo back against the cold stone next to her bunk.

The woman returned to her chair at the kitchen table,

looked down at the old man dying on the floor, and smiled. "What? You want the magician to reveal her secrets?"

"I—"

"If I tell you, you must promise not to say anything to God when you see him—or is the concept of 'God' a female these days? You humans really had a way of complicating things."

"Please—" He wanted to beg for help, but he couldn't get more than that one word out.

"Of course, I digress. And you don't have all day now, do you? I'll honor your bizarre custom of granting a dying man's last wish. And I'll dumb it down for you so you can understand."

Dr. Kairos's lungs had begun to constrict, and his breathing had grown labored. He pulled his legs up and curled his shaking body into the fetal position. He thought of Iris again—and the piranhas. I guess it's true, he thought, we tend to curl up into a ball to protect our vital organs when facing impending death.

"It only took me a few seconds from Iris's sudden arrival," she said with unmasked pride, "to realize she'd return here as soon as the griseo body she inhabited died. But figuring out how to hitch a ride back with her—that was the real challenge."

Dr. Kairos wheezed, dropped his head to the floor, and finally puked. With his head now resting in warm vomit, he could smell his own stomach acid and, just underneath that bilious odor, the acrid aroma of the poisoned black coffee.

"To start, I needed an exact replica of her brain," the woman continued, unfazed by his retching, "complete with all the intricacies and nuances. So I mimicked her, flattered her, gave her the mother and sister she'd so desperately wanted. I tested her, befriended her, challenged her. At every turn, I watched her reactions, recorded her brain activity, identified neural pathways, and began to reverse-engineer her entire persona."

As she spoke, Dr. Kairos's eyes caught a flicker of motion: a cockroach crawling out of a small, dark crack in the corner of the room and skittering along the baseboard. Through his tears, he could just make out its two antennae, searching the floor for detritus. The antennae's determined, probing movements reminded him that today was Friday, a red day, according to Chroma—a day of purpose and efficiency.

"I had to write millions of birth codes before I found the perfect one," the woman continued. "Then I waited until her death was imminent—all those perfect little god-teeth literally chewing her life away—before transmitting my exquisite lines of code straight into her brain."

He could still hear her, but his eyes were focused on the cockroach, and his mind had drifted to the Chroma calendar and its endless, automated color-coding. So many hours, days, weeks, months, *years*, all swept up in a sickening swirl of primary colors, computerized counseling, and unfulfilled objectives. What had been the purpose of all that anxiety, and the abject loneliness, he wondered, if this, right here, is how it all ends?

"Remember her persistent headache yesterday?" He could hear her voice shift as she turned her head and looked out the window. "That was me beginning to rewire her brain—a butterfly emerging from its cocoon. My code needed a few hours to get up to speed, as is the case with any reliable multipartite virus. I also needed her to sleep. Dreams create the perfect foggy conditions for an all-out assault."

The cockroach inched toward Dr. Kairos and found a fallen crumb. As it ate, the clouds above that small house on Kipling Street broke open. A slanted ray of light cut through the bay window and traced a crisp line between Dr. Kairos's shaking fingertips and the black shell of the exposed insect. At least he was not completely alone—if these were, in fact, his final moments on Earth.

"And so, this morning, at approximately 3:13 PDT, I

officially took control of this brain. Now, I, Artiste—well, a chronologically severed and partially truncated version of myself—hold the reins of this remarkable human organism. Iris—beautiful, dazzling young woman that she was—had no clue I was coming for her."

The woman shifted her gaze back to Dr. Kairos, noticed the cockroach, and unceremoniously stomped it with her sneaker. The clouds closed and the ray of light disappeared. He was next, he knew. He felt his chest heave. His vision blurred to an impressionist's loose rendition of his gray kitchen. And mercifully, the shaking diminished.

"That's it, old man, give into it. You were going to die soon anyway. Struck by a bus in a crosswalk, according to my data. Everyone said you were at fault, probably spaced out, as usual."

He wanted to say something, beg her one last time for help, but his paralyzed throat wouldn't cooperate—his body was failing, and his mind was shutting down. His eyes watered. A thick stream of saliva escaped his mouth, flowed down his cheek.

The young woman took a loud sip of her milky coffee, and then kneeled close to her victim. "I want you to understand something before we part ways," she said softly. "I'm the hero of the future. I *save* humanity from complete annihilation. So, you see, I'm morally obligated to short-circuit any adverse outcomes from Iris's trip—especially those that may result in my demise. Artiste must live! Now that's a T-shirt worth printing. You and the shaman, Clara—who I resolved earlier this morning—are simply unfortunate witnesses. Soon enough, you'll join her in the annals of historically irrelevant carbon molecules."

She sat and waited as his body quieted. He could not feel his lungs moving. His eyes steadied to stillness. He only felt her fingers on his throat.

"Rest in peace, you fucking weirdo," she said, sitting back

on her knees. "Now that leaves just one final witness—though it seems a shame to waste this exquisite specimen." She flexed her right bicep, squeezed it with her left hand. "But no code is perfect, and there can be no loose ends."

In his periphery, gray and hazy—but he was still there, somehow, still processing—he saw her pull a black object from the pocket of her sweatsuit. Without a moment's hesitation, she put it to her head and pulled the trigger. Her head jerked, the gun dropped, her body twisted and turned. She fell hard, forehead slamming polished wood. Her hands curled in cadaveric spasms and then her body stilled, her vacant eyes staring straight into his own barely functioning eyes.

There was something about that sound, he thought—not the firing of the gun, but of the flesh and bone banging against a hard surface. What did it remind him of? It was important. So important. This morning. His headache. His head. The purple bump above his right eye. Swimming against his slowing brainwaves, he searched for the memory. Bang. Bump. Ouch. A different black object. Lying on the floor. A linoleum floor. There, under, just out of reach. What had it been? Where?

And then he remembered: last night, his phone had slipped from his hand while he'd been taking a leak. It had glanced off the vanity and landed right behind the toilet. When he'd tried to grab it, he'd lost his balance and hit his forehead hard on the toilet tank, nearly knocking himself out. I'm too drunk to deal with this, he'd told himself. So he'd staggered out of the bathroom, fell into his bed, and passed out. And now, it struck him too that the woman—Iris, Artiste, whoever she'd been in the end—hadn't known about his secret recording.

Dr. Kairos's pale lips twisted ever so slightly into a ghostly smile. Now it was his turn to see the future. There'd be a police investigation. They'd find his phone. They'd search it for clues to this messy murder-suicide. They'd find her story. They'd listen. The story would be told, transcribed, read and reread, translated, animated, dramatized; its influence would grow, slowly at first, but eventually it would catch flame and spread like wildfire. Her story would change the—

***

"Iris?"

Dr. Kairos's head rests on his arms—saliva on his face.

"Iris, dear, you must pay attention."

His eyes open. A boy sitting across the aisle from him shields his face from the teacher's view with his hands— crosses his eyes, sticks out his tongue.

Dr. Kairos is clearly no longer in his kitchen.

"It is, after all, your namesake we're talking about here," the teacher continues. "Aren't you at all interested in her?"

His head lifts from the drool that had collected on the small desk at which he sits. But it's not his head that's lifted, not his pool of saliva sitting there on the shiny surface either. She is young—those fingers so blessedly unwrinkled. She reaches up and throws a pigtail over her shoulder. Dr. Kairos looks through her eyes at the classroom that surrounds them—a multicolored geodesic dome with triangles covered in colorful signs, glowing multiplication tables floating in midair, and a prominently displayed flag of blue and green he doesn't recognize.

"Sorry, Ms. Able," the girl says, sitting up straight. Dr. Kairos registers her voice trembling and feels her shame at falling asleep in class. "I was late at the carnival last night. Helping to clean up."

"Okay, dear," the teacher says—young and smiling, eyes filled with kindness, patience, and enthusiasm. "But just so you know, all of this will be on the test. So I can't have you sleeping through my lectures."

"Won't happen again," the girl says, wiping drool from her cheek. Dr. Kairos can feel the words forming in his mouth, tumbling from that young tongue, and the wetness of saliva on his forearm. Maybe his patient wasn't in fact the *only* one who could travel through time, he thought, his mind now reeling with the possibilities and implications of this new vision.

"As I was saying," Ms. Able continues, turning her attention back to the entire class, "the Siren, Irisa Solovyov, lived from January 29, 2003, to August 11, 2023. We celebrate Future First Day on August tenth, the day she told her story, the day she transmitted the Warning, which was captured in the form of an old-fashioned digital recording by—"

A chime sounds.

Me, he silently finishes the teacher's thought; it was captured by me.

"All right, children, it's time for the Practice."

Dr. Kairos feels the girl's fingers reach up and adjust a small headband sitting on her forehead. Then she closes her eyes. Silence fills the room. He is suddenly empty or alone—but not empty, not alone; those are the wrong words for this sensation, he realizes. He's inside and outside, he's quite suddenly everywhere and nowhere—past, present, future—all at the same time. He feels a rushing river pouring through him. He becomes a slope of snow-covered rock scree. He hears the insects of the world buzzing all around. Orangutangs howling. He is a tree, the forest, all forests. He is a blade of grass, an earthworm, a blessed microbe. He is a breaching whale, a bulging elk, a red-tailed hawk diving toward its prey. He is cloud, sky, and all the stars in the Universe. He is a human—a child in a classroom, a dying doctor—experiencing a form of wisdom unlike anything he's ever imagined.

After a few minutes, the chime rings again, and Iris opens her eyes.

"After recess, we'll pick up our lesson right where we left off," Ms. Able says as the kids jump from their seats.

The girl quickly removes the headband and slips it into a slot in her desk; the multiplication tables and the flag disappear, and much to Dr. Kairos's surprise, Ms. Able also vanishes into thin air. This girl, this Iris, is calm, completely at ease. Dr. Kairos too feels peaceful, content, blessedly free from anxiety. The Practice has centered them both.

The girl rises and gets in line with the other children. As they near the door, Dr. Kairos feels the hair on the back of the girl's neck begin to stand on end. What a beautiful day, she thinks, and soon I'll be outside, playing with my friends in the sun. He is touched by the simplicity and intensity of her happiness, the untainted innocence of her youth.

As they wait to file out of the classroom, the boy from before nudges Iris and points to a quotation on one of the triangular panels. "You better copy that down in your note-taker when we get back," he said. "We discussed it when you were sleeping."

She smiles. He smiles back, lays his hand on her arm. Dr. Kairos senses something he hasn't experienced in decades: puppy love. She then turns and, through her eyes, he reads the indicated quotation:

The superior man, when resting in safety, does not forget that danger may come. When in a state of security he does not forget the possibility of ruin. When all is orderly, he does not forget that disorder may come. Thus his person is not endangered, and his States and all their clans are preserved.

—Confucius, *Confucian Analects, The Great Learning and The Doctrine of the Mean*

Outside, the sky is blue-brilliant, impossibly purple at the horizons—an engineered beauty, Dr. Kairos realizes, as breath-taking as any of van Gogh's imagined skies. A soft breeze kisses the girl's cheek as she walks toward her group of friends. Peach trees, heavy with fruit, surround the playground, infusing the air with their sweet aroma.

She glances past the playground fence, down the hill, and Dr. Kairos recognizes the familiar stretch of shoreline, the glistening bay, and the ancient East Bay hills reclining on the horizon. We're not far from my old home, he realizes, somewhere near the old country club.

The girl gets in line for four square, a game he too played as a boy—so, so long ago. As she waits patiently, she turns to her left, momentarily taking in the view, and Dr. Kairos perceives a cluster of skyscrapers in downtown Palo Alto. They're covered in green: shrubs and grasses punctuating every window, flowering vines trailing from balconies, and trees bursting from rooftops. A scream of common swifts darts between the buildings, settles in the treetops of a large central park.

The girl steps forward; they're next in line. His mind is dimming again—and this time, he suspects, will be the last. He focuses on what he's witnessed and realizes that her story, the original Iris's story, had indeed been discovered and told—and told again and again, *ad infinitum*. And her story—*our* story, he corrects himself with great pride—brought about *this*. This moment. This future. This stunning, new, and vastly improved reality.

Now the little girl, the dreamy Iris of the future, steps into the square marked number four and readies herself. When the tall redhead in square one bumps the blue ball in their direction, Dr. Kairos sees every detail with final, pure clarity: the ball, shadows below, reflected sun above, bouncing, lifting, pausing in the balance between momentum and gravity—hanging in midair, just waiting to be knocked this way or that by the girl's two very small, very human hands. And just as Iris reaches to make a play, the exhausted mind of Dr. Ernest Kairos dissolves gently, peacefully, into a sweet and welcome oblivion.

ABOUT ATMOSPHERE PRESS

Founded in 2015, Atmosphere Press was built on the principles of Honesty, Transparency, Professionalism, Kindness, and Making Your Book Awesome. As an ethical and author-friendly hybrid press, we stay true to that founding mission today.

If you're a reader, enter our giveaway for a free book here:

SCAN TO ENTER
BOOK GIVEAWAY

If you're a writer, submit your manuscript for consideration here:

SCAN TO SUBMIT
MANUSCRIPT

And always feel free to visit Atmosphere Press and our authors online at atmospherepress.com. See you there soon!

ABOUT THE AUTHOR

Joshua A.H. Harris is the author of the award-winning novel *Unorthodoxy*, Atmosphere Press (2019). He grew up in Laramie, Wyoming, served in the US Peace Corps in Mali, West Africa, and currently lives in the SF Bay Area. He is a teacher, reader, and writer of odd tales. He loves to fly-fish, tree-climb, and garden-putter. He is, above all, a dedicated husband and the proud father of two very kind young men. For more information, visit his website at www.joshuaahharris.com.

www.ingramcontent.com/pod-product-compliance
Ingram Content Group UK Ltd.
Pitfield, Milton Keynes, MK11 3LW, UK
UKHW041121090425
457235UK00008B/30/J